Peace of Time

Rosalind Rendle

DEDICATION

To my mother, Christine Herring, herself a published author, who encouraged me to write a book.

1 CHAPTER

Summer 2010

Why did this have to be happening to her in August? The first of this month was Lammas day, in ancient times traditionally a day for foretelling marriages and trying out partners for eleven days before deciding whether to go with it or part forever. 'What was that all about?' Jenny thought. Nowadays, of all the months in the year, this was supposed to be her chill-out zone, not a time for life-changing decisions, for goodness sake!

'Men talk of killing time, while time quietly kills them.' She wondered who had said that; somebody clever, more than a couple of centuries ago. How true though. Jenny's night had been constantly broken. She was feeling tense and uncharacteristically grumpy. During the long hours of darkness, she'd put the light on and had tried reading but that hadn't worked too well. She just could not concentrate. She'd listened to some music on her smart-phone, dozing off and then jerking awake again and again until she'd finally turned it off. Every time she had looked at the clock the numbers had only seemed to kill a little of her night. Now she had awoken early, too early. She lay restlessly trying to decide whether to get up or roll around some more.

Goethe, no, that other bloke he had been friendly with….Schiller, was that the fellow who said those wise words so long ago? Those carefree days of college when she had studied such things with enthusiasm and curiosity seemed a long time ago, although it was really only five years since she had left to start her teaching career. Right now she was too worn down by all her emotions to follow that train of thought any more. Oh it didn't matter anyway, thought Jenny, as she clouted her pillow and turned again. This was hopeless. She glanced at the clock for the thousandth time and decided she might as well get up even though it was only seven am. She wasn't meeting Mike until eleven o'clock but for all the good lying in was doing, she decided she might as well push back the covers and haul herself up.

Thinking of the day ahead and the meeting they had set up, it seemed impossible that after the months of anguish, as well as the mixed events more recently, it had all come down to this single morning.

As the shower ran until it was hot enough, Jenny ran downstairs and switched on the kettle to begin boiling. She tried, yet again, to decide what to wear. Something informal but smart was called for, she felt; nothing too schoolish, though, that wouldn't help the atmosphere at all but what pride she had left would not allow her to be too casual. She needed to look confident even if she didn't feel it. She continued this train of thought as the hot shower water cascaded over her skin. She stood for longer than usual trying to wash away all her tiredness and indecision. This was so out of character. She used to know just where she was going and how her life would stretch ahead on its pre-ordained course – with some influence from her, of course. Had she been too set to allow Mike a proper and full place in her plans? She genuinely didn't think so. He had thought it was a good idea to apply to her present school after three years in her first job. It was a sideways move but was closer to home so less petrol money meant a small increase and they had needed every penny then. She liked the school, the head was a good one and most of the staff was really friendly. Her promotion there had come in good time too. Was that when it all started to go wrong at home though? She filed her thoughts away as she had tried to do so many times, before she started treading that well-worn circular route.

Having towelled herself dry she threw

on her dressing gown, went down and made a cup of tea and again returned to the bedroom to dry her hair and choose the all-important outfit. She liked this room. Despite the waterfall that had been shed quietly into the pillow here, she'd had moments of contentment too, more recently. The colours were calming and serene. Jenny moved to the window which was framed by the delphinium blue and grey fabric which matched the blue of one wall behind the bed. The colours were cool but the sun, for most of the day in this room, brightened it. She never closed the curtains at night. When sleep eluded her she liked to watch the stars as they travelled silently across the sky. There was something consoling in their constancy. Now, she opened the window and breathed in the fresh air. It was a real sapphire and gold morning. Looking down on the garden she saw that the wide flower bed she had created against the neighbours' fence was a rebellion of colour. She was only a casual gardener, managing fertilizer and dead-heading. Here she had achieved planting of spring bulbs with perennials that followed; now a riot of black-eyed Susan, phlox, salvia and hemerocallis. She reflected on the common name for this last one – day lily, here today and gone tomorrow, seemed like a metaphor she thought morosely. Then she drew herself up, typically. The smell of the garden on the already warm morning air was delicious. What-ever happened later she had to believe that it would be the right thing for her, at any rate. This wasn't being selfish. Now, she knew, it was self-preservation. Jenny had tried living her life just to please others and realised that whilst compromise was often necessary, giving all she was, as well as all she had, to someone else was not always best. She turned to pull up the duvet and straighten the pillows. She had treated herself to the white cotton covers when, for what she thought was a different life, she needed new bedding covers and she still liked the crisp white freshness of them in her blue and white room.

Jenny dried her hair with care, and turning in front of the mirror the light from the window emphasised the auburn tints that enlivened the brown. She opened the wardrobe doors. She had been undecided between the blue flowered dress that her Mum said brought out the colour of her eyes, or the red blouse and black A-line skirt she had bought recently, in a fit of rebellion. Really, she knew all along that it would be the dress. The colour was vibrant but not aggressive and she hoped that the tie at the back, drawing in the waist, suited her slender figure. She chose a fine silver chain to fasten above the V of the neckline and some plain silver studs for her ears that emphasised her new tidy haircut and slim neck. She had a few good pieces of jewellery but they all seemed to have one connotation or another. This had to be a neutral affair. She didn't wear nail varnish. Her job in the classroom was not suited to that at all and anyway she really couldn't be bothered with all that palaver every other day. A simple pair of grey flat sandals, with three small diamantes on the front of each, saw her finished. She glanced at her watch. Oh my goodness it was still only eight thirty! As she surveyed herself in the long mirror, Jenny hoped it was the correct effect that she had created – enough to give her confidence for the decision she would have to make, the reasons to explain clearly and then the determination to carry it through.

She was mooching around restlessly into the living room; back to the bedroom; casually stroking Fudge's head; wondering what to do when, just as she finished her cooling cup of tea, the phone rang. "I bet that's Mum" she said aloud to Fudge, her small white and tabby cat. One day more than a year ago, just when she needed something to care for in her life, more than at any other time, Fudge had adopted her as quite a young kitten. Having asked around the neighbours and finally visited the vet for all the necessaries, Fudge had determinedly made her home with Jenny. "Oh Fudge! I really don't know if I can cope with this call right now".

Jenny knew her Mum had been almost ill with worry for her but sometimes it was too claustrophobic and there were some things that were just too difficult to discuss with her Mum. For that, she felt certain guilt but it was easier to lean on her good friend Pat when she needed someone. Right now though she knew Mum had her very best interests at the heart of her concern and so instead of ignoring the call she hastened to answer the insistent ringing.

As she lifted the phone, Jenny took a deep breath. "Hello."

"How are you doing?" came the reply

"Oh Pat. Thanks so much for ringing. I thought it might have been Mum and I'm not sure I can deal with that right now. I know that's mean."

"I can understand that. Maybe you have to look to your own needs today of all days, rather than hers. I'm sure she'll tell you she understands when you next call her" said Pat at the other end of the line. "Are you nearly ready?"

"I *am* ready and kicking my heels now, wondering how to kill the time"

"Come up for a quick cup of tea if you want. Both boys are out on their bikes already, so it'll be just us"

"Thanks, Pat. You read my mind. You're a great friend. I'll be there in two minutes."

Gratefully, Jenny grabbed her bag, keys and a cardigan and pulling the door shut behind her she ran into the sunshine and hurried up the road to her friend's house, relieved to have some more purposeful action than she had hitherto managed that morning. Pat lived in a small semi, very similar to her own but there were four of them again now and it was crowded. The two boys were growing and expanding, in all ways, very quickly. She raised her hand to knock just as the door opened. Pat had anticipated her arrival and gave her a warm, smiling welcome.

They had first met the day that Jenny and Mike had moved in, five years ago. Anticipating their need for reviving coffee, Pat had appeared from up the road with a tray of everything they could want. They had shared half an hour of chatting and drinking and then, ever sensitive, Pat had left them to get on. Although she was ten years older and further along the road in terms of family responsibilities, Pat had been a steadfast friend to Jenny since that day. Her warmth and understanding had been invaluable. She seemed to know intuitively when to ask and when to listen. Her husband, Doug, was a manager at the local leisure centre. Mike and the others always teased him about combing his hair at every opportunity and it seemed that he could not pass a mirror or shop window without checking his reflection. However, they had been friends since that first week. Mike and Doug still got on well and with Diana and her partner, Greg, who had also been friends of Pat and Doug's, they had been a constant 'sixsome' for several years; going out for the occasional meal but more often sharing an evening of playing a board-game and snacks with a couple of bottles of wine. That way Pat and Doug didn't need to get a baby-sitter. It was all different now of course!

"So…." said Pat, leaving the conversation hanging, as they moved towards the kitchen. She knew Jenny may want to share her feelings but was equally content to wait in companionable silence. Right now, the kettle in Pat's kitchen was hissing and flagging its readiness for the teapot. They more often than not sat at the table in the kitchen. It seemed the right place to be, amongst the slight chaos, rather than in the living room where the sofa and chairs meant they were less intimate in their chatter. Frequently the children were in the other room too, watching television or playing games. She sat and glanced around as Pat poured the tea. Everything was as it should be. Ben's and Joe's school art on the wall next to a large, smart wall mounted plate;

the colour scheme behind them slightly resonant of the 1980s; the empty cake tins draining next to the sink; the fruit dish over-flowing with apples and oranges onto the counter next to some letters. It didn't matter, it was right. There was always a homely smell in Pat's kitchen too; baking or toast or bacon. The atmosphere was comfortable, with a warm personality and a ready sense of reality.

"I've been like a cat on the proverbial tin roof." Jenny smiled self-consciously.

"Well you look lovely. Just right"

"Thanks" Jenny looked relieved. "I've lain awake half the night wondering what to wear, what to say, whether to be five minutes late or to arrive before he does so I can arrange myself artfully on a bench" she laughed, half-heartedly.

"It's the country park, right?" asked Pat as she parked her comfortable frame onto a kitchen chair and put a mug of tea before each of them.

"Yes, it seemed like neutral territory. We didn't want to meet in a pub where everyone can hear what's going on. A restaurant's out in case one of us wants to leave before we've finished eating, and how do you manage the money? That could be very awkward. It's just as well it's good weather though. Doing this, walking about in the rain, would be far too dramatic, not so say uncomfortable. Who would sit in whose car if we just stayed in the car-park? It's a territory thing isn't it?" Jenny realised she was gabbling, justifying to herself what was happening.

Well, it seems the perfect place and yes, the weather has come up trumps for once" agreed Pat.

They sipped their tea in companionable silence for a minute. "So how is everyone here?" asked Jenny, thinking to move away from the subject of herself for a bit of light relief for a while.

"Oh, we're all fine. The boys are loving the holidays so far and as it's early days I'm not having to invent activities yet. Doug may take them swimming tomorrow though. He's busy, of course, as it's holidays he's got all the summer activities on top of the regular stuff and he's short of a life-guard so he's doing a bit extra there, too."

"And what about you?" asked Jenny. "You don't look quite so tired".

Only last year Pat's short brown hair had seemed to lose it's swing and bounce and the grey had been beneath her eyes as much as in them.

"I'm more in a routine again now," Pat replied. "I'm feeling a bit more relaxed these days." She paused as she seemed to evaluate what she had just said and then added "Well I've decided to reign in my emotions and be more independent. Marriage is not all it's cracked up to be, for me anyway, and I'm no longer relying on it! There are times when the boys are bickering or something like that and I get wound up, of course, but overall it's fine. I get some time to do my own thing when Doug takes them out for the odd day here and there and in the holidays, when Mum has them. I'm more self-reliant and I know that I can't rely on Doug anymore so that's how it is. I'm not looking for more these days."

It all sounded a bit lonely and loveless to Jenny. "Do you feel lonely, though?" she asked.

"Not really. I have an amount of companionship while he's here that I didn't have when I was on my own for that while. I don't believe in the myths of marriage anymore and so I shan't be disappointed another time. It's a relief, to be honest, to know where I stand. I know who comes first with Doug and that's Doug! I feel more self-confident and know that I could cope on my own and so I can relax. As it is, the boys have a father and know nothing of what's gone on and I can manage."

This just does not sound good Jenny thought, with feeling. It all sounded sad and not a full existence. She changed tack again "How is your Mum?"

"She's great and she's so helpful. To be honest it's given her a new lease of life, since dad died, to be with the boys more and she's always got something up her sleeve to help entertain them. She's coming down next week to stay for a while so you'll see her then. Your Mum will be there for you too, you know, if/when you need her." Pat reminded Jenny.

"I know but I can't help feeling Dad prefers her there. She's in the background though and that's good. I don't know what I would do without you though. I'm so lucky we met, Pat.

"Me too." Pat laughed wryly. "It goes both ways."

"Well, I'd better think about going" Jenny said reluctantly. Now the time was finally closing in upon her she had a moment of under-confidence and foreboding. She sat un-moving and sighed. "Oh Lord! What am I going to do?" she panicked, her voice rising.

"Whoa, Jenny! Take a deep breath.

You'll be fine. Even if you don't know this minute, I promise, you will when you get there."

Jenny's voice ascended again in her anxiety "Why did this happen to us? It wasn't meant to be like this. What did I do wrong?"

"Who says you did? It's complicated isn't it? It really is not that simple. There's several of you involved in this and you each have a view and a part. OK, some have been more proactive and some have suffered more. Who is to say who has agonised and who has grieved? I can't say, Jenny. Look, when you get back, I *will* be here. Just go slowly and drive carefully, for goodness sake!"

"Oh Pat, thank you" breathed Jenny.

She stood to leave, thinking again, how lucky she was to have this friend, so calm and competent. She knew Pat had had her moments too and she had been there for her at those times, but she doubted she had been so wise and steady.

At the front door she impulsively planted a light kiss on Pat's cheek. Theirs had not been that sort of demonstrative friendship and tears sprang to Pat's eyes. "Go now" she said carefully "and take care".

Jenny turned to wave at the end of the path and retraced her steps towards her own home and the car but much more slowly than she had come in the other direction earlier.

She opened the car door and sat in. Putting the key in the ignition, she stayed still for several moments calming her racing thoughts, breathing deeply. She'd hyperventilate next she thought and grimaced to herself. Well, she couldn't delay any longer. She'd drive slowly and maybe stroll in the park before arriving at the bench next to the lake.

The little car was one of Jenny's favourite things. It gave her independence and freedom. She turned up the music on the CD player and let the smooth tones of her favourite singer wash around her. She wound down the window and felt the warm breeze sweep over her face as she drove. The journey was an easy one, avoiding the town centre, and she arrived without incident.

Parking was easy too, at this time of day, even though it was holiday time. Jenny got out of the car and having locked it she nodded to the security attendant and strolled reluctantly towards the park. Mothers had brought their children to use the swings and climbing frames. One baby didn't like the swing and was crying loudly. She could hear the cries and shrieks of excitement from others. Two little girls were racing each other towards the play-house and its slide. She knew some would have brought picnics, too, in order to spend the day in the pleasant balmy air. It was a perfect day for all that. The hardy were already splashing in the shallows of the beach area and Jenny stood for a moment watching the children who were so carefree and unaware of anything but their own enjoyment of the moment. As she moved on she could hear the water birds racketing across the other side. No doubt some mothers had brought bread with which their off-spring could feed the ducks and geese. After a short stroll along the footpath towards the water-sports centre Jenny found a bench sheltered by bushes and facing the water. She sat for a moment to gather her thoughts. A light breeze ruffled the water. A small sailing dingy, a Mirror with its red sail and distinctive M logo, was out on the lake. It looked like a couple of teenagers sailing. It was perfect for them with its stable buoyancy, small size and 'stich and glue' construction. Jenny remembered doing the same thing in her pre-college days. She remembered sailing with her dad too and being tipped into the water on more than one occasion when he sailed too close to the wind and then made a bad manoeuvre. It had been exhilarating though. She closed her eyes. A blackbird was singing somewhere not too far away. Then she got a sudden whiff of chips from the Centre café. It was time to move on, find the agreed bench and to meet Mike again.

She took a deep breath as she stood and she walked as composedly as she could toward the bench on the far side of the lake. As she had planned, it was not busy over there she could see. She could even see the bench - empty at the moment. Everyone else preferred the leisure activities on this side.

With every step hear heart was pounding. A dozen questions raced through her mind. What should she say? What should she do? How would he react? What would he say? What if he didn't even come? Stop! She had to calm down! This was Mike. They had been together for years before all this collapsed her world. The bench was out of sight for a few moments, as bushes growing at the edge of the lake hid it from view as she passed.

Then suddenly she saw it again and he was there, not sitting, but standing and she could see his rangy figure walking back and forth. From this distance she couldn't see the detail of his dark hair, just longer than was fashionable, nor could she see, of course, his dark eyes or the crinkles at the corners that she had found so attractive. She thought he was as nervous as she was though. She could see that, as he put his hand to the back of his neck as he paced.

This was it then…. the moment to communicate her decision!

CHAPTER 2

24 months earlier

The end of the summer holidays came quickly that year as always but Jenny was particularly looking forward to this start of the September term, however, since she was starting at Holly Road School for the first time. It was a professional day first and the children would be in the next day. During the day-times of the holidays, when Mike had been at work, she had been preparing for several weeks now, labelling books and making drawer names for her new class. There had been some lesson preparation too, of course, but most of that would be during this afternoon with her partner teacher, Sally Harrison. She knew Sally had been teaching about the same length of time as herself but although they had spoken on the phone they hadn't yet met properly. Sally had been away at the end of the holidays and she for a week at the beginning so hooking up had been difficult.

Jenny drove into the school car park. The journey was short; one of the reasons she had applied for the job in the first place. A much shorter journey meant less petrol money and that was as good as a much needed pay rise for her and Mike. He had been keen on the move when she had applied. She had been up early and was ready in good time, excited to be going back to the place at which she had been interviewed all that time ago. She'd had to hand in her notice, at her previous school, by the last day of May and the interviews had been before that half term. Now September, it had been a long time to wait to take up her post and she was eager to get started. The day was cloudy but rain seemed to be holding off which was an optimistic sign. She climbed out of her car, having been sure not to park right outside the front door in what looked like anyone else's space. She didn't want to upset someone on her first day so until she got the lie of the land she would be circumspect. She lifted a bag and a large box from the boot and staggered towards the main entrance. As she was about to put the box down to open the door, someone got to it before her and she lurched through. "Thanks, this is really heavy" she said gratefully.

"We meet again", said Sheila who was the deputy headteacher. "It's lovely to have you here and I hope you will settle in happily"

"I'm sure I shall"

"Would you like me to help you carry

and I'll remind you where your class will be. Sheila took Jenny's bag in her solid grasp. Sorry we can't have teachers in when the caretaker's not here. I know in some schools you can do that but it's because of the central alarm system. Jim took his holiday late this year. Anyway I'm sure you'll catch up. The classroom assistants are really good here and often stay on a bit to help out."

Jenny followed Sheila down the corridor and when she arrived in the room that was to be her class her tummy did a flip and she was both nervous and excited all in one. It smelt like all classrooms seemed to - a mixture of cleaning fluid, polish and just something unique to schools, though not unpleasant, just familiar. She took in the arrangement of tables and straight away started thinking what she needed to move. She needed to make it hers somehow. Sheila stood back and let her take it all in. "We'll all be meeting in the staffroom in about half an hour" she said "Will you find your way back alright? Nearly opposite the front door."

"Yes, that's fine and thanks for carrying that" Jenny added as she took her bag from Sheila's capable hands

"Sally will be next door at any moment" added Sheila. "I'm sure she'll re-introduce herself when she arrives and you'll be able to come down with her"

Jenny felt that would be a good idea. She didn't totally relish the thought of entering the staffroom for the first time alone. She remembered that feeling when everyone's conversation stopped as they would all turn simultaneously to see the new-comer.

"Well, I'll leave you to it and see you soon" A smile appeared on her broad face as she left.

As she surveyed her space, Jenny secretly hugged herself with happiness. She immediately started sliding tables around into groups that suited her teaching style and would benefit the pupils that she had already put into sets on paper. She didn't hear another person come into the room and jumped as she turned to pull another table.

"Hi," said Sally with a smile in her voice. "Here we are again. It doesn't seem long since I was pulling backing paper off the walls and tidying away for the holidays. I'm Sally, by the way. It seems a while since we spoke on the telephone though. We're to be partners in crime, so to speak"

"Jenny", she answered as she stuck out her hand. It felt a slightly awkward moment but Jenny knew she would be friends with this girl with the bouncy pony tail and cheerful voice.

"I'm glad it was you who got the job. I like it here a lot but they're all older than me and it'll be good to be working with you", Sally said. "I see you've started to get settled in. It's always good to make the room feel like your own. I'll pop back in about twenty minutes and we'll go to the staff room together if you like"

"That would be perfect," breathed Jenny with a sigh of relief.

As they walked up the corridor shortly after, Sally chattered inconsequentially which enabled Jenny to take stock of her surroundings. Some of last term's work was left on the boards to make it feel welcoming for this new school year. The colours were cheerful and the work from all ages of the pupils was delightful and well-presented. The school smelt clean and the floors were shiny. Jenny felt she had made a good move coming here. On their way they passed the caretaker who smiled a somewhat toothless grin and said "Hi ladies, no glitter this term, *please.*"

"Hello, Jim. We've planned it for next week" said Sally laughingly "... and this is Jenny Lucas. She'll be using it too, so there'll be twice as much to hoover up!"

"Pleased to meet you, Jenny"

"...and you. I promise to be good. I know that 'grime' doesn't pay!"

"The old ones are the best ones" he smiled at her slightly feeble joke and she grinned back, feeling more relaxed.

As they entered the staff room Jenny could see that several people were there before them. Two or three were getting tea and coffee organised for everyone and some were already seated. She and Sally took two chairs by the windows and Sheila asked them what they would like to drink. Sally explained that all the staff joined in equally in most things like this which made for an easy going atmosphere.

"How's your Mum, Sally" asked one teacher from a seat at the end.

"She's much the same I suppose" replied Sally. "... although she's in the wheelchair most of the day now. I've got Age Concern to thank for a lot. While I'm here someone comes in to clean now and they are organising transport for her to keep her appointments. I am worried about her being on her own most of the day though"

"Well, I'm glad I don't have to cope with all that" said this teacher.

Jenny was a little surprised that someone would voice their opinion so bluntly although it sounded like Sally did have a lot on her plate. However, she seemed to be a very sunny, cheery person. Jenny knew Sally lived with her mother, just the two of them, so she did have heavy responsibilities.

Sally introduced the teacher, who had asked after her Mum and one other, to Jenny. She was Lesley, a year 4 teacher, and Joan who worked with her in that year group. They were sitting next to each other. They clearly got on together well as they resumed their whispering conversation. Just as Jenny was being informally introduced to several others the door opened and Graham Lockwood, the headteacher, arrived for the staff meeting of the morning. He welcomed Jenny and the session started.

▢▢▢▢▢▢▢▢▢

A couple of weeks later Jenny already felt very settled at Holly Road School. The class of six year olds were delightful and even young and grubby Billy Hollis was likeable. Although he had his moments, she had got the measure of him quite quickly now that the 'honeymoon' period of settling in was done. She enjoyed the stimulation of lesson planning with another teacher and the routines of staff room and playground were generally enjoyable too.

In was nearly six o'clock on the Friday

of her third week when she arrived home. Time had flown by after school as she marked the last few maths books she hadn't quite got done in class time with the children; pasted and trimmed some children's work onto backing paper and planned how she was going to arrange it; making question labels and placing the work on the display board. This was par for the course at this school and she loved every minute of it. It was the type of school that was buzzing with enthusiasm and whilst she was tired at this end of the week she was exhilarated too.

"Hi, I'm home", she called as she took her key out of the front door and pushed it shut again behind her with her foot. Her hands were full of yet another box of books and bits, a bag of tools – paper trimmer, stapler, glue and she also had her handbag.

Jenny new Mike was already home by his car parked on the road outside their modern small semi-detached house. "I'm in the bedroom," came the reply. Jenny dumped her stuff in the corner of the living room and went upstairs to say hello to her husband.

On entering the bedroom she gave him a quick kiss as he stood by the window looking out at the small garden below and plonked down onto the bed. "Phew, I'm whacked" she said, "but I've had a great day. You'll never guess what Sian Day said just before break this morning. She was nearly crying and when I asked her what was wrong she said 'I don't want to be a teacher anymore.' When I asked her why not she said 'I don't want eyes in the back of my head and my Mum says you must have eyes in the back of your head to know what we are all up to all the time'. I nearly laughed but didn't. I managed to cheer her up and explained that my head was normal."

There was little response from Mike, just a half-hearted smile.

"How was your day?" Jenny asked, perhaps a little too brightly.

"OK, I suppose" Mike answered, not turning. "You're late again." Jenny didn't like the sound of that statement.

"Well you know what it's like, difficult to get away sometimes, so much to do."

"Yes, I know that by now. Anyway, what's up this evening, anything?" he asked, turning to edge around the bed.

"Nothing much", she replied. "I've got some work to do at some point" she cringed inwardly, "but I don't need to do it tonight. I could leave it until tomorrow or Sunday morning. What about going down the road for a drink later?"

"I'm just tired'" he said "what's for

tea?"

"I've no idea at the moment but I'll go and look" she said conciliatorily.

Jenny knew that Mike was not enjoying his work, as she was. He was a manager at a major insurance broker in town. It was a large office and he had to deal with commercial and personal lines but if he wasn't sorting out problems created by his staff he felt he was chasing problems for clients. That's how he described it anyway. Jenny tried hard to understand what he did on a daily basis but it did seem complicated sometimes. However, he always wanted to be the best and it seemed to her that he put pressure upon himself sometimes, too much. She knew he had a big presentation evening coming up when he would need to show his technical knowledge of products on offer, but Jenny thought that sounded like an exciting thing to be under-taking.

"How is the planning going for your presentation evening?" Jenny asked, genuinely interested in his work.

Mike exhaled "Oh I suppose it's OK. Let's not talk about work now though. It's Friday, for goodness sake"

"Shall we have a glass of wine while I sort tea?" she asked, biting her tongue.

"I think I'll go to the gym" Mike said as he opened the wardrobe door to retrieve his bag which had his kit and shower stuff in it.

"Right" said Jenny, "Are you eating when you get home then? Only I'm starving already"

"I'll get something myself, later"

Jenny followed Mike down the stairs.

"See you in a bit, then" he said as he disappeared out of the door.

"Right," sighed Jenny to the door which was already closed.

It was three hours later when Jenny heard the front door open and Mike arrived home. In his hands he held a bunch of flowers that he had clearly bought in the all night supermarket. Jenny didn't mind that. She was touched that he had bought them for her and took it for the apology it clearly was intended to be.

"They are lovely" she said "Thank you" and she kissed him lightly. No more was said of the tensions of earlier. Jenny acknowledged that this was Mike's awkward way of saying sorry for his earlier surly attitude.

September turned into October and already there were signs of autumn. Jenny needed a coat now, especially for playground duty. This particular morning the low sky made her feel sad for the departed and carefree days of summer. In the front garden the fuchsia flowers bobbed in the brisk breeze like teardrops as she hurried up the path to her car. She didn't think they would last much longer. A few fallen leaves eddied around and around in a never-ending dizzying whirl in the corner by the gate, caught in their own vortex. As she arrived at school and parked, the first drops of drizzle were starting to beat against her wind-screen. What a grey and depressing hour. Jenny hoped it didn't presage a bad day. This was Thursday and Jenny usually really like Thursdays. She had a parent helper who came in to her class and an extra pair of hands and eyes was always welcome. She wasn't to know what lay ahead.

Hurrying indoors she passed the staff room as normal. Not for her the delaying tactics of some schools where teachers were drawn there before the children arrived. She recognised the hushed voices of Lesley and Joan and the clatter of plates and cutlery as they presumably emptied the dishwasher. Jenny had no desire to join that duo. She had done much of the classroom preparation before leaving the previous evening so she just had some books to take out of her bag from the night's work at home to place ready for one group of children, who would be working with Sian's Mum this morning. As she switched on her laptop and started loading the programme for the interactive whiteboard her door opened and Sheila popped her head round. She looked uncharacteristically rather grim and serious. "Christopher Mayhew, Charlie's Dad, is here to see you. You can use my room: might be best." She came further into the room and hurriedly whispered "Charlie's had an accident. I don't know the detail. Christopher seems quite distressed! He asked specifically for you"

Charlie Mayhew was a child in Jenny's class. He was a delightful little boy with a round face, bright green eyes, and very curly hair. He was quite small for his age but could stand up for himself when required. Jenny was very fond of all the children in her care but the fact that Charlie's Mum had died when he was only just three years old ensured that she had a special regard for him and his courageous cheerfulness. She had reflected, when they met, that he probably only had hazy memories of his Mum but a week after Jenny had taken over the class he had brought a photograph of her for 'show and tell' on that Friday and Jenny's heart had flipped. She remembered now how she had caught her breath, plumbed the depths of her sensitivity and smilingly achieved the best tone of normality and made the right noises for both Charlie and the other children.

Hastening back up the corridor now, Jenny greeted Christopher Mayhew. As she shook his hand she could see that something serious was amiss and so without hesitation she placed her other hand warmly under his elbow. "Come this way" she said as she led the way into Sheila's small office next door to the staff room.

"It's Charlie," he said before she had closed the door. "He was knocked off his bike yesterday after school."

Jenny took a sharp intake of breath and said quietly, "tell me what happened." She indicated the chairs and they sat opposite each other, Charlie's dad on the edge of his.

She saw that he was completely shaken. "He's in hospital. He's got to stay for a while. I've come from there now but I have to get back". It explained the shadows under his green eyes and the pallor she could clearly see. "He was on his bike and he rode out in-front of a delivery van. He skidded, fell off and hit his head on the kerb. There was so much blood. I shouldn't have let him ride out like that. It's all my fault. I shouldn't have let him out but all the children ride their bikes up and down the close." Mr. Mayhew rubbed his face with the heels of both hands and Jenny could see he was really tired and close to tears. He hadn't had time to shave and his wavy, dark hair was tousled. "He's fractured his skull. It's all my fault", he repeated.

Jenny was nearly moved to tears too, but she held herself together and said "Mr. Mayhew, Christopher, you had to let him out to play with the others at his age and your Close is safer than many places."

"I kept looking out of the window while I was getting things together for his tea. No-one normally comes into the close at that time of day. I always make sure he's in before people come home from work and I finish my work so I can come and get him from school and give him attention. He had his helmet on when I last looked out of the window, so I don't know what happened there."

"I know you look after Charlie really well," said Jenny reassuringly. "What have the doctors said?"

"Well, I called the ambulance because of the blood. Then in the ambulance he started vomiting such a lot and they're keeping him in. I have stayed overnight with him. He's had x-rays, of course, and a CAT scan last night. They put some dye into him and I had to say if he was allergic to shell-fish but I didn't know. At his age he won't eat anything like that. They asked so many more questions as well. They've put in a line to drain some pressure. He was asleep so the nurse said I should come home and get some things.

Just then the door opened and Sheila spoke urgently. "Christopher they want you back as soon as you can. Charlie's fine", she added when she saw his expression "but they think he may need a small operation"

"Oh, my Lord! I have to go" Christopher shot up out of his chair "Sorry," he said.

"Let us know what ….." Jenny said but the door closed before she could finish. As she watched him go, Christopher turned and gave her a quick wave, before running on towards his car.

"The hospital just telephoned here," Sheila explained as he left. "He must have told them he was calling in. He does such a great job" she added "This seems so unfair with everything else he has had to cope with. Are you OK?" Sheila asked as she saw Jenny's expression

"Yes, oh, yes, I'm fine" Jenny said, although she felt shaken herself. Charlie was such a lovely little boy; she desperately hoped he would be alright.

The previous week at her first parents' evening in this school Jenny discovered that Christopher Mayhew was a financial adviser who largely worked from home. She knew he managed his appointments and subsequent paperwork to fit in with Charlie's schooling. This way he was able to help his son with reading and be there for play activities after school. He took his role as sole parent carer very seriously and tried hard to be father, mother and everything else to Charlie. It must have been very difficult indeed managing his own grief when his wife had died of cancer whilst coping with the feelings of his young son, never mind all the day to day work and caring that he had. The lad was always clean, well fed, seemed happy and from what Charlie told her at school, his dad always seemed to find the time to take him swimming or to visit his grand-parents at the weekends.

As she slowly walked back towards her classroom, Jenny called in next door to tell Sally what had happened. Sally was as shocked as Jenny was herself. She gasped as she put her hand to her mouth. "Oh, no! That's dreadful, poor man. He does so much and copes so well. I really admire him. I've always thought we have so much in common, him and me. I have to look after my Mum and he has to look after Charlie, both of us on our own. It's hard to get out and meet other people. Oh this is awful." Jenny told her the details that she knew and assured Sally she would let her know when she knew more.

The day wore on in much the usual way but Jenny felt a heaviness that was hard to disguise and, unusually, she was glad when the time came for the children to leave at the end of the school day.

Before she left for home there was a telephone call for Jenny. Christopher was at the other end of the line when she got to the school office. The sound was echoing and hollow and Jenny guessed he was using his mobile phone, perhaps from the foyer at the hospital. She was correct. "How is he?" she asked immediately, dreading the answer in case the news was bad.

"He's had an operation. The doctor had to take away part of his skull and remove a blood clot." There was a strange, stifled sound and then a long pause.

"Christopher, are you OK? Is Charlie alright?"

"Sorry," he continued after several seconds, "the clot was pushing his brain, but they say he will be alright, but I don't know."

"Is anyone with you, Christopher, to help you?" Jenny asked because she could hear the distress in his voice.

"Yes, well my Mum's on her way" he answered.

"Christopher, it sounds positive; believe that," Jenny said, and then after a pause she added "Thank you *so* much for letting me know."

"I have to go now. I don't want to be away from his bed"

"Of course. If there's anything you need or I can help with *please* do let me know straight away."

"Thanks, Mrs. Lucas. Bye" The phone went dead and Jenny sank onto the secretary's empty chair. She sat for several moments willing everything to be alright before heaving herself up. She called in to Sally to relay the latest news. Sheila and Mr. Lockwood the headteacher had left for the day. She knew she would also need to tell them tomorrow.

"I'd really like to visit after school tomorrow" Jenny said to Sally. "Do you think it would be alright to do that? Even if I can't see Charlie, I do feel I'd like to be there to offer some support"

"I'd like to come too" Sally said straight away. "I'm sure it will be okay and if we can't see Charlie at least his family will know we are there in case they want anything fetching".

With that thought, Jenny headed for home.

3 CHAPTER

That evening Jenny was home before Mike and as she made herself a much craved cup of tea she really hoped he would be home soon. She needed to share her day and the upset she felt. She had some lesson preparation to do but was finding it difficult to get motivated. She needed to share her troubled mind and new that if she started her work for the next day she wouldn't get very far with it. On the other hand, she thought with a sigh, perhaps it would help to settle her so she took her tea into the living room and went to get the set of books out of her bag and take them to the table. She had just arranged her things and opened the first book when she heard Mike's key in the front door.

"Hi", he said as he came into the room and gave her a small kiss on her cheek.

"Mike, I'm really glad you're here. I heard about the most awful thing today. One of my children has had an accident and is in hospital with a fractured skull."

"Nasty." he said frowning. "I've had a

crap day too."

"His name is Charlie and his Mum died three years ago so now he is on his own with just his Dad, and now this has happened"

Mike wandered away into the kitchen and shouted through "So how long will he be in hospital? One less for you to worry about"

"What?" said Jenny, "One less for me to worry about!" she said incredulously as she got up to follow him into the kitchen.

"Well, you're always saying your class is too big. One less, for a while!"

"Mike, I can't believe you just said that! He's got a fractured skull. They've taken some of his skull away to remove a big blood clot. It's awful. And I'm not *always* saying my class is too big"

"Sorry," Mike looked slightly sheepish, "but I've had a dreadful day. Colin in the office has completely messed up with one of our big clients. This guy has a massive account through us and he's fuming. I've had him shouting in my ear down the phone on and off all day. I think I've begun to pacify him now but I've got to talk to Colin tomorrow…….again. It's not the first time"

"I'm sorry you've had a rough time" Jenny said, disappointed. Perhaps she had timed her news badly. Was she being too involved with a pupil and his circumstances? She had a few moments of reflection while Mike made himself a cup of tea too. No! She really didn't think so. This wasn't some angry hiccup over money; this was life and death – literally. She had one more try. "Mike this child is seriously ill and his family circumstances are already dreadful." She wanted, no needed, some sympathy and understanding here. She had tried hard to be diplomatic recently. She understood that Mike's work was draining and he was finding it demanding and problematical but her work was important too.

She lifted her chin and said "I shall be a bit late tomorrow. I'm going to the hospital to visit."

"That's a bit above and beyond isn't it?" he replied.

"No, it's not. It's what any teacher would do in the circumstances." she answered somewhat shortly.

"Well, I know you get paid more than me but it doesn't mean you have to live and breathe the flaming job" he said moodily.

This was sounding suspiciously like an argument brewing and Jenny slid away from that whenever she could with Mike. She was far more confident in other aspects of her life. She could deal with difficult circumstances at work and could face up to colleagues or people in other aspects of her life far better than with her own husband. She had never even considered that as she earned more than him it would be any kind of relevant detail, never mind a problem. Their money went into one shared pot so why was he bringing it up now?

"I've already said I'll go with Sally tomorrow but I'll try not to be too late" she said in a conciliatory voice, although quietly she felt resentful of Mike's attitude.

I told Doug I'd be at the gym this evening by six-thirty, Mike announced. I could do with a good work-out and get this day out of my system," he added. I'll get something to eat after, so don't wait" and with that he poured the rest of his tea away and went to collect his bag from the wardrobe upstairs and left, banging the front door behind him.

□□□□□□□□

The next day, as soon as was decently possible after the children had left in the afternoon, Jenny gathered her bags together and went to Sally next door. "I'm off to the hospital" she said, "Do you still want to come?"

"Yes, absolutely," she replied. "I've just got to put this away, and I'll be there. I'll see you at the front door in two minutes."

"Are you sure you don't mind driving?" Sally asked. "I'm not keen unless I know exactly where I'm going and it's at the other hospital that Mum usually has her appointments" she smiled.

"No problem," said Jenny as they walked together towards her car. "I love driving. Just sling your stuff in here with mine," as she opened the boot.

As they pulled away Jenny asked after Sally's Mum. "She needs a lot more care these days. It's arthritis so she can do less and less. I get her up in the morning and get her sorted and into her wheel-chair. We've had some alterations done to the house so she can get about and we've got grab handles everywhere so she can use the bathroom, and so on. I do worry though because if she had a fall she has got a mobile phone and one of those BT panic button things but she would still have to wait and if she hurt herself ......," she tailed off "She's on her own a lot."

"It sounds really tricky for you trying to balance everything." Jenny was sympathetic.

"Everyone who has a job has their own balancing act" Sally said intuitively.

"That's certainly true to an extent and since we're on the subject you don't think this visit is over the top in terms of taking an interest in what happens to a pupil out of school do you?"

"Certainly not," said Sally, clearly. "Why do you ask that?"

"Well Mike and I sort of had words about it last night."

"There you are you see; the balancing act"

Reassured, Jenny smiled. "Well that's how I saw it and then I had a crisis of confidence"

"Christopher Mayhew is a wonder of modern man" Sally grinned. "He has such a lot to balance and he seems to managed amazingly well and here's us worrying about what we have to do"

"Absolutely", said Jenny, feeling relieved and now completely justified.

Having arrived at the hospital they went to the reception desk to ask where to go. They used the lift to the floor for the paediatric intensive care unit and pressed the buzzer at the security door. The nurse who came to answer their request went and returned after a minute to say that she had consulted with Charlie's father who had said it was fine for them to visit. They both used the hand wash at the door and entered. There were eight beds in the ward but only two were occupied and Jenny saw Charlie straight away. Christopher was at his bedside, looking extremely tired. When he saw them he came straight over. Charlie was sleeping and so he was able to have a quiet word. He explained that the doctors had removed part of his skull to remove the blood clot that had depressed his brain by about two centimetres. Jenny was horrified and it must have shown on her face.

"Things are much better now though," Christopher added quickly. "He's most likely going to be fine and they say he will probably move to a more normal ward very soon."

"Oh, that is such a relief" said Jenny, hoping that was true and they weren't just making comforting noises for Christopher's benefit.

Sally added "I can't imagine what you have been through but that is such good news"

"They're have fitted his bones back together with a titanium plate apparently" Christopher added, "He's sleeping at the moment but do go and see him. I'll wait over here because they don't want more than two people at a time, although it is quite quiet in here at the moment"

Jenny and Sally moved to Charlie's bedside. "Poor little mite" Sally whispered. Jenny touched his forehead and gently smoothed the little bit of hair she could see poking under the gauzy bandages that were wound around his head. There were a lot of tubes and pieces of equipment which all seemed quite scary when neither of them really knew what each machine was for, but the care and help he was receiving was clearly truly amazing. He stirred in his sleep and the corner of his mouth almost smiled. It reminded Jenny of the 'windy' smiles a tiny baby gives and her heart fluttered.

Sally left the bed-side to move across to where Christopher was watching them. She touched his arm and spoke warmly to him, reassuring and being reassured in the conversation.

Jenny stayed watching Charlie's little sleeping form, taking comfort from the news that Christopher had told them when they arrived.

They didn't stay long at the hospital. Jenny knew Christopher needed to be with his son but she was glad they had gone. As they said their goodbyes, Sally led the way towards the door beyond the nurses' station. Christopher gently caught Jenny's arm and said "Mrs. Lucas, thank you for your commitment and interest. It means a lot to both of us. My mother's at home now and she wanted me to express her gratitude too."

"Please, it's Jenny, and really I'm not

doing anything special at all. I can't help but be involved. It all sounds a little more positive today. Let me know what happens won't you?"

"I will. They'll do another scan in the morning and we'll know more then."

They said their goodbyes. "I'm really glad we came," said Jenny to Sally who clearly agreed with her.

□□□□□□□□

A few days later Jenny was home from school comparatively early when there was a knock at the door. When she answered it, Pat was standing wrapped in her coat and shivering slightly in the fresh autumn breeze. Hopefully, "Hi!" she said. "Is this a convenient time for a chinwag? I've just dropped the boys at the leisure centre with Doug. He's giving them a swimming session which is great for all of them."

"Anytime is a convenient time for a chinwag," laughed Jenny. "Come on in and I'll put the kettle on. We've got at least an hour before Mike gets home. It seems ages since we had a good natter."

"That's what I was thinking" said Pat. "I wanted to hear all about how the job is going. I saw your car home a bit earlier so thought I'd pop round. There's something I need to sound you out about too." She added mysteriously.

They went into the kitchen where Jenny made coffee for them both. Where Pat had a table in her kitchen, Jenny had a large chest freezer, which was ideal for monthly shopping when she was busy with work. Since Jenny and Mike had yet to start a family she and Pat went into the living room where they could sit comfortably on their own, unlike in Pat's house where there were generally the two boys playing. The small table clung to the wall so they each settled into the corner of a sofa. Placing her mug on the floor beside her, Pat shrugged out of her jacket. "It's getting quite chilly out there now. Summer is well and truly gone. You've been at this school for several weeks now. How's it going?"

Jenny told her about Charlie's accident. The last time she had spoken to Christopher Mayhew, however, the news had been much more positive. Charlie was now in the usual children's ward and Christopher was hoping he would be home before too long. His mother and he had been taking it in turns to stay at the hospital, although Christopher had told Jenny that she was having to leave for her own home again and Jenny thought she would probably have gone by now. All this she relayed to Pat. "This Christopher certainly has a job and a half" she said sympathetically. "I bet he's glad for any help he can get."

Jenny was reluctant to tell Pat of her disagreement with Mike over her visit to the hospital. It seemed disloyal, somehow, but in the end it was Pat who brought it up. "I gather from Doug that Mike was not too pleased about you visiting"

"Oh so they've been gossiping have they!" Jenny remarked feeling disgruntled that she had just felt guilty about whether to say anything to Pat and there was Mike telling Doug everything. Well so much for loyalty! With that she proceeded to tell about her crisis of confidence following the words she and Mike had and how Sally had assured her it was the right thing to do. Pat then added vociferously "I think it was absolutely appropriate. Okay it's not within the job description but it's compassionate and where would we be without a bit of generosity!"

Jenny was mildly surprised at the vehemence that Pat was showing on her behalf. She also thought how tired Pat looked. She had grey smudges beneath her eyes and even her short bobbed hair looked weary.

"Anyway, how is the rest of school going? Are you enjoying it there?"

"Most of the staff are really great; friendly, hardworking, supportive. There are a couple of teachers who seem to like to mutter in the corner" Jenny recounted "but they don't really affect me too much. The head teacher seems to know his stuff. He's quite high profile round the school which is good but he larks with the children too, so they like him. Mind you, he can have a good voice on him though, if they mess him around. He did an excellent assembly the other day. She launched into the detail enthusiastically. He asked for a volunteer to come and try something really tasty and to guess what it was. Well you can guarantee one of the Year 6 boys will always go for it. He blind-folded the lad. Then he produced two tins, one was dog food and one was chocolate custard. He took the dog food tin and gave the boy a spoonful of it."

At this point Pat's face was incredulous and somewhat horrified.

"You can imagine the reaction of the children," Jenny continued "but of course, really, the boy in fact, tasted the custard. The Head had swopped the labels over. He made lots of it, asking the boy if he was enjoying it and would he like some more and so on. Eventually he told the school what he had done and what was really happening, the whole point being that you can't tell from the outside what the inside is really like – just like people. Great! The whole school had been in a bit of uproar but he got them back on side in the blink of an eye. Such skill!"

"I imagine the children will remember that point for a long time" Pat said. She could see how animated Jenny was in recounting all this — somewhat different from the telling of the disagreement with Mike just now. "I can see you are really enjoying the work"

"Yes, I really am" said Jenny, "but what about you. Is there anything wrong, Pat? What did you want to sound me out about?" Jenny wondered if they were getting to the nitty-gritty of Pat's visit. It was unusual for her to pop around on a week day during term time.

Pat looked down, avoiding Jenny's concerned gaze.

"Pat? If you'd rather not say that's fine, of course, but it's not like you to be so down."

With that, tears came to Pat's eyes and she rummaged up her sleeve for a tissue "I think, well I'm sure really, that Doug's up to his old tricks again. He's doing a lot of long shifts and seems so distant and…., I don't know, shifty. The other day I came back from the shop round the corner and he rang off the phone really abruptly with the old chestnut of a wrong number. He *never* leaves his mobile lying around and he *always* used to. You remember I know these signs!"

Jenny had heard from Pat in the past

that Doug had an affair shortly after their first son was born. She had discussed it at length with Jenny and come to the conclusion that he just hadn't been ready to be a new dad. The reality had not been what he had been expecting and he realised, too late, that babies take up an inordinate amount of time. Pat had blamed herself too. She had said that perhaps she devoted too much time to the new child and not enough to Doug. Perhaps she had not paid enough attention to her looks and figure following the birth. Jenny privately wondered about this last point, however. She gathered that money had been tight; Pat had been incredibly tired with a baby who didn't sleep at night and cried much of the day. Anyway who was to say where the main problem lay. You could never fully judge accurately someone else's marriage from the outside looking in. She did understand some of the fall-out that Pat still suffered to this day, though. She was inclined to blame herself for every small thing that went wrong and she certainly ran circles around Doug to keep him happy.

Jenny had liked Doug but he was very vain. She privately thought it went with sporting types who thought 'body beautiful' was too high in their estimation. She felt she had seen it all too often on television where so many professional sports people liked the trophy wife too. Perhaps that was a generalisation though so she kept those thoughts to herself!

"Have you confronted him at all?"

"No not yet. What do you think I should do? If I don't say anything perhaps it will just blow over. Maybe I'm being over-imaginative because it happened before. I thought we were getting on so well. During the summer we went out for several days with the boys – down to the lake and so on – and we had some really great times." Then she blurted out "It's just constantly on my mind."

"I really don't understand it. Maybe some men need constant reassurance of their appeal, or maybe it's just the fun of the chase. You really need to know if he is seeing someone else though don't you." Jenny asked, "….or you'll drive yourself round the bend."

"I suppose so" Pat sighed.

"How are things in the bedroom department?" Jenny hazarded.

"Definitely not brilliant, but I put that down to him being so busy and tired."

Jenny looked quizzically at her friend. "Okay" said Pat "I'm being naïve and kidding myself aren't I? I'm making excuses for what is blatantly obvious to anyone else."

Just then Jenny's mobile rang. "I'll

ignore that" she said.

"No get it" Pat snuffled "I need to visit the loo anyway to do a quick repair job."

As she got up Jenny reached for her phone and saw that it was Diana calling. They were friends but Jenny hadn't spoken to her in what seemed like ages, although it was probably only about three or four weeks.

"Hello, Di."

"Hi! How are you, haven't seen you in ages," the voice echoed Jenny's thought. "How is the job going?" Jenny really didn't feel like a repeat conversation at this moment. Her mind was on Pat's news and she certainly wouldn't discuss that with Diana even if Pat had not been just down the hall-way.

"It's fine, I'm really enjoying it. It's very full on."

"I heard you were really busy"

"Oh? Who's been telling tales – out of school, so to speak?" Jenny laughed.

"I bumped into Mike at the gym and he was telling me."

"Right, he didn't say"

"Well it was only a quick conversation. I was really phoning to see if you could use some fabric I've got; in the classroom, or in the school somewhere. There are four lots each of three metres. It's like lining material. My Mum was having a clear-out so I took them."

"That's great" Jenny said. "I can certainly put them to good use I'm sure. Thanks"

"I'll put them in the car, drop them round soon then, or give them to Doug or Mike to deliver if I bump into either of them again."

"I didn't know you had become a keen keep-fitter" Jenny said.

"Well, you know......" answered Diana ambiguously.

Just then Pat came back into the room so Jenny finished her call and thought little more about it, in her concern.

"There I'm all mopped up and back on track" Pat said as she came through the door. Jenny smiled at her and thinking to normalise the moment she said "That was Diana on the phone. She's got some fabric I can use in school. Her Mum gave it to her and she thought of me which is really kind of her. She can be thoughtful like that."

"Mmm" said Pat somewhat vaguely.

"Do you want another coffee?"

"No, I better be going. They'll all be home soon."

"Are the boys okay?" asked Jenny.

"They know nothing and I'm fairly sure they haven't picked up any vibes. They both seem normal enough."

As Pat put on her coat, Jenny said "Let me know what happens won't you? I hate to think of you so unhappy"

Just then the front door opened and Mike arrived home from work.

"Hello" he said.

"Hello and goodbye" replied Pat with her head down. "Just off, see you both soon" and Jenny saw her to the front door, giving her arm a friendly squeeze as she left. Pat turned and gave a half smile which didn't quite reach her eyes.

"She seemed eager to be gone" Mike observed.

"Did you know she and Doug were having problems?" Jenny asked.

After a hesitation he answered "Yes, I did"

"Why didn't you say?"

"He asked me not to."

"Is he seeing someone else?"

"He didn't want me to say because he thought you would tell Pat."

"Well she has a good idea already. Who is it?"

"It's some-one who works at the pool side. I don't really know." he said abstractedly.

I bet you know a lot more than you're telling me thought Jenny. "I can't bear to see such a good friend so upset" she said. "How long has it been going on?"

"Look I really don't know much about it. A few weeks, I suppose."

"Oh hell's bell's" sighed Jenny, feeling absolutely dreadful for her friend.

It seemed that she'd had nothing but sad, bad news recently.

4 CHAPTER

The week-end was a mix of the mundane and the ordinary. The normal household work Jenny did on Saturday while Mike was at the gym again and the school lesson planning she had, she did on Sunday morning, as usual. Mike was somewhat surly most of the weekend. Jenny tried hard to be cheerful and chatty but began to wonder if she was making the atmosphere worse so on Sunday afternoon she sat and read quietly and generally did her own thing. This was something she so rarely did she almost felt guilty sitting around. Mike went out into the garden and did some sort of tidying up, vaguely hoeing around the plants and sorting out the shed. The he came indoors and fixed the wobbly handle on the kitchen drawer. 'Well, at least a row was getting all those little outstanding jobs!' she thought wryly. During the evening they skirted around each other politely.

By Monday morning Jenny was feeling distinctly mutinous. She didn't really know what she should do for the best to create a better mood at home, and not really sure whether she had done anything amiss to provoke this atmosphere anyway. The more she considered it the more certain she was that she did nothing wrong in going to the hospital to visit Charlie and both Sally and especially Pat had supported that opinion, erasing any doubts she may have had. Mike's words regarding her earnings had upset her more than she realised at the time and as the day wore on she began to feel increasingly rebellious. By the end of the day she had unilaterally decided she would visit the hospital again. She genuinely wondered how Charlie was and felt certain that Christopher Mayhew deserved a little support.

When the school day ended and she had made a good start on her preparations for the next day's work, she packed up her things and left for the hospital. Sally had an after-school club so on this occasion she was going on her own.

During the drive she became more and more positive that she was doing the right thing until, with a thump on the steering wheel, she announced aloud to the fresh air "Stuff it! Why ever not?"

Arriving at the hospital she again made enquiries at the desk for the ward than Charlie was now in. Having ascertained the information she needed she headed for the stairs rather than the lift. The exercise would help to calm her racing mind. She strode along the corridor, passing several doors to sluice rooms, wards and offices on one side whilst large windows on the other looked over a rather sad internal courtyard where pebble beds and large yucca plants looked somewhat neglected. The anonymities of a large hospital were always a mystery. There was a kind of hush but muted noises behind doors made her wonder what happiness or pain was going on. She was passing the cafeteria when, through the long thin windows, she spotted Christopher sitting with a coffee cup in front of him. It was quiet at this time of day and he looked slightly forlorn sitting on his own there in the large echoing room. She pushed the door but he didn't even turn his head to see who was entering, so deep in thought did he appear.

As she went across to his table he saw her approaching and his expression became much more animated as he rose to greet her. He had only just started his coffee. "Let me get you one".

"No, no," she replied "I'll go." She headed to the counter where she bought herself a welcome cup of tea and returned to join Christopher. She sat and asked "How is Charlie? It seems like good news that he is in the regular children's ward."

"We're waiting to see Mr. Power when he does his rounds tomorrow morning and I'm hoping he'll say Charlie can come home"

"That's such good news. I wasn't sure if I'd be able to visit at this time of day or where you'd both be but thought I'd risk it," she said.

"I shall be very glad to be home, I have to say. Hospital food is quite good and it means I have been able to spend most of my time on the ward, but it has been quite hard, all this," he frowned as he spoke.

"It must have been really tough" said Jenny. "Never mind all the worry."

"I shall have to get into the habit of cooking again and doing cleaning things. The house is a bit of a tip to be honest. It's quite hard trying to keep Charlie entertained with things that he can do without being too boisterous. It' going to be a test, when I get him home, to do the household things as well." He shrugged smiled to himself.

"Life must be quite tricky at the best of times without all this" Jenny acknowledged. "Has your Mum gone home or is she still around?"

"She had to go. When she realised Charlie was off the danger list, I could tell she thought she needed to go so I told her we'd be fine. She has a part-time job at the Sue Ryder charity shop. It's voluntary but other people have to do her sessions if she's not there. Dad is quite capable on his own, sorting himself out at home after work, but I told her to go. They're both so great and help out such a lot, but we'll okay, I'm sure. It's been a steep learning curve, being on my own and doing everything, but generally we seem to muddle through."

"Better than that, from my short view." Jenny said vigorously.

"I need to get back to doing some work somehow too. It's been such a relief to be able to work from home, but I normally do that when Charlie's at school. The money hasn't been making itself the last couple of weeks!" Christopher smiled to himself again in his shy way, but the smile was hardly expansive.

This guy certainly has a bowl full of problems Jenny thought to herself.

"Enough about me." Christopher said hastily and slightly embarrassed for telling so much of him-self. "You are really busy too and I imagine you came to see Charlie. I do appreciate you coming, a lot. He'll be really excited to see you. I know it's not been that long but I do get a lot of 'Mrs. Lucas said...' when he's not in school"

Jenny gently acknowledged that this was the way of many young children and they both rose to go and visit the little boy.

Christopher rang the buzzer and when a nurse pushed the ward door he allowed Jenny to precede him through it. Having both stopped to use the obligatory hand rinse from the dispenser just inside the door, Christopher then led the way to Charlie's bed-side. The room was quite large with several beds. The walls were brightly painted with large murals of cartoon characters. Even the floor had a large picture in the middle. There were some small child sized tables with different coloured tops and chairs to match. Several of the beds had soft toys on them. It did still have a faint hospital smell, however. That seemed in inevitable.

Charlie's little face beamed the biggest smile as she approached. How different this visit from the last! He was kneeling up with a tray of cars on the bed in front of him. His head was still wrapped in a gauzy bandage which now had stickers all around it. Jenny handed him the little parcel she had brought and he eagerly tore the paper off. It was only a small box of lego to make a transformer. She thought it would make one of the ugliest things she had seen but she knew they were all the rage with the boys in her class. Christopher was clearly moved to see his little son so happy and revitalised.

Jenny spent over half an hour playing with Charlie and chatting easily with Christopher. When she glanced at her watch she was surprised at how the interval has rushed by. That thing called time!

"I better go," she said. "I still have some school work to do at home before tomorrow, and my husband will think I've disappeared." If he notices I'm not there, she thought to herself.

"I'll walk to the door with you. What do you say, Charlie?"

"Bye-bye. I want to come back to school, tomorrow."

"Well, maybe not tomorrow, but soon and perhaps I'll be able to come and see you again," Jenny said

"Thank you for my present." The boy added, whilst not really looking up from playing with it.

"You chose the right thing there" said Christopher, and then to Charlie "I'll be back in a minute, lad, and then we'll see if we can put that together shall we?"

At the door Jenny had what she thought was a brain-wave to help him, but she wasn't sure if Christopher would accept.

Hesitantly she suggested, "I'd really like to cook some freezer meals for the two of you. It wouldn't be any extra work because I'd be doing food for Mike and me. I could just do a bit extra. It might just help to get you through the next few days until you get back into some sort of routine."

As anticipated Christopher was full of concern about the idea. "I really couldn't put you out like that."

"Well as, I say, it wouldn't be any extra work. I really wouldn't offer if it was going to be a big trouble. I'd just like to help. What is this life if we can't do a small service for someone when it might be needed?" She smiled diffidently. I understand if you'd rather I didn't. It was just an idea."

"If you really are sure, it would be a massive help. I'd be able to give so much more attention to Charlie. Really, you must only do meals for a day or two though, just so we get home and I get sorted out."

"That's absolutely fine," Jenny reassured him "I'll drop them round the day after tomorrow. You should definitely be home then by the sounds of it. If there's anything different to that, just leave me a message at school. Will you be OK for tomorrow if you go home then?"

"I'm sure I can find sausage, chips and beans or something. Thank you again, *so* much."

"I'll see you then. Bye." Jenny left,

feeling she was doing something useful that truly would not take her much extra time. As she walked down the corridor she turned to see Christopher Mayhew watching her go. She smiled and lifted her hand in a small wave back.

⬜⬜⬜⬜⬜⬜⬜⬜

On the way home, Jenny flashed into the local big supermarket. What on earth did people do before twenty-four hour shopping? It was as busy as ever. She rushed around, dodging the home shopper trolleys and those re-stacking shelves, buying things that she could use. She tried to think of nourishing things and that she thought a little boy would eat. She bought chicken to make nuggets, and fish to make fingers and minced beef for some meatballs. She added several other ingredients: eggs, bread for crumbs and semolina to make a coating and having decided she had enough to supplement what she could find at home, she queued up at the check-out and waited restlessly, aware that time was creeping onwards quickly and the queue in front seemed to be creeping only slowly. When she finally got to the checkout the till girl was bright and breezy and Jenny responded in like manner, although a moment before she had been feeling tense and rushed. She decided the lass must really enjoy her job too and was silently grateful to her. She hurried home and although she was later than usual, she wasn't really thinking about that anymore. Rather, her mind was sprinting around what she would make first and fitting it in with making tea for Mike and her and the other tasks she needed to complete this evening. She had become remarkably adept at multi-tasking since leaving college, starting a job and being married

When she arrived at home she hauled her school bags and shopping into the house, feeling mildly surprised that she had still beaten Mike home.

She got straight on with her voluntary task, feeling enervated to be doing something useful. She had done the basic preparation for the nuggets and fish fingers by the time the front door opened and Mike arrived home.

"I'm in the kitchen" she called. "You've had a long day. Do you fancy a glass of wine?"

"I'll get one in a bit, I just need to shower first, I think. You look busy. What are you doing?" he frowned as he asked.

"I'm making a few freezer meals" Jenny answered ambiguously. She suddenly wondered what Mike's reaction was going to be.

Shan't be long and then I'll get those drinks," he shouted from the bathroom.

As he returned, having showered and

changed, Jenny was just frying up the chicken nuggets. "That's a lot for two," Mike observed.

"I'm doing a few extra for Christopher Mayhew and Charlie." Jenny internally winced. "I went to the hospital to see how Charlie was getting on and Christopher said he was hoping they would be able to go home tomorrow."

"So why are you cooking for them then?" asked Mike quietly.

"Look, Mike," he started defensively, "he's on his own trying to hold down a job, care for a sick little boy all on his own because his wife *died*. It's just a small neighbourly service."

"That's all is it and who's paying for all this extra food; you on your mighty big salary, or me on my lowly one?"

Oh, Lord here we go, thought Jenny, but she was determined to put her point of view calmly and openly this time. "Mine, if you like," she said but I'm sure he'll pay me back. Anyway, as I said it's just a neighbourly thing to do."

"And what else are you doing for him, to be neighbourly" he asked sarcastically.

"What's that supposed to mean?" she asked.

"Well, since he's on his own maybe there's something else he'd like you to do for him, or with him!"

"Mike!" Jenny was horrified. "There's nothing going on, nor would I like there to be. How can you doubt me in that way or doubt that you are the one on my mind and in my heart. Everything I do is with awareness of you." She turned off the gas under the pan and immediately went to him and tried to put her arms around him. He turned from her. "Look at me," she said. "Believe me when I say it's you I love and I have no desire to be with anyone else." She felt this was a little like emotional blackmail, on his part. All she was doing was cooking a bit of food. Why was he making this an issue and such a big deal?

"OK, fair enough, sorry," Mike conceded, "but I still don't see why you are doing this. He's just a kid in your class, for goodness sake!"

"Well I've decided to help out, just for this week, so that's how it is. It doesn't need to affect you. Our tea is here too" she said as she turned and switched the gas back on. "It'll be ready in ten minutes."

"I don't think I'm hungry at the moment" he said huffily.

"Well what about that glass of wine?"

Jenny asked trying to mend fences, again.

"I don't think so, not if I'm driving."

"What do you mean if you're driving? Where are you going?" she asked puzzled. "You didn't say you were out."

"Well I don't think I need to ask," said Mike argumentatively. "I've only just decided, anyway. I think I'll go to the gym since you're so busy."

"But I've got your tea ready here, too" said Jenny.

"I'll have it later, or you can add it to Christopher Mayhew's, that seems appropriate" he added acerbically.

"Oh for goodness sake," Jenny raised her voice now. She felt like saying 'grow up, you're not the only one who needs attention' but wisely she kept that thought to her-self.

With that she turned to carry on with her task and as she did so Mike left the room. Five minutes later, she heard the front door slam.

"Damn it!" Jenny exploded to thin air.

□□□□□□□□

Later in the evening, since there was still no sign of Mike, Jenny decided to telephone Pat. The boys would be in bed and

70

she thought Doug would probably be out, given the current circumstances so, hopefully, there would be the chance for a good talk and some advice to help her decide if she was being too stubborn or not. They had spoken since Pat's latest news on the telephone and Jenny knew that Pat was coping in her own way. She'd had practice previously and Jenny knew she was trying to hold it all together for the children; a cliché perhaps, but usually clichés were based in fact. Pat still hadn't tackled Doug to find out for definite if he was seeing someone else. It was almost as if to hide her head in the sand was less hurtful than knowing the worst.

The phone rang several times and Jenny was beginning to wonder if she had tried at a bad time when a breathless Pat finally picked up. "Hello." She puffed into the hand-set.

"Hi, Pat, it's Jenny. Have I called at a bad time?"

"No, no not at all. I was just upstairs tucking in the boys, but they're all snug now. I love them lots but this is the best moment of the day, when they are tucked up and I can put my feet up, especially at the moment."

Without any further pre-amble, Jenny said, "I think I need some advice." Then, feeling she had been a bit heartless, she added "...if it's convenient, or I can call another time. I'm sure you've earned some peace and quiet."

"It's fine, always ready for a chat. What's up? You sound a bit tense!"

"Mike and I have had a good few words and he's stormed out. It's all because I've cooked a few freezer meals for Christopher Mayhew and Charlie because I think Charlie's coming out of hospital tomorrow." Jenny explained how sorry she felt for Christopher and his situation and that she was only trying to be helpful. "Mike completely flipped and suggested I was having some kind of fling, for goodness sake! I would never do that. I made promises when we got married and they mean a lot to me. On top of that he's made comments again about the fact that I earn a bit more than him. That's certainly never mattered to me and I didn't think it was important to him either. We just have a shared account."

"When did all that side of things seem to start?" asked Pat.

"Definitely when I started this job" answered Jenny, "but he knew the salary before I got it and he was all in favour of the move. It's no more than I was getting before. I've always earned a little more than him."

"Sound like he's feeling unhappy for some

reason," Pat said. "Any ideas why?"

"The only thing I can think of is that he's very unhappy at work at the moment. That smacks of childish jealousy to me!" Jenny said crossly.

"Maybe, but perhaps he's feeling a bit insecure," Pat added intuitively.

"What's he got to feel insecure about?"

"Perhaps he feels he's not providing enough for you, not just money, but happiness too, and what with this thing with Christopher, as well, maybe he's lacking a bit of confidence."

"You could be right," said Jenny feeling slightly less irritable and more mollified.

"Try giving him a bit more time."

"I do try to listen to his troubles, but I suppose I have been a bit wrapped up in work recently. It's all so new and good fun."

"That sounds part of the trouble to me," Pat observed. "It's all going so well for you, he probably is a bit jealous, that's only human nature, no matter how you might like to think he should be happy with you. Then this thing with Christopher Mayhew is just adding to his insecurity"

"You are always so wise, Pat"

"Not in my own life, though." She said, unhappily. "I'm as sure as I can be that Doug's at it again."

"You still haven't tackled him, then!"

"No, I'm hoping he'll get over it. It's probably me not doing enough to please. I really think he loves us in his own way."

Jenny thought that Pat was doing herself down, but then how was she to know. It really was impossible to know exactly what was going on inside someone else's marriage. It seemed you can have an idea but really only the two people involved knew the whole truth. Having thought that, she then wondered if each person really knew the whole of the other person actually involved either. Surely it wasn't right for Pat to be in this situation. It was all so complicated, especially when there were children and a whole raft of other responsibilities.

"Relationships!" said Jenny. "Well, thanks for listening, Pat, and if you need a friendly ear at *any* time, come round or call, won't you?"

"I will, I'm fine, but thanks anyway. Speak soon. Let me know how it goes."

With that Jenny ended the call and went to have a quick shower. After, wrapped in her dressing gown, she was feeling peckish but couldn't decide whether to eat now or hope that Mike came home soon and she could make it up to him. She'd had time to think things through, having listened to Pat's advice.

Very soon after, he returned. She hastened to meet him in the hall way and flung her arms around him. Taken a little by surprise, Mike dropped his bag and his arms, in turn encircled, Jenny's waist and he kissed her tenderly and long.

"I hate it if we argue," she whispered.

"Me, too" he responded, taking her hand and leading her to the foot of the stairs.

All thought of food gone, she followed him up whilst he held her hand behind him as they went. Pushing the bedroom door open they fell onto the bed and Mike kissed her more forcefully, pulling open her dressing gown and enclosing her breast with his warm hand. Jenny responded readily, cradling his head in her hand and running her other hand down his cheek, pulling him to her. They gained mutual comfort from their love-making, each giving and taking pleasure. This time there was no giggling or laughing, no teasing, no joking. There was an intensity born from their earlier disagreement and a need to confirm their relationship. He came within her with a passion that matched her own certainty that she loved him and him alone. After, she told him again that she loved him and he responded in kind. For now, at least, all was well again.

5 CHAPTER

A couple of days later all was still well between Jenny and Mike. Trust was restored and things were as normal. Whilst they were grabbing a breakfast cup of tea together and finishing toast, Jenny hesitated but eventually said "Mike, the food I made for Christopher Mayhew….."

"I know," he responded, "you need to take it to him."

"Is that OK? I'm not staying or going in or anything, just delivering."
"Yes, it's fine. I know I was an arse! I trust you, Jenny. I know you wouldn't do anything behind my back," he smiled self-consciously.

"In fact, I shall ask Sally if she wants to come too. She came to the hospital, that first time. I think she more than likes him, you know!"

"If you want to, but don't worry about it anymore." Mike responded equitably.

"I'll see you later then," said Jenny giving him a quick kiss. She quickly loaded her freezer meals into a bag, planning to transfer them into the school freezer to wait until the end of the day. She then gathered her school bags ready to leave the house.

"See you tonight. Love you!" she called from the door but as there was no response she guessed Mike was re-reading something in the paper he had beside his place at the worktop. She shrugged and smiling she pulled the door shut thinking of the single-mindedness of men, sometimes, and how different from women they were – thankfully. It must come from the hunter /gatherer era when they needed to concentrate solely on one thing.

Driving to school Jenny contemplated her situation. She was still slightly uneasy about Mike's recent reactions when she thought hard about it but she had to be honest with herself and thought that really everything seemed to be back to normal. Perhaps she had been too wrapped up in her own work and the needs of others. After all, they loved each other, had shared so much together and were good friends as well as lovers.

The school day was without particular note – pleasant but just a regular day. Jenny had spoken to Sally at lunchtime and she was really keen to accompany her to see Christopher and Charlie Mayhew and to deliver the meals. She had the feeling Sally had been a little put out over the reason for the visit. Jenny had the distinct thought that her colleague fancied Christopher and maybe wished she had thought of something practical to do to help out, as Jenny had. It was just the way it had happened though. There was certainly no thought of competition in Jenny's offer. It had been a natural response to someone else's need. In the car, travelling to the house after work, her suspicions were confirmed when Sally said as much. The journey took longer than expected because at well gone five o'clock the traffic was starting to build up. The children could take a footbridge to school but although it wasn't far, Jenny had to turn right across quite a busy road and then take a few turns into the local estate. This gave them the opportunity to exchange a few words.

"I would like to help Christopher Mayhew more," Sally said wistfully. "I admire him and what he does for Charlie" said Sally. "From my experience, I know how difficult and lonely it can be, caring for someone when you are on your own."

"He does a good job." Jenny responded. "Charlie is a delightful little boy. He's always chatty and confident without being overly so. I hope this incident won't inhibit him in any way."

As they arrived in the right road Sally kept an eye on the house numbers as Jenny slowly drove. This was the first time either of them had been down this way. It was a cul-de-sac and not very long so they quite quickly found where they needed to be. Jenny retrieved her cool bag of food from the boot and Sally opened the gate and preceded her up the path. The front garden was small. There were no flowers but the small patch of grass was cut and the edges trimmed neatly. Sally knocked and when Christopher came to the door Jenny planned to hand over her bag on the step, enquire after Charlie's health and beat a retreat. That was not quite to be, however.

The door opened and Christopher smiled when he saw who it was. Jenny moved to hold her bag forwards and opened her mouth to make a greeting but Sally almost leaped forwards to explain why they were there.

"Oh, yes, Mrs. Lucas, Jenny," he added catching her eye "said she would be bringing me a food parcel," he grinned. "Come in."

"Thank you" said Sally, before Jenny could say a word.

"I really can't stay long," Jenny added. "Is Charlie up and about?"

"He certainly is," Christopher stated. "It's hard keeping him calm enough. He would love to go out to play, but I think that's a bridge too far at the moment. I'm going to have to be careful not to mollycoddle him, though, I think."

They were shown into a living room which showed signs of being well lived in! "I'm really sorry we're not tidier," said Christopher self-consciously.

"I'm sure you have more important things to do" Jenny said "and anyway it's much better to see this than a sterile unfriendly place."

"I'll call Charlie. He's up in his room playing with his cars. Please, sit down," he said, hastily removing a computer magazine from one chair and sliding a collection of lego further along the sofa. Jenny recognised the transformer model she had given Charlie in the hospital and was gratified to know that he had been playing with it. Just as they sat down, the door flew open and Charlie burst into the room.

Both Jenny and Sally were shocked to see him. He had no bandages on now and his hair to one side had been shaved off. His scars were still quite livid, but he was clearly his normal exuberant self. Both the teachers said hello trying hard not to let their feelings show and Jenny slid down off the sofa to sit on the floor, taking pieces of the ugly lego figure in her hand. "I see you've been making him. Will you show me how he 'transforms'?" Charlie came and sat down on the floor next to her and Jenny was quite touched when he snuggled in against her to complete the figure. While Charlie happily demonstrated his skill to Jenny, Sally asked Christopher. "What is the next step for Charlie?"

"He has to go to see the doctors as an out-patient next week, Miss Tate," explained Christopher "but they seem very pleased so far."

Jenny glanced at Sally just to see her slanting her gaze sideways up to where Christopher was standing. "Please, call me Sally" she said.

Christopher cleared his throat and there was a pause. Then he spoke again. "We had the nurse calling round this morning and they've given me a leaflet of information – things to look out for and things to tell other people, like school."

"When do you think he might be able to come back?" Sally asked.

"I think I need to come and talk to Mr. Lockhart about it. What do you think Jenny? He'll be in your care and I don't want to be unfair to you by expecting too much."

"I think if you can come into school and the three of us discuss the things that he will be able to do or not do and we can take it from there."

Charlie continued to play and the conversation appeared to pass him by. "At the hospital they indicated that he may be able to come back soon but perhaps part-time. Do you think that might be an option, Jenny?"

"I don't see why not. Ring the office when you're ready and we'll fix up a meeting," she responded.

"I want to come back to school," Charlie joined in. So much for children not being aware, thought Jenny. You had to be so careful what was said in front of them, no matter how young.

"I'm sure it won't be too long," Jenny addressed him "but you want to be able to do things in school without getting too tired."

She didn't want to give him the idea that he needed to be overly careful although he did, a bit, nor did she want him to think everyone would be watching him closely, although she was sure they would!

"Is there anything you need?" asked Sally of Christopher, hopefully.

"No, we're fine now," Christopher replied, smiling at her, and then he turned to Jenny and added "Thank you so much for what you have done. That is a tremendous help."

"It was really no problem," Jenny

answered. She certainly did not add that it had caused ructions at home with Mike, or that she had been really disappointed with that reaction. "I'm afraid I shall need to be going in a minute." Thinking of her previous problems made Jenny suddenly aware of time passing quickly. She stood to gather her bag and move towards the door.

"I haven't even offered you a tea or coffee when you have been so thoughtful and helpful." Christopher said sounding somewhat mortified.

"Please, don't even think of it, but I really must be off." She turned and spoke to Charlie whose little round face was looking up at her. "We'll see you soon, won't we?" He silently nodded, looking tired now, and probably ready for his tea, bath and bed.

"Ring school when you're ready" Jenny repeated as she opened the front door, "and see you soon."

As they followed the short front path both she and Sally waved to Charlie who was at the window.

Jenny dropped Sally off at the school so that she could collect her own car and then she hurried home, aware that Mike was probably there before her.

As she pulled up at the kerb outside the house she could see Mike just going in through the front door.

"Hello," she called out as she went in too. "How are you? How was your day?"

"Hi, not bad." Mike answered as he came and gave her a kiss on her cheek. "Mind you I thought the rollicking I had to give Colin the other week would have woken him up a bit but I'm still fielding problems he's made. I'm going to set him targets and start some disciplinary stuff if he can't sort himself out." He moved towards the stairs on his way to get changed out of his work suit. "I'm really getting fed up with him." With that he took the stairs two at a time.

Jenny, having dumped her bags in the corner of the living room, went into the kitchen to start tea. Oh well, she thought, no questions was better than the third degree regarding her activities of the day. Maybe she would get the chance to share her day later!

□□□□□□□□□

It was Saturday morning, later that week. Since Mike was out at his usual gym session, Jenny had done some basic housework and put the washing on so she decided to walk to the paper shop. She wanted, no needed she decided, a bar of chocolate and she would see if they had the Times Educational Supplement. She read it from time to time to keep up with the constant changes and innovations in her work. They had it in the staffroom but as soon as anyone opened it everyone else immediately thought they were job-hunting and she wanted to avoid that kind of rumour since nothing could be further from the truth. She hadn't been there long and anyway she was really enjoying being at Holly Road School. It was a chilly but bright late autumn day so she wrapped up and left the house. It was the sort of day that was uplifting. Although the wind was blowing the sun was low and bright and the sky was blue. Bundles of leaves had collected in odd corners where they had been swirled around but they were dry and crisp. As she walked briskly Jenny hummed the tune to the last song she had heard on the radio as she turned it off before leaving the house. She didn't know the words but the title of Christine Aguilera's 'Keeps Gettin' Better' seemed appropriate and optimistic and as she hummed she gave the occasional hop over the piles of leaves.

It wasn't far to the little parade of shops. She wondered how some of them managed to keep going. The little hardware shop was amazing in the varied stock that it kept. It had everything from buckets and disinfectant to hammers and boxes of nails, washers and screws. It was a really old-fashioned family run business and Mr. Goble, who always wore his well-worn, long, green apron, and his son were always friendly and helpful. It was useful to have a chemist and a little bakers shop too, but an aquarium shop? Jenny didn't think that would last long. However it was to the newsagents-cum-post office that she headed now.

It was quite busy and having found her paper she went to browse the bars and packets of sweets. She could smell the chocolate and her mouth watered. She couldn't decide whether to choose a bar with a crunch or one that she could sink her teeth into and push around her mouth with her tongue. She had been really tired by the end of the week and so perhaps that was the cause of her current craving. She selected something chewy and tasty and went to pay. There was quite a queue and who else should be there, just ahead of her, but Pat. Jenny could see instantly that her friend was not well. She looked pale and oh so tired. "Hello, Pat. I just nipped round for a pick-me-up" said Jenny waving her chocolate.

"I think I need something like that, only times it by ten" smiled Pat, always the optimist. 'Times it by a thousand more like,' Jenny thought.

"I'll just pay for this and see you outside, if you've time," she said. "We could walk back together." As she hurried outside, Pat was waiting for her. "Where are the boys?" Jenny asked.

"They are away at Mum's for the whole

weekend. She came to collect them. She said she wanted to take them to the woods near her for the day because they are having some kind of event there. I didn't argue. They'll all have a great time. Apparently there're all kinds of activities going on and some 'making' thing. Mum's fantastic like that, she'll get stuck right in with them. She just senses when I could do with a break and I know she enjoys it too. It helps to keep her active now that she's on her own since Dad died."

"I have to say, you look like you could do with the break," Jenny remarked. "Is there anything I can do?"

"No, no. It's just the on-going saga of Doug and me. I'm not sure I can take much more though. I think the boys are taking note of me looking like death warmed up and that's not helping the situation with Doug, of course, either. A bit of a vicious circle really!" She shrugged deprecatingly and sighed.

"Maybe you both need a little time apart for thinking," Jenny said tentatively. Could or would he consider that?"

"I suppose he could go to his Mum's or he's got a good friend at work he might ask. Huh, a male friend that is! I think he loves us in his way but at the moment I feel so useless. I just keep thinking if he loves us why does he persist when he *must* know it's hurting us so much. How does he rationalise it all? I'm feeling it must be partly my fault as well, of course, otherwise why would he do it? I feel a total failure, you know. I can't even keep my husband contented. I'm clearly just not enough. After the last time I told myself we were both too young to have settled. He needed to sow some oats, as they say. I made excuses, I suppose, but perhaps he wishes now he had never got married to me. I just don't satisfy him."

"He must realise you know about his affair, surely, although maybe, Pat, he thinks you don't and so he'll carry on until you confront him. Maybe he's kidding himself that no-one is harmed if it's all covert still and he can persuade himself that you don't know. I don't pretend to understand the deep psychology of it. Maybe he's reassuring himself that he can still do it, be attractive to the opposite sex. Perhaps it's the fun of the chase. I really don't know but I do think you need to talk." offered Jenny.

"I just keep thinking he'll get over it and we can go back to how we were. I can't make him want me. He has to do that for himself."

Jenny thought, it'll never go back to how you were, but she kept that thought to herself for the time being. The last thing

Pat needed was defeatist chatter. "Yes, but if he's kidding himself that he's not hurting you he has no reason to leave her alone! I really think you need to talk, or one of you, probably you, is going to be ill, and then what will the boys do?"

"You're right, Jenny. I need to say all this to Doug, don't I?"

By this time they had arrived at Jenny's house. "Do you want to come in for a cuppa?" she asked.

"I think I'll get home. Strike while it's hot and all that." Pat replied. "Since the boys are away perhaps this is the day to have that discussion with Doug."

"If there's anything I can do, just call me," said Jenny "and let me know how you get on."

"I certainly will, and thanks."

Pat hurried on down the road and Jenny wondered if she would follow through with her new resolve. She was thinking you either had to be a very special kind of person to put up with that or maybe just too timid to face up to it and ditch him. Jenny didn't have children though, and perhaps that made a difference.

As she put her key in the front door she thought how lucky she was not to be in the position in which Pat had found herself.

Mike was still not home from his Saturday morning session at the gym although it was 12.30 and she was expecting that he would be. Perhaps, she thought, he had gone on to do the shopping at the supermarket. Sometimes he did do that which was great. She didn't enjoy that task at all. Trying to decide what to buy for dinner on Tuesday or Wednesday when it was a Saturday morning was definitely not in her mental vocabulary! She could guarantee that she would meet parents and children from school too. Most were fine and just gave her a friendly greeting, but there was always the one who made some smart remark about the bottle of wine she might have in her trolley or the fattening treat she had popped in.

However, when Mike came in she discovered what he had been doing and it wasn't the shopping. He was in a fine and lively mood and straight away put the kettle on for a coffee.

"How was the gym session?" she asked.

"Fine" he answered. "I ran 5k on the treadmill and cycled 20k on the bike, so I went for a quick pint in the hotel bar. Diana was there." He said casually. "She was waiting for Greg to come from work but he was late."

"How was she? I haven't seen her for ages" said Jenny.

"She was OK. She's had her hair cut differently, looked quite smart"

"Since when did you notice peoples' changes in fashion?" Jenny teased, but Mike ignored her comment and finished making the coffee, whistling quietly to himself as he did so.

"We'll have to do the shopping this afternoon," said Jenny. "Not very exciting, I know, but needs must."

"Yes, I suppose so. Diana invited us to go for dinner sometime soon. We didn't fix any date but I said you would get in touch and fix it up."

"That'll be something to look forward to." Jenny exclaimed happily. "She said she'd speak to Pat too," he added.

"I'm not sure what's happening there. I bumped into her at the paper shop this morning and she really didn't look good. Things between her and Doug seem to be going from bad to worse. I suppose you know all about that though." Jenny remarked.

"Well, we'll see then," Mike avoided any more conversation on that point.

"I don't know how I would cope if you were to cheat on me," Jenny said wistfully. "You'd tell me though wouldn't you, rather than be deceitful?"

"Have an affair? Of course I wouldn't do that!" Mike laughed loudly. "Where did that come from? I expect us to grow old together."

6 CHAPTER

The weekend had been lazy and non-eventful but relaxed and enjoyable too. Another Monday morning came all too soon. The morning's teaching went well, with many of the children having good sessions in maths and then English It was lunch-time before Jenny knew it. Time certainly passed quickly here. It was both satisfying and enjoyable. She went, with her lunch box and feeling buoyant, to the staff room at quarter to one, having prepared her classroom for the afternoon and a whole half an hour ahead of her to eat her pack-up.

Only Joan and Lesley were there before her. This was not unusual. The two other teachers were having a whispered conversation when she entered which appeared to stop abruptly. She made herself a drink of hot black-currant juice rather than tea and settled on a seat by the window to eat her lunch. Smiling, she asked if they had a good morning, just to make conversation really and she got a brief nod and a grunt that passed for assent. Oh well, she thought, I've made an effort. Joan turned away from her slightly to ask Lesley a question and Jenny felt decidedly cut out of the conversation, so she ate her lunch in silence until the door opened and several others came in.

"Well, you lot are quiet today," announced deputy headteacher Sheila expansively as she made herself a cup of tea. Sally, who had arrived at the same time, smiled and came and sat next to Jenny.

Jenny stood up to throw her lunch rubbish in the bin. As she did so her skirt caught on her mug sending it flying across the carpet sending the dregs everywhere. "Oh shoot!" she exploded, rushing to the sink for some paper towel and a cloth.

"That'll be there for posterity," said Joan

"One to remember you by" added Lesley rather meanly as Jenny knelt on the floor alternately dabbing and rubbing. It was clear that, although the stain was fading, it was looking distinctly like a permanent fixture. "I'll bring some special cleaning fluid in tomorrow," she said desperately, "but I'm really sorry everyone." Fortunately it hadn't been a whole mug full but there was a definite pink tinge on the grey carpet.

"Never mind, Jenny" Sheila consoled her, "Maybe it will encourage Graham to spend the money and change the carpet before too long. It's well overdue."

"Thanks," said Jenny "I'm so sorry, I feel dreadful about it."

"Phew," said one of the others, thankfully changing the subject "I've had a right session with John Daley so when he said he was going to tell his Dad of me for being mean I said I'd welcome the opportunity to tell his Dad all about the fact that he hit Stephen Black and used the 'f' word in my maths lesson!"

"Times have certainly changed" said Sheila. When I started teaching in the late 70s I was advised to get a plimsoll ready for boys like him. I had a pair of shoes I called my pair of 'wackers' most days. They were very flexible and just the job. Mind you, I never used them on legs after about two thirty in the afternoon because they left a red mark. There had to be time for that to fade a bit. Crikey, that was awful by today's thinking. It was quite normal and acceptable then."

"Did you really do that?" asked Sally.

"Yes, the head teacher advised it. Seems incredible now, doesn't it? I remember taking one real horror to the head one day because he was just terrorising everyone, throwing books and pencils and you name it. I regretted it though. The head wacked him so hard on his back-side the boy shot across the office. Darren, the boy's name was. I felt really bad about it afterwards. Mind you I only had to threaten a visit the next time and he stopped kicking the other boy."

Jenny was thankful for a change in the conversation and the mood was certainly lighter after Sheila's history lesson. Joan and Lesley were a right pair sometimes. Typical in a staff room, such a cross-section, she supposed. What had started as quite a good day had turned a little sour.

Just then the door opened and Graham Lockwood came in. No-one mentioned the stained carpet but Lesley nudged Joan's arm and Jenny could have sworn she smirked as she looked at the stain. Mr. Lockwood pinned a new notice on the staff room board. "Some of you may be interested in this," he said, and without further discussion he left. Joan stood to look at the new piece of paper and leaning over the chairs to peer more closely she let out an exclamation, "Well, well, he's clearly got some money from somewhere, but not for a new carpet!"

"Go on then," Sally said. "Share it out."

"He's advertising for an internal promotion; one extra salary point for a home/school liaison responsibility."

"I suppose he never did replace Peter's point when he left and you didn't get it when you came, did you Jenny," Joan said pointedly.

Jenny could have sloshed her one. This lunch time had been one dig after another.

"What have I done to deserve that?" she asked Sally on their way back to the classroom just before the end of the lunch hour.

"Nothing, nothing at all," Sally reassured her. "She's been like that with all of us in turn. You're just the lucky winner at the moment."

"Do you think you'll apply for this point that's on offer?" Jenny asked her friend. You've been here awhile and I'm sure you have the experience."

"It's tempting," Sally replied "but I'll have to think about it. It would be more hours after or even before school and I've got Mum to consider," she sighed.

Jenny felt really sorry for Sally at that moment. Just when she could be advancing her career, she had too many other responsibilities holding her back. It must have been very frustrating for her at times but she put such a brave face upon it all. Jenny admired her commitment.

As the afternoon disappeared quickly under the weight of a lively technology session using fabric and materials as well as a watering can to find the best material to make a waterproof coat for Talented Ted, the school mascot, playtime arrived in no time at all. Jenny was not on duty and normally she didn't bother to go to the staff room at this time but stayed in her room making preparations for the last session. This afternoon, however, she was thirsty since half her drink had ended on the floor. As she entered the room and found it empty her eye was caught by the head's new notice on the board. At this stage in her career it would not be unreasonable to consider going for it but she hadn't been here that long and she really didn't know if she would be in with a shout. Perhaps she should go and discuss it with Mr. Lockwood. He had written that suggestion for anyone who might be interested. She decided to discuss it with Mike first. That would be politic, especially if it meant a few more hours, and then she would go and see Graham Lockwood.

At the end of the day Jenny saw the children out and stood with them until all had been claimed by their adult. As she was waiting with the last two children Mrs. Jones came marching across the playground to her with Johnny in tow. "I want a word with you," she said forcefully. I know what this is going to be about, thought Jenny to herself.

"If you'd like to go into the classroom,

Mrs. Jones I'll be with you just as soon as these two children have been collected."

As soon as possible Jenny went to speak to Mrs. Jones. "I'm fed up with my Johnny being bullied by Ian Williams," she said. She continued to shout at Jenny for some minutes. Jenny knew that Mrs. Jones needed to voice it all before it was possible for her to get a word in edgeways. She spewed her point of view in a never-ending stream. Eventually Jenny was able to ask Johnny what he thought had happened. Parents frequently came when children had argued. More often than not it wasn't a case of constant aggression or teasing which might be genuine bullying but just a childish scrap. However, such an allegation needed to be taken seriously and Jenny knew she would need to talk to both boys in the morning. She promised Mrs. Jones that she would act and get back to her after school the next day. Finally the worried and angry parent had calmed down and eventually left in a reasonably pleasant mood. This wasn't the first time Jenny had felt the wrath of such a parent and she knew it wouldn't be the last. Just a perfect end to the day though!

She was just packing up her bags when there was a knock on the classroom door. She shouted "Come in," as she turned to the door and Christopher Mayhew came in.

"I've brought your storage boxes back.

I've transferred the last of the food into another box."

"Thank you" said Jenny, pleased that this, at least, was a pleasant conversation.

"Are you still OK for Charlie to come in part-time soon?" he asked.

Jenny, Christopher and Graham Lockwood had had a meeting several days ago and decided on a protocol for Charlie's re-entry to school. "Absolutely" Jenny nodded enthusiastically. "I'm really looking forward to having him here again.

"I am so grateful to you for all your kindness" Christopher reiterated. "I've just finished reading this." He produced a paperback from the bag in which he had brought the plastic boxes. I really enjoyed it. I don't know if it's up your street.

"Thank you," said Jenny. She was aware that Christopher must feel a little indebted to her and this was probably his way of showing his thanks. "I've read two of his before" she added, "but not this one. I couldn't put the last one down. Do you need it back in a hurry because this one may take me a little longer to read? During term time I only manage a few pages each night before I drop off to sleep."

He smiled "No rush!"

With that, he thanked her again and left.

Jenny picked up her bags once more, took her coat from the hook behind the door and followed in Christopher's footsteps towards the front entrance. At least she had a smile on her face now.

Sheila had just come out of her office and was standing at the front door. She was looking out towards the car park. As Jenny arrived she could see what Sheila was watching. Sally was beside Christopher, standing next to his car. She must have been in the car park when he emerged from the school and joined him. "I think we have a blossoming romance there," Sheila remarked.

"I think Sally feels they have quite a lot of shared experience," Jenny said, smiling. "I'm not sure if Christopher is interested or not though," she added, thinking back to the visit they had both made to Christopher Mayhew's house recently.

"Well it's clear she's got the hots for him, look at her!" Certainly Sally was looking quite coquettish next to Christopher, laughing and standing quite close. Sure enough, he moved away slightly but she reached out and lightly touched his arm, before removing her hand and moving away herself with what was clearly a smiling goodbye. Jenny was unsure what to make of the exchange. She was fairly sure Sally would not say no to a relationship with Christopher Mayhew, but would he reciprocate? She really was not convinced. It would need to be a very strong feeling on his part, Jenny thought, to continue with someone when he had, by all accounts, been very happily married and with a such young son. She hoped Sally was not on a destination course to be hurt and disappointed.

All thoughts of Sally and Christopher were dispelled as Jenny headed home with the advertisement for the internal promotion upper-most in her mind.

□□□□□□□□

On this occasion she arrived home before Mike and she prepared in her head how she would present the information and her point of view. Briefly, it shot through her mind that she shouldn't need to prepare any kind of argument. If she decided to go for the job because she was confident she could do it and wanted it, she should do it. However, living with someone else seemed always to hold an element of compromise but that was fine if the compromise was equal.

He arrived home shortly after Jenny and, for once, Mike told her he'd had a good day, landing a major contract that would go down very well when he had his annual one-to-one appraisal. It was Jenny's turn to want to share her problems of the day but on this occasion she refrained, not wanting to put a dampener on the calm atmosphere.

Jenny had decided to wait until after tea to have her discussion. After a meal and a glass of wine they should both be more relaxed and ready for an open discussion.

Once they had eaten, shared some of the day's events and cleared away the dishes, Mike headed for the living room and the television. She headed him off by saying "Can we have a family conference?"

"That sounds a bit serious," Mike observed, and Jenny mentally kicked herself for getting it wrong, especially after all her abstract preparation. Perhaps that was the problem; too much planning on her part. It really shouldn't be and probably wasn't necessary.

"No not at all," she laughed. "It's just that an internal promotion has come up at school."

"What does it involve?" asked Mike, naturally enough.

"I don't think it will be too many more hours because I'm not doing quite as many as when I first started since I know the routines better. It will also mean a bit more money of course and the joint account can always do with that. We could perhaps afford to decorate the living room and buy a new flat screen television."

"Hmmm," said Mike. This was the tricky

bit for Jenny, the money thing! "Well it's up to you" he continued. "The money will always come in handy."

"I think I'll talk to Mr. Lockwood tomorrow and find out exactly how he sees it going. I'll need to write an application letter and probably go through another interview. I should imagine there will be more than my application to consider."
"Why who else might apply?" Mike asked.

"I imagine Sally will, I don't know who else. Joan is the only other person who possibly could, though, I think."

"What old crabby knickers?" Mike laughed. He had heard her name in several contexts when Jenny had told him different things that had gone on in the staff room.

"Oh Mike! Yes, the very one, but she has loads of experience at the school. I would have thought she might have got a responsibility point before but who knows?" Jenny replied contemplatively.

"It sounds like you have decided to apply already from the way you just said you'd talk to the headteacher about it," Mike observed.

"Well, I possibly will, but I need to talk to him anyway to find out more details. I'll sleep on it 'til then."

□□□□□□□□

The next day Jenny decided she would definitely talk to Graham Lockwood. She really felt she hadn't been at the school very long to be throwing her cap into the ring and if he felt that too then it would be a waste of her time and his. He wouldn't tell her she couldn't or shouldn't apply but Jenny was sure he would give her some sort of coded message if he felt it was too early. First thing, she knocked on his door. She knew he was in before her because his car was parked in front of the main entrance.

"Hello, come in," he called.

"'Morning," Jenny said. I wondered if I might have a word about the responsibility point you have advertised on the board."

"OK. Fine, but can we do it after school? I've got a meeting with the finance committee this morning and I've got some last minute figures to present to them; extra information that's just come in from the office."

"Yes, of course," said Jenny, thinking 'rats, I shall have to control my impatience all day, now, having worked myself up to this!'

After school Jenny saw the children out and caught Mrs. Jones to let her know the outcome of her findings regarding the incident on the previous day between her son and Ian Williams. As was frequently the case, in her experience, Jenny was not too surprised to find that Mrs. Jones really was not worried anymore. Having got it off her chest yesterday Johnny and Ian had become good friends again and Mrs. Jones was eager to get to the shops to get tea for her family organised. Jenny then hurried along to the head's office.

"I believe I can do this increased role but the thing is," Jenny said as soon as she was settled in one of the chairs opposite Graham Lockwood, "I haven't been here very long and if you think I'm being presumptuous and there is no chance of me being ready for this promotion I'd rather not go for it."

"Jenny, you have made a very good start here and as you know the observations of your classroom practice have been graded as very good and with several elements of outstanding. Remind me how long you were in your last post."

"Three years," Jenny responded.

"Well it seems to me entirely appropriate that you put in an application, then. There may well be more than one person applying. Two others are seeing me about it. Whether they'll both put in for it, of course, I have no idea yet."

Jenny asked for some more information regarding the role, so that she could better judge what to include in her letter of application, but she was very encouraged by Graham's words.

"Some schools need a full time post for this if they have mainly hard to reach parents but here we have very few, as you know. However we need someone to organise workshops, help remove barriers, encourage parents as co-educators and so forth." Jenny nodded, her mind already buzzing with ideas. "I've prepared a paper, a sort of job description but clearly the list could be endless. Give it some thought and if you decide to apply I need the letter in by a week on Friday. There's no sense in hanging around.

"Thanks," said Jenny. "That's put me in the picture well. I'm sure I will be applying now."

She left the room closing the door behind her. She had difficulty not to hop, skip and jump down the corridor. This sounded right up her street and she was really excited by the thought of the endless possibilities. She knew she was personable and got on well with the parents and she'd had some experience of working with outside agencies like social services and other provider groups in her previous placement. She was extremely keen to get home and share all the potential with Mike. He would surely see the opportunities that this would provide for her.

When she got back to the classroom, Sally heard her arrive and popped her head round the door. She recognised the paper that Jenny had in her hand. "I've got one of those but it seems like an awful lot of extra work to me."

"I don't know," said Jenny "it seems quite exciting and Graham said for the more major things like meetings there might be some classroom cover now and again. Otherwise it would be fitting it around everything else, certainly. You could do it though, I'm sure."

"I'm not sure I can do it just now, what with Mum and everything. She's on her own a lot as it is and she's not getting any better. She's finding it increasingly difficult even to hold a cup"

On the way home Jenny had plenty to think about. She wanted to share her excitement with Mike. She was already planning things to include in her letter. It did seem as though Sally was going to pass up the opportunity. Although she was genuinely sorry for her friend and felt she could do the job it would certainly help her if Sally didn't apply. She immediately felt guilty about the thought. She wondered who else might go for it.

☐☐☐☐☐☐☐☐☐

On arriving home, Jenny found the house

in darkness. It felt decidedly chilly too and somehow seemed unwelcoming. She switched on the wall lights and turned up the heating. Pulling the curtains and switching on the glow of the old-fashioned electric fire, with its coal effect, in the living room made it seem a lot cosier. She wondered when Mike would be home because she was hungry. She thought he would be in very shortly; he usually was around this time and so she started to prepare some pasta and a sauce. That would be quite quick, easy and tasty. By the time she had added the chorizo, mushrooms and onion Jenny's tummy was rumbling and she was beginning to wonder where he was.

Time dragged on and Jenny realised she had begun clock watching. She decided to eat before the meal really had become a disaster, so she poured some boiling water over some of the pasta and re-heated the sauce. Having finished her solitary meal and put the plates and pans in the dishwasher she pondered on what to do next.

Having been elated with the thought of the new role of responsibility at work, Jenny now became quite deflated because she had so wanted to share the possibilities with Mike and get his opinion on the job prospects. 'Where is he?' she thought to herself disconsolately. She decided to get the job description and make some notes that might be useful if indeed she was going to apply.

A full hour later, Jenny had more than three full pages of notes that she considered would enable her to form a clear letter of application. Looking at the clock she was surprised how late it had become. She was becoming seriously worried about Mike's absence and started to imagine all sorts of gory details, worrying herself even more. It was now gone eight o'clock and still there was no sign and no word. He had his mobile phone. Why had he not used it? Had his car gone off the road and no-one had noticed? Maybe he was injured some-where and the hospital or police hadn't had time to inform her. She spoke firmly to herself before her imagination went any more wild. It was only just after eight, so not really that late. Maybe he was working and had forgotten the time. 'Don't be daft, Jenny' she thought to herself. He never works this late. 'On the other hand maybe he had gone for a drink with one of his work mates' she counter-argued with herself! 'Then why had he not blinking well telephoned her?' She started to consider who she might telephone to see if she could track him down, but then those friends she might call would start to worry too and the police wouldn't be at all interested yet. She was probably just being foolish!

It was after nine o'clock when she finally heard the key in the lock.

"Hi!" called Mike as if it was three hours ago and she had not been going mentally mad for much of those three hours.

As she had been so concerned for him and her worries had started festering in her mind, Jenny was considerably less than amused to hear him so chirpy.

"I imagined you lying in a ditch or on life support at the hospital," she exploded. "Where have you been?"

"What do you mean, where have I been?" he answered belligerently, all signs of jauntiness disappearing.

"Mike, I was really worried," Jenny said more calmly. "I thought you must have had an accident."

"I only went to the gym. I met somebody I know and stayed for a swift half."

"…but you always come home first and you almost never stay on in the bar. Who did you meet?" Jenny asked, just as half an after-thought, intending to get back onto a more even keel of conversation.

"Just a friend," he responded in a desultory fashion, and then somewhat more antagonistically "You needn't start checking up on me!"

"I wasn't checking up!" Jenny said feeling aggrieved. "I was worried!" she added, raising her voice, now too. "For goodness sake, you are never this late without phoning me."

"Well there's a first time for everything," Mike rasped back and stormed out of the room.

Jenny sat down heavily. She detested arguing and tears came to her eyes. She didn't understand what was going on here at all. After mending the fences from their previous argument this was like ten steps backwards. They rarely had words of disagreement and never so violently as these last couple of times.

7 CHAPTER

When Jenny went up to bed Mike had gone up before her and seemed to be asleep. She wondered if he was pretending but wasn't prepared to continue the argument or raise the demons again, so she quietly undressed and climbed in beside him. It was a long time before sleep came and after a good half hour, from his breathing, she was sure Mike definitely was sleeping before her. She tossed about but couldn't relax enough to drop off to sleep her-self. Silently she got up again and went down stairs to make a warm milk drink. She sat in the living room sipping it and thinking. Eventually she yawned and climbed the stairs wearily to try sleeping again. It was some time later that Jenny finally dropped into an exhausted slumber.

She awoke early and patiently waited for Mike to wake too. She controlled the urge to toss and turn and awake him artificially and when he did open his eyes she was tired again but there was no time to drop back off to sleep. They looked at each other but it was Jenny who broke the silence and spoke first.

"Are we friends again?" she asked unhappily.

"I wasn't aware that we weren't friends" he answered.

This threw Jenny, since they had gone to sleep on a blazing row.

"OK, let's just forget it then," she added, feeling that there was a lot more to be said but Mike was clearly not prepared to clear the air easily. With that, Jenny got out of bed and headed for the shower. By the time she had finished, Mike had risen too. They were like ships that passed in the night; he going into the bathroom as she was coming out; she finishing getting dressed and going downstairs as he came out of the bathroom. Downstairs was a similar affair with each of them getting something to eat in a fairly stilted manner. Jenny made Mike a conciliatory cup of tea. He thanked her politely, took a couple of sips and said he had to go. He kissed her briefly on her cheek but Jenny felt that he was just going through the motions. She was at a loss to know what to do and started analysing her reactions from the previous evening. This continued as she collected her things, left the house and drove to work.

Once she arrived, however, she became immersed in the activities of the day and time flew by as normal. By lunch-time, Jenny was feeling much better and more confident that when she got home, with time apart, all would be on a more even keel. Before going to the staff room, Jenny called next door to see if Sally was ready to eat.

"How's it going?" she asked her friend.

"Oh! Hello Jenny. I'm going for lunch any minute now. Are you ready for that?"

"I came to see if you were going now. I feel like congenial company today. I'm a bit fed up with the terrible two-some having a snipe at every opportunity."

Sally grinned in her usual up-beat way. "Let's go then. I'm feeling good today and ready for anyone!"

"What's the 'good', then?" asked Jenny.

"I've got a date this weekend," Sally happily divulged.

"Wow, come on then, dish the dirt!" laughed Jenny.

"You'll never guess who," said Sally mysteriously.

"Don't keep me in suspense. I can't guess so let me know!"

"None other than Mr. Christopher Mayhew!" Sally said delightedly.

Jenny was a little surprised but never-the-less pleased for her friend. Thoughts of exchanged glances and brief conversations that she had witnessed flitted through Jenny's mind. She was also pleased that Christopher was dipping his toes in the social sea again after all he had obviously been through in the last few years.

"Good for both of you," Jenny said warmly. "So what are you doing or where are you going?"

"Well, of course, there's Charlie so I'm meeting them both at the café in the park to start with, on Saturday, and we'll take it from there."

"I really hope you have a good time and it works well." Jenny meant it too. "Changing the subject, have you decided whether to go for this internal promotion? If you'd rather not say that's fine, you don't have to tell me."

"I have decided and I don't mind saying," Sally answered. "I'm definitely not going for it. I feel I have so much on my plate at the moment with Mum and other personal stuff. I really don't think I could do it justice. You are the best candidate by a mile so good luck to you if you're going for it," Sally said cheerfully.

"Thanks," answered Jenny. She assumed now, 'other personal stuff' meant a blossoming relationship as well as the problems with her mother's illness.

After school, Jenny was just packing up her bags, having prepared most of the classroom for the following day, when there was a knock on the door. She turned as it opened and Christopher Mayhew walked in with Charlie in tow.

"I just popped in to say that we saw the doctor at the hospital again today. He's very pleased with Charlie's progress and is confident that he'll be fine for part-time school next week."

"That's excellent news," Jenny said and crouching down to Charlie's height she added to him "I'm really looking forward to having you back in our class and so are the other children. They've missed you a lot."

He beamed at her and when she rose and turned to Christopher she saw the same large smile reflected on is face too. She could certainly see the father/son resemblance in the eyes. Whilst he wasn't exactly traditionally 'good-looking' Christopher had a kind, comfortable face with fine green eyes that twinkled when he smiled. The crinkles at the corners made Jenny aware that for a long time during his life he must have smiled a lot. Of course Charlie's rounded baby face had not yet acquired the chiselled features of his father and Charlie's paler curls had matured on his dad to attractive wavy brown hair. Christopher was clearly loyal and hard-working and she could understand Sally being attracted to him. He was indeed very appealing.

When Jenny arrived home she was immediately transported back to the atmosphere of the previous night and even this morning which had not been good. She followed her routine upon arrival, making the house warm and cosy now that it was dark so early and the wind was bitingly cold outside. She was trying to dispel the mordant feel indoors too. Eventually, Mike came home too but instead of rushing to meet him this time, she waited until he came into the living room. "Hi," she said as normally as possible, whilst feeling ridiculously nervous.

"Hi, he replied. "Have you started dinner or shall I get on with it?"

"I haven't got that far yet. I've only just got in too."

"OK, I'll crack on with it then." It was as if nothing at all had happened the previous night. They took it in turns to cook without any particular routine about it so it was not particularly conciliatory for Mike to cook. It was just as if nothing had happened. Had Jenny placed too much importance upon their words of the previous evening? Had she imagined the atmosphere this morning?

Following their meal, during which they equally chatted about their respective day, Mike turned on the television and Jenny got out some school work – children's writing that she was going to mount for a wall display. She could have left it for Jodie, her teaching assistant, but she thought she might as well get it done so that Jodie could put it up the next day.

As she was sticking and trimming the work the telephone rang. Since she was closer to it she picked up the handset to discover Diana at the other end.

"It's been such a long time since we saw each other," Diana said following the usual greetings. "I bumped into Mike the other day and we talked about dinner one evening. I've spoken to Pat and she and Doug can come a week on Saturday. She says they can get a baby-sitter, one of the swimming teachers at Doug's work. Can you do then too?

"A week on Saturday," Jenny said out loud, turning to Mike and raising her eye-brows in a question. "It's Diana," she said waggling the phone at Mike.

"That sounds great, just hang on while I double check Mike has nothing on then." Mike nodded agreement and turned back to the TV.

"I'm imagining Mike with 'nothing on' now," laughed Diana at her own risqué joke.

"I wasn't sure if Pat and Doug would make it," she continued. "When I asked her she seemed quite distracted."

"She's had some problems lately." Jenny said obscurely. She didn't want to discuss Pat's problems and she didn't know how much Diana knew.

"I know about all that," Diana clarified. "Why she doesn't just confront him if she's not happy, I don't know," she said in her typically forthright way.

"She assured me she was going to but I think she's frightened to do that," Jenny said. She had spoken to Pat just a couple of days ago so knew that her friend had not followed through with her determination. When she had arrived home that Saturday morning having seen Jenny at the local shops, Doug had been out so her new-found resolve had faded away. When he returned with paint for the boys' bedroom and plans to build a toy chest she began to wonder if it was over and the need for confrontation was past. He also wanted to discuss the possibilities of upgrading the windows at the front for uPVC ones. If he was planning long-term house improvements then surely he had got over his distraction? Jenny really didn't understand how Doug could kid himself he was a happy family man with all those responsibilities and still mess around behind Pat's back.

"Anyway, it'll be lovely to see you all. We haven't done that for a while, now," Jenny said, to bring that part of the conversation to a close. She was uncomfortable discussing Pat's and Doug's problems. It seemed disloyal, somehow. "Do you want me to bring anything?"

"Oh no! Our treat this time," said Diana generously. It was not unusual for each couple to provide one of the courses for a get-together. "Bring a bottle, if you want."

"Yes, of course, we'll do that! That goes without saying" Jenny laughed. "We'll probably walk round so we don't need to worry about driving."

Diana and Greg lived about twenty minutes' walk away from Mike and Jenny. It was a large flat in an old, converted building which they had bought together about five years ago. They were as yet to formalise their relationship but as there were no children there seemed no pressing rush and they had been together now for a couple of years longer than the time they had been living there. They were a constant and Jenny, whilst still feeling that Pat qualified as her 'best' friend, if adults had such a thing, liked Diana for her kindness and liveliness. You didn't have to work too hard when Diana was around since she was spirited and sometimes seemed eccentric. She was always talkative. Her

long, auburn hair seemed to epitomise her
temperament, and her buxom figure, her
larger than life personality. She didn't
qualify as beautiful or even pretty but her
vivacity made her attractive and easy
company. She was often outlandish in what
she said and did but somehow seemed to get
away with it where in another woman it would
be crass or unappealing. Whilst they were
friendly, Jenny sometimes privately thought
Diana was a bit 'obvious', especially around
men but she was clearly alluring and
generally good fun. She was consistently
friendly with women too, and through Pat,
Jenny had met and liked her. Greg was
slightly older than the others but he was a
gentle man whose character was evident in
his compassionate, grey eyes and quiet
smile. He was the exact opposite of Diana in
many ways and he was often content to sit
and let her take centre stage. Their
relationship seemed to work, thought Jenny
at this point in time. She liked Greg as
well and it felt as if he often seemed to
nurture her as he would a child without
diminishing her as an adult. He was
dependable, kind and caring. She felt he was
ever trustworthy.

□□□□□□□□

The week-end came round quickly. Jenny
was looking forward to going out that
evening. It was a while since the six of
them had got together and Diana and Greg

were always good company. She decided on something warm to wear. She felt she needed to be cosy, especially if they were walking around to Diana's and Greg's house for their dinner date. The weather had a typical late autumn chill. The wind seemed never ending but fortunately the promised rain had held off all day. She chose a chunky sweater with a large collar in a rich, deep rust colour that went well with her mid-length skirt and brown boots. She knew the colour warmed her skin tone and the bias cut of the skirt was flattering. By the time she had done her hair and make-up and added a pair of long earrings she felt 'good to go'. Both she and Mike wrapped up in their long coats and with scarves and gloves they faced the weather. When they were ready to go they stepped out into the chill air but still tensed up against the cold. Whilst the wind was cutting the sky was filled with stars, not that easy to see, however, because of the street lights. Jenny remembered their last holiday. They'd had a long weekend in the Dales at a small bed and breakfast that they had found as they drove. It had been a good choice with excellent, filling food, heavy old-fashioned furniture and cosy thick duvet on the big bed. The stars, in the wide sky above the village had been so bright and clear to see. Whilst only earlier this year, it seemed a long time ago. Now, with heads down they hurried along the road towards their target. They could have got a lift with Doug and Pat but he was collecting their sitter so they decided to work up an appetite with the brisk walk. They were pleased to arrive and with glowing faces greeted Greg with wide smiles when he opened the door. Handing over the clinking bag they had brought with them "One bottle of white and some beers," smiled Mike.

"Let the party begin, then" added Greg taking coats at the same time. They went through to greet Pat and Doug.

"Hiya you two," greeted Mike. Doug stood and shook his hand and leant in to kiss Jenny on her cold cheeks. Pat rose too and gave Jenny a quick, firm hug and kissed Mike hello.

"It's really chilly out there," said Mike rubbing his hands together.

"Did you walk?" asked Greg.

"Yes, safer that way. Can't afford to lose my license at the moment! Need the work, need the money. Mind you with Jenny's earnings I could move to being a 'kept' man."

Jenny glanced across at him but she could detect no malice in his comment this time.

Just then Diana appeared from the kitchen. "Hello both of you" she raised her voice expansively and with arms out wide she embraced them both at the same time. "Well you two haven't been to hell and back. You're freezing. Come and sit on the sofa by the fire and Greg will sort out drinks. You look cosy, Jenny and lovely too."

Unlike Jenny, Diana could have been dressed for summer. Her off the shoulder gathered blouse was bright red, a brave colour that somehow enhanced the colour of her hair. She wore several heavy gold chains around her neck. Her skirt was a modest length but when she sat down the high split revealed a good pair of legs. "Just as well I don't have to go out tonight," she laughed looking down at herself.

"We came in the car" said Doug, "One of us has to take the baby-sitter home later. I imagine it will be me," he added, "I doubt Pat will be able to drive later."

"Well, I do believe it's my turn, so I *shall* probably make the most of it!" she said determinedly

"I'm sure I can abstain if you insist, though" she said, not smiling.

"What can I get everyone to drink?" asked Greg, who then busied himself with the task while everyone generally exchanged casual conversation to cover the awkward pause that had followed the short exchange between Doug and Pat.

After a while Diana announced that

dinner must be ready and disappeared into the kitchen. She called them to be served and they all went across to the dining area where the table was aglow with candles. The light bouncing off the glassware, cutlery and warm colour of the mahogany table with the scarlet serviettes, gave the area a convivial luminosity as they all sat. It occurred to Jenny that the colours mirrored Diana herself giving her radiance too. Very clever! Jenny considered herself an adequate cook, who could pull something reasonable out of the oven when required, but the smell emanating from Diana's kitchen was wonderful and Jenny had no doubt something special would arrive at any moment. The starter was not only delicious but looked amazing too. The warm goat's cheese on bruschetta was just the right depth of flavour and the lightly baked figs and cool salad leaves with dressing looked and tasted perfect with it. Everyone complimented Diana and conversation flowed with the wine. There was a slight awkwardness when Doug pointed out that the last starter that Pat had produced was not a patch on this one but she laughed it off well.

"So Mike, have you been toning up your muscles much at the gym?" asked Diana "I rather think you have," she laughed. Mike looked somewhat mortified but carried on the banter with a degree of restraint, Jenny observed. Everyone else laughed indulgently.

This was characteristic of Diana.

The evening progressed. Diana and Greg had really gone to town on both food and drink. Doug tried to impress everyone with his wine knowledge but well and truly had the mickey taken from him by everyone. This was so typical of Doug and they were all used to him. He took it in good part generally. Mike was unusually quiet and Jenny quietly asked him if he was OK while there was a general milling around between the starter and main courses. "I'm fine," he answered but he didn't seem so to Jenny. Following a hefty portion of delicious chicken cacciatore and vegetables that were typically al dente no one felt like moving much. Diana was her usual dynamic self and there was a lot of laughter between her and Doug and Greg. Normally Mike would have joined in while Pat and Jenny were content to sit back and listen or laugh, knowing that they couldn't compete with this level of banter but comfortable to know that it was not expected from either of them.

However, this evening, on occasions there was the odd snipe between Pat and Doug too, when the teasing seemed a bit near the knuckle. During the chocolate crèmes brulees dessert, some- time later, Jenny said "This is truly delicious. I could get used to eating like this but I'd be like a balloon in no time at all."

Doug responded with "Pat keeps trying to lose weight but it keeps finding her."

Diana took the sting out with her likening the comment to herself and when Pat re-joined Doug's comment with "To belittle is to be little," everyone laughed but it seemed unaccustomedly false somehow.

After dinner, with the coffee, they played cards for a while with tokens and matchsticks but it was somewhat desultory. Eventually the evening broke up with Pat announcing they had to get the baby-sitter home and Doug yawning and saying he had to be up early anyway. Jenny and Mike re-wrapped for their walk home but accepted the lift offered by Doug. "I can drop you off and then take the sitter home," he said.

There was the usual thank you and the four friends left Diana and Greg who stood on the step, peeking out into the cold to wave good-bye. They were all quiet in the car but the journey wasn't far anyway.

"Speak to you soon," said Jenny as she and Mike got out.

"Cheers," said Mike. "I'll give you a call about that squash game, you know, the one we spoke about the other day," Mike added to Doug.

"You didn't say you'd thought of playing squash," Jenny said as they walked up the path. She was thinking the way Mike had reminded Doug sounded a bit conspiratorial.

Once indoors Jenny and Mike took off their coats. "I'm tired and ready for bed," said Mike.

"Me too," Jenny replied. "That was a good meal but there were a lot too many undercurrents in the atmosphere, wasn't there?"

Mike didn't reply. "You were quiet tonight. Did you feel the atmosphere too?" she pursued.

"It seemed fine to me. I told you earlier I was fine."

"Well Pat and Doug were on edge."

"I suppose so," Mike agreed in a half-hearted way. It was clear he did not want to talk about the situation between her friend and his. He clearly knew exactly what was going on but wasn't prepared to share much, even with Jenny. "Diana was on form, as usual" Jenny continued. "Did she embarrass you when she commented about you working out and toning up at the gym? You were very non-committal about that one."

"I told you, I'm fine with it all, I wasn't quiet, I'm not ill, I'm quite alright." Mike snapped.

"Hey," Jenny said. "I don't mean anything by it. I was only making conversation about the evening."

"I'm just a bit tired now, that's all" said Mike, heading up the stairs.

Thinking to change the subject, Jenny asked Mike about the squash session as they climbed the stairs. Mike sighed loudly and Jenny thought, somewhat dramatically. "It's not finalised yet, just an idea that Doug and I were talking about, as soon as it is I'll check it out with you. OK?" he added. Jenny still tried hard to make conversation. Perhaps it was the wine talking and maybe she should have left it there, but she desperately wanted, indeed needed the re-assurance of a normal happy conversation.

8 CHAPTER

The next week was to be Charlie's re-introduction to school. Jenny was genuinely looking forward to having him back in her class but she was also a little apprehensive. She wasn't sure how the other children would react to the sight of his injury. She remembered her response to seeing him and the expression on Sally's face when seeing his loss of hair and the livid scars that were so evident. Children could be very, very kind and considerate to those in need but they also spoke as they found and comments could be hurtful and unhelpful to Charlie's self-esteem. In addition she was slightly unsure of his capabilities and how tired he might become. Still, all that would become clear. She would be in regular contact with Christopher and he would be on the end of the phone should there be any problems or questions. The meeting that she'd had with him and Graham Lockwood had been helpful and the paper from the hospital, via the nurse, had been informative. That was for the afternoon, though. She had a morning of busy activity and lunchtime to have, first.

For morning playtime she walked towards the staff room with Sally. "I'm dying to know how you got on with your date on Saturday afternoon," she said at the first opportunity. "You met at the café in the park didn't you?"

Sally answered with animation, her eyes shining and her blonde pony-tail characteristically bobbing as she walked. "We had a really great time. I was a bit nervous. It's a long time since I had a date and with Charlie there too it had the potential to be tricky. I took along some bread for the water birds and we all fed those for a time. Charlie was quiet to start with but after a while of chucking bread he loosened up a bit. Mind you those birds can be quite grabbing and aggressive. He was understandably an bit nervous and was jumping about and running away. He's certainly lively enough again," she said. "We went inside for a coffee after that. It was a bit chilly," she continued. "They have a small display of flora and fauna type of stuff and some push button and feel in the box activities especially for children so we did those together. Charlie was chatty and fun by then. He seems quite well, now. It's amazing. So actually he helped break the ice. I really felt Christopher and I made a good connection. I talked for ages really easily."

"Did he tell you about his wife?" Jenny asked. "I think it was breast cancer about three or four years ago."

"No, we didn't touch on much personal stuff. Just chatter really. I guess that'll come. It's quite hard for both of us, I think."

"Of course, you've got plenty of time. That all sounds great," Jenny responded warmly. Perhaps her concerns for Sally were going to be un-founded, although she noted that Sally had said she chatted easily rather than 'we'. "Are you seeing him again?"

"Yes, as a matter of fact, he's asked me to go to the cinema with him next weekend. He told me he hasn't been for literally years but his Mum is going to come and take Charlie back to her house for the day and he's going to sleep there." Sally answered diffidently.

"Wow" Jenny exclaimed.

"It doesn't mean anything much," Sally said hastily. "I shan't be late out because I have to get Mum to bed.

"Of course," said Jenny, "but you can still have a good evening without Christopher being too anxious about

Charlie."

"Yes, I'm really looking forward to it. We seem to get on really well and have such a lot in common."

After play-time a typically busy morning followed. Jenny was hungry by the time she entered the staff-room again at lunch-time. She just had half an hour to eat her packed lunch, have a quick coffee and meet the children out on the playground for the afternoon session. Joan and Lesley were in their corner and several others were arriving at the same time as Jenny. There was a general melee as people got themselves a hot drink or poured for each other. The level of noise rose until everyone was settled in their usual places. Jenny joined Sally and shared some casual conversation about the morning while she ate.

The room was emptying again, for which Jenny was grateful when the next conversation ensued, as it turned out. She had just finished her apple and rose to throw the core away saying "Right, time to get back, I guess." She was thinking about Charlie's return again and wondering how he would settle into the routines of the classroom after such a long and disruptive break, when a voice from the corner piped up.

"It's Mike, isn't it – your husband?" Joan enquired.

"Yes, that's right, "Jenny responded, wondering where this was leading.

"Tall, dark hair, red swimming shorts?"

"Yes," Jenny confirmed.

"I thought it must be him," Joan added enigmatically. "I only met him that day he dropped you off for your interview but I thought it was him," she added. She turned at that point and murmured to her friend.

It didn't seem as if she was going to say anything else. Jenny was sure she was doing it deliberately and waiting for she, Jenny, to ask to what she was referring. It was the sort of ploy Joan loved to make. A bit of a 'power play' Jenny supposed. She was sorely tempted to let her stew and not rise to the bait. She moved to put her mug in the dishwasher while she contemplated what her next move should be. In the end, the silence was clearly driving Joan mad and she just could not resist it. Jenny felt it was one small battle she had won but this feeling was quickly taken from her with Joan's next words.

"Only I saw him in the swimming pool at the leisure centre on Saturday morning," she said.

"He quite often goes to the gym there, said Jenny as pleasantly as possible. "He's turning into a right keep fit enthusiast," she added.

"Well, he certainly looked enthusiastic," Joan said, "but it wasn't keep fit he was particularly interested in, I wouldn't have said."

"What do you mean?" Jenny could no longer resist asking.

"The curvaceous red head seemed to be taking his enthusiasm readily enough," Joan couldn't help smiling.

Jenny physically felt her breath leave her body in a rush and her heart pounded erratically. Then she managed to restrain her-self and said calmly "He told me he had met Diana. She's a good friend of both of us. We had dinner with her and her partner as it happens, just this week-end." So put that in your nasty little mind, thought Jenny, and choke on it!

All this time, Lesley, Joan's only real supporter looked down at her hands in her lap and refused to be drawn into the conversation. It seemed that she drew the line at some things.

As she headed back up the corridor to her classroom, Jenny felt quite shaken. She didn't believe Mike would have over-stepped any lines but she was really angry that Joan had seen fit to be so spiteful and insinuating. Then Jenny thought, perhaps

Joan had guessed she would be applying for the internal promotion and felt it might be a way to put Jenny down and feel less confident. Perhaps she was under-confident herself and needed to boost that. Anyway, of all the small-minded tricks! If Jenny wasn't careful she could let this nasty intimation affect her confidence just as Joan was hoping. She wasn't going to let herself fall for it she thought with determination.

As Jenny arrived in her classroom she headed for the out-side door onto the playground. It was nearly time for the whistle and children were tidying away the play equipment. She could see her teaching assistant Jodie, shepherding children in various directions, because Jodie was also the senior midday supervisor. Jenny went outside to meet the children and take them into the classroom from the playground. Most children stayed at school for lunch but one or two went home and Jenny greeted their parents with a sunny smile as she welcomed all the children in. Christopher Mayhew was there, too, with Charlie. The little boy was wearing a baseball cap so the full extent of his recovering injury was masked. All thoughts of the horrid lunch time conversation evaporated instantly. Her mind turned to that morning when she had spoken to her class about his imminent return and described how he might look. She didn't want the shock of that to provoke unwanted comments from the children. Several of her class and one or two from Sally's parallel class were clustered around Charlie and his Dad on the playground and as the whistle went for the children to line up, several tried to take his hand. Jenny was well aware that some of the children, both older and younger ones, would try to 'mother' him, seeing his injury as a need for that. There were several issues for which she might need to be ready. The whole school had been prepared for his return during departmental assemblies, too. As far as Jenny was concerned she wanted his re-introduction to school to be as normal as possible whilst she would be aware of keeping an eye upon him, without him realising it. This, she had discussed with Christopher when she had met him with Graham Lockward previously.

Certainly the raw lividness of Charlie's scars was less and his Dad must have taken him to the barber because he sported a very short hair-cut. His adorable curls had all gone now so that the shaved part was significantly less noticeable than when Jenny had visited his home with Sally. He had suddenly lost his little baby boy look and seemed older. However, he leaned against her as his Dad spoke to Jenny.

"He has been really looking forward to this afternoon," Christopher said as Jenny greeted him. Christopher bent to kiss his son goodbye and indicated he should join the line. After the lad had moved away Christopher added "I'll be on the end of the phone if you need me at all."

Jenny quite understood his anxiety and made to re-assure him. "I know you'll be there but I'm sure he'll be fine. Try not to worry, although I'm sure you will anyway." They laughed together for a moment, each understanding the other. With that, the whistle went and it was time for the afternoon session to begin. Christopher spotted Sally in the distance and gave her a wave before he turned and headed for the side of the school and the gate.

Jenny took her class indoors and as they hung up their jackets and hats she hovered in the doorway to ensure good order. The children knew her expectations now and responded positively to her calming, positive comments. As they came to sit on the carpet ready for registration she caught several children staring at Charlie's head, but no-one said anything. Jenny had decided to bite the bullet and have it out in the open, so after saying good afternoon to each child as she called their names she welcomed Charlie back to the classroom. She had decided previously, and this had been ratified by the information leaflet, that she would enable Charlie to talk about his time in hospital and allow the others to ask some questions if they wanted. This should de-mystify the experience for all of them and help Charlie to be accepted as he looked now. Some questions were very perceptive from her group of six year olds as well as the usual one or two predictable and immature ones like 'did it hurt?' Charlie spoke openly and with confidence about his hospital experience. Jenny didn't allow them to dwell too long, though, before she moved the session on. They all had a good afternoon. It was perfectly normal without Charlie needing anything in particular. The other children, having had the opportunity to talk carried on and ignored his looks and particular needs. They had no PE and at playtime he stayed indoors with Jenny. They read a book together and then he wanted to play with some of the classroom toys. Since playtimes were unwinding times for children she was content to leave him to his own devices for a while and Jenny got on with her own work, companionably silent.

By the time the afternoon was over Jenny was confident that Charlie was going to continue to flourish at school. She took her class to the door after she had waited for each child to do their own coat up and collect their things, and then let them out to meet their parents and carers. Christopher was there to greet Charlie and having given him a hug and exchanged a quick word with him he came towards Jenny.

"Come in," she said, holding the door wider. "I shan't be a minute. I just need to make sure they are all collected," she indicated the remaining children.

Two minutes later she joined him in the warmth of the classroom.

"The smell of these places always transports me back to my own schooling," said Christopher.

"Good days?" enquired Jenny.

"Hmm, not ever- so" he replied. "I remember being scared of several teachers and hating the school toilets," he laughed. "So different here, for Charlie. He loves it, and you! How has he been today?"

Jenny smiled at the compliment. "Charlie would you go and put this away for me in the three bears home corner, please?" Jenny asked the little boy so that he was out of ear-shot of their conversation. "Truly he's been fine." Jenny went on to explain that they had all shared a discussion about Charlie's accident and his stay in hospital. "I'm afraid I also took the opportunity for a bit of propaganda for promoting safety too," Jenny said. "We talked about wearing bike helmets and road awareness. The Year 6's do a bike course here at school but it makes you wonder if that's too late. He stayed indoors with me at playtime," she explained and told Christopher about that too.

"I really don't want to put you to extra work," Christopher said, looking worried.

"I don't usually leave the classroom in the afternoon break," Jenny explained "and when it's my turn for duty one of the other teachers or our teaching assistant will look after him. He'll have to go onto the playground before too long but this week it's probably better that he stays in. We'll stick to what we agreed about PE and at the end of the week we'll decide how he's been and whether he's ready for all day.

"If we can take it as it comes like we said, that would be great," Christopher responded. "I really can't thank you enough for your kindness."

"Really," Jenny assured him, "it's a pleasure to help in any way. Are you ready to go with your Dad, Charlie? I was just telling him what we chatted about when you came into school after lunch. Have you had a good afternoon, do you think?" Jenny didn't want Charlie to think he was totally excluded from their discussion when it was about him. Children could be so perceptive and he had probably had his ears wagging in the home corner.

With that, Charlie carried on chattering away to his Dad as they moved towards the internal door and up the corridor to the front entrance. Jenny followed them through the door and stood talking to them both on the step for several minutes. Conversation flowed between the three of them very easily and there was quite a bit of laughter too.

"Oh, I almost forgot, I've nearly finished the book you leant me," Jenny said. Charlie had drifted away to the footpath and was kneeling down peering into the flower bed. A further conversation ensued between Jenny and Christopher about the book and then they joined Charlie to discover what he was looking at, sharing his interest in an exceedingly long worm that he had discovered.

Eventually, they all stood and said their goodbyes. Jenny reassured Christopher that she would keep in touch and he thanked her again.

She shivered as she turned to the front door. It was very wintery and she had stood chatting without her coat on, not realising how cold it was. She thought she would collect a warming cup of tea to take back to the classroom so she headed for the staffroom. When she arrived Sally was there before her.

"Hello," Jenny said to her friend. "I've just been chatting to Christopher about Charlie but it's really cold out there," she said.

"I saw you." Sally stated. "I thought he might have popped in to say hello to me too."

"I guess his mind was on Charlie. I think that's understandable, though," Jenny said equably.

"Well, of course, but he could have just said hello, all the same," Sally persisted.

Jenny tried hard to think of a way to phrase what she was thinking. "Sometimes it's hard to separate work form personal stuff. I'm sure he was seeing this visit as work," she tried to be diplomatic, referring to Christopher rather than Sally herself.

"You and he looked like you were getting along well, though," Sally observed sounding worried.

"He's just a worried parent of a poorly little boy in my class," Jenny reassured her friend. Changing the subject and trying to sound positive she asked "What are you going to see at the weekend when you go to the pictures?"

"I don't know yet, we still need to decide. I looked up the cinema on the internet last night to see the synopses and times. Perhaps I'll catch him tomorrow and ask what he fancies seeing." She answered brightening.

□□□□□□□□□

Jenny still had to finalise her letter of application for the internal promotion so that evening she set her mind to completing it. The pages of notes she had made previously were a help but she needed to be aware of being concise and not rambling. She knew now that Sally was not applying but rumour had it there would be one other candidate. Sheila had dropped that much information to her, although she hadn't said who. All would become clear after the closing date but Jenny thought the only other likely candidate could be Joan. Only one other could possibly have been in a position to apply and she had made it clear, as had Sally, that she definitely would not be going for it. With the end of her pen tapping her cheek Jenny contemplated the prospect. Joan had been at the school for quite a while and as one of the older, established members of staff it would be a little surprising that she had not thought of promotion before, despite the fact that she had the knowledge. Perhaps it was just the convenience of it, a job in her own school should she choose to apply. However, as Jenny had discovered, she might have experience and knowledge but her people skills left something to be desired and that was the crux of this job.

As Jenny finished her application letter she asked Mike to read it and check it over for her. There would be nothing worse than making a foolish spelling error. As he finished he said "I think the job is yours. Having read this how could they even think of giving it to one of the gruesome twosome, even if she applies."

"It all needs to be accurate. I can't blag any evidence like I could if I was applying from another school. They know me and exactly what I can and have done. Do you think it's concise enough?"

"Yes," he answered it's a good letter, like I say, I think it's yours." Jenny smiled at Mike's praise. She had sometimes shared Joan's gems with him. She debated whether to tell him now that he had been spotted at the swimming pool, flirting with Diana. "You'll never guess her latest pearl of wisdom. Jenny launched into the story of the staffroom discussion from earlier, making it clear to Mike that she knew he would not do anything wrong with their mutual friend.

"Ridiculous," he barked and reaching down to the side of the sofa he retrieved his newspaper and dived behind it, from where he said "the woman should be locked up."

"Jenny almost jumped at his vociferous response, but she guessed he must be quite angry as she had been.

9 CHAPTER

The day of the interview dawned and had the promise of being bright and clear. Although it was still dark the stars were intense and the forecast was good for the time of year. The wind seemed to have died at last and the day before had been beautiful, if cold. This must be a good omen, thought Jenny. She knew now that she and Joan were the only candidates for the internal promotion. She felt confident but nothing was guaranteed in this life and so she would still need to do the best interview she could. For her pride this was also necessary. She wanted to know she had been given the job on proper merit and not by default because the other candidate was even worse than herself. Also as an internal candidate, pressure seemed greater because she couldn't just walk away if she wasn't given the job.

She was awake early and tried to clear her mind of the imaginary conversations that were whizzing around in her brain. No matter how many of these she had, rationally, she knew that no part of the interview would follow her prepared fictional route. Jenny didn't want to wake Mike up early so she crept out of bed and wrapping her dressing gown around herself she tiptoed down the stairs silently in the dark. She pushed the kitchen door closed and filled the kettle, switching it on to make a warming cup of tea. As she waited for it to boil she re-read her letter of application in preparation for the day ahead. She didn't need to go into school as normal so in fact, she had plenty of time to prepare. She had left everything ready for the supply teacher and as her name, Lucas, came after Joan's alphabetically, she knew her interview was second. By lunchtime it would all be over. Whichever way it went an afternoon of normal teaching would take her mind off it and she could be at home with Mike to await the result. Graham had said he would telephone by early evening so that the two candidates had time to adjust before seeing everyone at school again. Inevitably there was going to be one disappointed person.

Mike staggered down sleepily three quarters of an hour later. "You were up early," he noted. Why was that?"

"Couldn't get interview questions out of my head," Jenny responded.

"Oh yes! I forgot! What time have you to be there?"

"My interview isn't until ten thirty, so I've got ages yet!" Jenny replied. How could Mike have forgotten this important day for her? Oh well, she thought, he seemed to have a lot on his mind, but she didn't know what, particularly, since he was not very communicative at the moment. She hoped it wasn't this new job and the extra money again. He had seemed alright about her applying; not over enthusiastic but quite alright!

After the interview it would be lunchtime followed by a regular teaching afternoon. Jenny didn't really want to come all the way home to change so she thought to wear something that could do for all events. In the end she decided to wear the outfit she had worn the other night to Diana's and Greg's dinner party. It was smart, warm but serviceable. After Mike had left for work, remembering to wish her well, she had a shower and got ready in a leisurely way. She read through her notes and had another quick look on the internet to reaffirm her ideas and then feeling as prepared as she could be, she locked the house and made her way to school.

On arrival, Jenny began to feel really nervous. She knew this was irrational because she already had a job here, one she enjoyed. It was no desperate thing for her to be doing, but she liked the idea of this role and it was one she knew she could do well. If Joan, of all people, got the position over her she knew she would be devastated. Thoughts of pride coming before a fall crept insidiously into her mind but she tried to relax and banish them. Whatever happened she would cope with it when it arose.......but she did want to do well and get it! She let the secretary know she had arrived and then she entered the staffroom which, thankfully, was empty. Some kind person, Sheila she imagined, had left a coffee pot, with milk, a plate of biscuits and pretty paper serviettes on a tray as a welcome. This was not normal fare for the staffroom and Jenny appreciated the touch, determining to thank the deputy head for this thoughtful move. She hadn't been sitting for more than about ten minutes when she heard movement in the corridor. This was sooner than she had expected. Thank goodness she had left it no later to leave home. It wasn't time yet for her own interview but she was ready should she be called early.

As the door opened Jenny's heart skipped a nervous beat. She hadn't touched the coffee but knew she would be ready for it when she came out of the interview. She didn't want to risk needing the loo during the questioning. That would be very distracting, she smiled to herself. A head popped around the door and the chair of governors, Mr. Davies, said "Hello, Jenny. I know we are early and if you want another few minutes that would be fine. Equally we can get straight on with it if you like."

Jenny had met David Davies at her last interview and he had been at the school, wandering round, on the evening of the parent/ teacher consultations. He had some fairly senior position at the post office and he also had a child in year four. She liked him. He was large and tubby and friendly but he was a conscientious governor and certainly seemed to know his stuff from what she had seen and from what others said.

"I'd really like to get on with it," Jenny replied.

"Are you feeling nervous?" David asked.

"I am a bit, this time." Jenny answered.

"Well, there are no trick questions," he said easily, as he led the way to the head's office. "We just want to find out how you see this role progressing and what you can bring to it."

He held the door to Graham Lockwood's office open for her to precede him into the room. As she entered Graham stood and welcomed her, indicating where she should sit. She put down her bag and made sure she placed her bottom right back on the seat, trying to look relaxed, as he said "Thanks for coming Jenny."

Once everyone was seated and opening welcomes had been voiced the substance of the interview began. They wanted to know, of course, what Jenny thought the role involved and then moved on to how she would implement some of her ideas. She managed to get the title of the government document "Every Child Matters" into the conversation and was confident that her ideas would reflect the Ofsted inspectorate's framework. She was convinced that the work would need to be child-centred and that positive partnerships between home and school should support children's development and learning. She knew that families needed to be identified at the earliest stage of a child's schooling and that families should be linked to specialised support if it was needed. Whilst all this was true Jenny was aware that it all sounded a bit bookish so, having pondered lengthily, the thing at home, she decided to add an anecdote to bring the theory into everyday reality. She spoke of a family she had known at her previous school where there had been twin girls. They had been vulnerable, having been fathered by their grandfather! Jenny detailed the influence she'd had in obtaining external support for the mother and her twins, both of whom were underachieving in school and who appeared frail and uncared for. She was able to talk about her professional relationship with the family and the care she took to deal with the various elements of the case with sensitive efficiency. Although their mother clearly loved them both dearly she found it difficult to know how best to cater for their needs. It was a powerful story that illustrated Jenny's previous experience and skill in dealing with such sensitive subjects.

Finally they asked her if she had any questions for them and Jenny took the opportunity to gain further information about resources that might be available to her. She knew she would need a small amount of money and a little non-contact time to achieve all that she would like to do. As the interview drew to a close, Jenny hoped fervently, that she had done enough to get the job. She wanted to continue to be able to support vulnerable families and to develop children in need but with the extra resources available to do that the possibilities were far greater. She thanked the interviewers for this opportunity and left the room.

When she entered the staffroom to make a cup of tea Jenny found she was shaking a little; reaction to the tension she must have been feeling. She wanted, so much, to be able to do this. She knew she had a little time before lunch time, when the mid-day supervisors would arrive and others would descend on the room, so she sat and went over the questions and her responses in her mind. She hoped she had done enough but it was only her best and the decision was her fate now.

⬜⬜⬜⬜⬜⬜⬜⬜

That evening she left school in good time and decided to call and see Pat on her way home. She was ready to share a good chat and felt she would get more joy there than at home with Mike. Pat's boys would be there but that was OK. They would be playing and she wanted to see for herself how Pat was too. That situation seemed to be draining all the vitality from her friend and she was worried about her. As she knocked on the door she could hear the boys playing some wild game. It was more difficult for them to let off steam in a small house when the weather was poor, although it had been better today.

Pat answered her knock just as a small car came hurtling up the wooden floor of the hallway. Ben and Joe had their 'hot wheels' set up at the far end and they were sliding and skidding and shrieking with fun as the cars sped from the stunt ramp along the floor.

"Come into bedlam," Pat smiled and raised her voice above the noise.

"I just thought I'd come and see how things are and tell you about my day," replied Jenny as she stepped around the game.

"You've had your interview, haven't you?" asked Pat. "I was going to ring you later but it's better to chat face to face. I told you to let me know."

They went into Pat's kitchen and she put the kettle on to boil. "I think it's safest in here," she said. "We can chat because the boys are completely engrossed in that. They've had a snack so they should be quite happy for a while and leave us to it. I wanted to tell you the latest as well," she said, looking away.

Jenny immediately wondered if there had been further developments in Pat's situation and put her own news on hold, determined to give her good friend whatever support was necessary.

As they settled at the familiar kitchen table, Jenny could see that Pat was anxious to get something out in the open. "What's happened?" she asked.

"Doug's gone," she said bluntly. Jenny felt a mixture of shock and relief for her friend.

"Well he's gone to stay with a guy who works at the leisure centre with him, just for a time, anyway. I suppose it's what people call a trial separation. I told him to go," she added almost as if she was surprised by her own decision.

"I can't help feeling it's a good thing, for now, anyway," Jenny replied. "It should give you both some time to consider things. How are you coping?" Jenny privately thought Pat looked better for it already.

"Oh, alright, I suppose."

"What have you told the boys?"

"I'm afraid I have just said that their Dad is on a course and can only visit at the weekend; that it will be just for a while."

"So what prompted you? Jenny asked. I know it can't have been easy.

"To be honest it's a bit of a relief. You were right, Jenny. It was all making me ill and that wasn't good for the boys was it? There's no doubt that he was shocked. I'm not sure whether that was because I had found out or whether because I had actually told him to go! He kept saying how sorry he was and that he loved us. Right at this moment, though I'm not sure I know what love is."

"Pat, I'm so sorry, and if there's anything, anything at all that I can do you must just ask. Whether it's baby-sitting or listening, or anything at all."

"I know Jenny, and just knowing that helps a lot."

"What do you think the prognosis will

be?" Jenny wanted to know. She knew it was slightly more complicated when children were involved, but she also thought Pat was better off without Doug. She thought it was quite a simple decision.

"I'm hoping the shock will be enough for him to really consider whether he will be better off on his own – or with her, I should say, or whether the grass really is not greener. It still needs cutting and tending even on the other side of the fence!" Pat managed half a smile but Jenny could see that it was a struggle. She couldn't understand how Pat could really consider having Doug back after the way he had treated her, although it seemed such a sad thing for a good relationship to falter like this. Perhaps it hadn't been such a good thing in the first place after all. Thank goodness she could rely on Mike, even if they did have the odd spat.

With that, Pat asked how the interview had gone. "Well," said Jenny, "I really do want this job now I've put in this much effort and the thought of Joan getting it has also spurred me on. I just hope I've done enough."

"I should be very surprised if you don't, if that's the only opposition," said Pat. Ben had been in Joan's class the previous year, and whilst he liked her well enough and had progressed satisfactorily,

Jenny knew that Pat had not particularly liked parents' evenings that year.

"I don't just want to get it because the opposition is duff though, either," said Jenny. "I'd like to think I got it because I'd earned it!"

"Of course, said Pat, "but I don't think they would give it to anyone who didn't deserve it. When do you expect to hear?"

"Someone is going to telephone this evening around seven o'clock. That's a lot longer than it normally takes but they thought as we are both internal candidates we would have time whichever way it goes to get over it before facing everyone tomorrow will be horrid for both of us really," answered Jenny.

"Yes, I suppose if you get it, it'll be hard to be overly happy and if you don't you have to brave it out."

"Exactly," grimaced Jenny.

With that the boys appeared, having exhausted both the game they were playing, and themselves. "Can we put the television on now?" asked Joe, the younger but always bolder brother.

"Yes, you can," responded their Mum but having glanced up at the clock she added "but only for half an hour and then its tea, bath and bed a bit earlier tonight." Turning to Jenny she explained that they had been out with Doug the previous evening and had been quite late in and to bed. "It's typical in our situation, isn't it? He gets to do all the fun stuff and I get to be the ogre who says 'early to bed'. Still I took them out for burger and chips the other night just so they could see me giving a treat too. It's all so un-natural though, and can't be that good for them." Pat looked worried.

"You're right but it's early days and you'll both find an equilibrium. So long as you both keep talking about that sort of thing and don't try to out-do each other," said Jenny, trying to be wise about something she really knew very little.

"You are wise," echoed Pat. "It's good to have a sounding board in you."

"Thank you," Jenny uttered warmly. She really valued this friendship. "I guess I better make a track, let you get on and go and see about tea. Mike will be in before long."

"How are things there?" asked Pat.

"Alright I suppose. He's a bit reticent at the moment and not keen to talk much. He really isn't enjoying his work but I'm trying not to gloat too much about mine, like you suggested."

"Be careful about my advice," smiled Pat. "I'm not the world's authority on married life am I?" she said ruefully.

With that Jenny got up and reached for her jacket off the back of the chair. "Try and keep smiling," she said "and don't forget to ask for help whenever you need it," she added.

"Goodbye boys," called Jenny as she passed the living room. Both boys were lying on cushions on the floor and turned to her as she went. Ben waved and Joe grinned and said "'Bye, Jenny," as she left.

"See you soon," she turned and said to Pat as she walked up the path.

□□□□□□□□

After Jenny arrived at home she realised it was going to be a long evening waiting for the results of her interview. She tried to imagine how she would behave as she entered the staffroom the next day both if she got the job and if she didn't. What would she say to Joan? How would she react with the rest of the staff? What would Graham Lockwood have to say to her? She supposed that the whole result thing would be a five minute conversation piece at school, however it turned out – she hoped! Then her mind turned to Mike. How would he react if she got the job? Would the extra money come further between them or would he be pleased and happy to redecorate the living room as she had suggested? Life seemed so complicated sometimes. Then there was Pat. How dreadful to be in such a situation as hers. She was wondering what to do next to make the time pass when the telephone's insistent sound broke into her thoughts. She picked it up abstractedly and was surprised to hear Greg's deep voice at the other end. "Hi, Honey" he said cheerfully

"Hello" said Jenny, wondering why Greg would be 'phoning her now.

"I gather you had your interview today. How did it go?"

"Oh, Greg! How kind of you to ask. I think it was alright but it's always difficult to know isn't it? As I came out I was thinking of other things I could or perhaps should have said."

"I think that's always the case but it doesn't really mean anything. So when do you expect to hear. I thought you might already know."

"Normally they tell you pretty much straight away but because it's an internal thing, I'm expecting a phone call this evening at about seven." Answered Jenny

"Well good luck, for that then. I think you would do the new job really well. You've got such good people skills and you work hard, lovely girl. Let us know how you do," and then he added "when you're ready of course."

"Thank you, Greg, and thanks again for asking," Jenny said appreciatively. He was such a lovely, gentle man.

As she wandered into the kitchen to think vaguely about food for dinner, Jenny reflected on the call and considered again what a very restful, considerate man Greg was.

It wasn't long before Mike arrived home. "So, how did it go?" he asked. Jenny remembered some of the questions she had been asked and tried to describe the answers she had given.

"I really don't know if it's enough, though."

"Well, the opposition isn't up too much is it?" Mike stated

"I know, but they may give it to neither of us if they feel I won't do it justice either," said Jenny gloomily.

"Let's have dinner" said Mike "You'll know soon enough, and then we can decide how to spend your millions!" he smiled. Jenny was glad for his level reflection as this point. She felt she couldn't have handled snide comments about earnings at this moment.

Dinner was a quiet affair with neither of them saying much but going through the motions of feeding themselves as a matter of necessity rather than enjoyment. Shortly after the chores of tidying up were done they settled in the living room in front of the television. Jenny felt distracted and wasn't concentrating on the programme when her mobile shrilled and made her jump. She glanced at Mike and leapt to her feet, moving to the hallway where the sound of the TV was muted.

"Hello, Jenny," said a voice at the other end. It was her Mum.

Jenny couldn't believe the timing. "Mum, I'll have to call you back. I'm really sorry but I'm waiting for school to call with the results of my interview."

"Sorry, Love. I was 'phoning to see how you did as you hadn't called."

"Well that's 'cos I don't know yet!" Jenny said in an exasperated voice. Then, cooling her frustration she said more calmly "I'll phone you as soon as I know but I'll really have to go now. They said they'd be 'phoning me about now with the result."

"OK, Jenny. Let us know darling, and good luck." The phone went dead and the call was ended.

Jenny returned to the living room as Mike turned to her with raised eyebrows in a silent question.

"It was Mum. Can you believe it? She was only calling to see what the result was" Jenny responded, smiling again now. "What timing!"

Just then the mobile resonated again, and again Jenny's heart bumped under ribs as she returned to the hallway.

"Hello, is that Jenny Lucas?"

"Yes, hello," responded Jenny.

"It's Dai Davies here," came a lilting voice at the other end. "Sorry to keep you waiting, Jenny but we have made a decision and the personnel committee of the Governors agree with that.

"Thank you for calling said Jenny; thinking 'just cut to the quick and never mind all the pleasantries'.

"We were very impressed with your answers and would like to offer you the job, Jenny," continued Mr. Davies

"Thank you so much," said Jenny breathing a large sigh of relief.

"Yes, your answers were exceptionally mature and sensibly realistic and so we have every faith in your abilities to take on this extra responsibility."

"Thank you," said Jenny again, suddenly feeling rather tongue tied.

"Graham will speak to you more in the next day or two, but in the meantime congratulations from us all on the Governing Body.

"I won't let you down," said Jenny feeling more and more ecstatic as she slowly acclimatised her mind to her success.

"Well, have a good evening, Jenny. Speak soon. Bye."

"Good-bye." Jenny disconnected the call and bounced into the living room with a broad smile of relief and pleasure on her face. Mike turned as the door re-opened.

"I got it!" Jenny's eyes sparkled as she announced her good news. "I'm so relieved. I was beginning to talk myself into not being too disappointed if I was unsuccessful."

"Well done," said Mike. "So when does all the extra work start?"

"After Christmas, officially, but as soon as I like I suppose. We'll be able to get that flat screen television for over Christmas though, won't we?" Jenny asked. "I won't get the first increased pay check until the end of January but we'll know it's coming. I better phone Mum back. Shall we open that bottle of bubbly we've had for ages when I've done that? I shan't be long."

With that, she went up to the bedroom to start telephoning several people, including Pat and Greg whom she knew were also waiting to share her good news.

10 CHAPTER

Once December arrived everything at school seemed to be geared to Christmas. Children's plays and concerts were a low key affair these days but songs till needed to be learnt and whilst costumes and practices were restricted to the week before the event children's activities took on a festive nature, whilst still holding an educational element!

Jenny felt festive too and one evening decided to telephone Pat with the suggestion of a girl's day out at the health and beauty centre in a nearby town. She didn't want to go to the local leisure centre because that is where Doug worked and she felt Pat would be more likely to come if she could book some beauty treatments and maybe a sauna or Jacuzzi session elsewhere. Anyway Jenny had no desire to see Doug at the moment. She was really angry with his behaviour and the upset he had caused. She hoped their day out could be arranged for a Saturday when Pat's mum, or Doug, might have the boys for the day. Maybe they could even have dinner out and make a real treat of a day. She went onto the web site for the centre to find out the information before speaking to the others. It had been months since she, Pat and Diana had had a girls' day out.

As she read the information she became more and more convinced it would do them all good. The weather had been dull recently. Pat had looked weary and dejected, and she was sure Diana would be up for it. The literature on line was encouraging. It spoke of a 'peaceful sanctuary which was calming and soothing'. The staff were 'trained therapists from some of the finest treatment houses'. Jenny was slightly cynical about some of the wording used but never-the-less, it sounded just what she was looking for. It was quite costly but there was a day's spa deal which included a glass of bubbly on arrival, a massage, facial, and lunch. It sounded perfect. She really fancied the 'tranquility scalp and shoulder massage'! She imagined snuggling into the complementary use of 'thick white towels and robes'.

Jenny phoned Pat and discussed the idea. Pat sounded really excited about it and was sure her Mum would have the boys if Doug couldn't or wouldn't. She imagined he would, though, because no matter what else he was up to he always had time for them. "I'll call Diana then and book it shall I?" asked Jenny.

"It sounds really great. I'm looking forward to it already!" sighed Pat.

With that, Jenny got straight onto the phone to Diana. She was quite surprised though when she finally got through. "Hi, Diana, it's Jenny." She explained what she had discovered and that Pat was very keen on the idea.

"Well..." hesitated Diana. "I'm not sure. I've had a stonking cold and I still feel ropey."

"It's another week yet and it sounds just the sort of thing to pick you up again, then," said Jenny cheerfully.

"You may be right but I've got loads to catch up on, so I think I'll skip this time. Sorry."

"Oh!" said Jenny, somewhat surprised. It was unlike Diana to miss something like this. She was usually the first to jump at such an opportunity. "OK, then. Maybe next time."

After a few pleasantries Jenny said that she hoped she felt better soon and hung up. She rang Pat back to say that it would be just the two of them. "That's fine, said Pat. We can still talk the hind leg off a donkey, just you and me," she laughed.

"We certainly can. I'll get straight on and book it then." When she ended her call to Pat she did just that.

That Saturday dawned dull, cold and grey, so Jenny was pleased that she had booked their girls' day out.

"What will you do today?" she asked Mike as she prepared to get out of bed.

"No plans," he answered vaguely, turning away as she got up.

There had been no more arguments, but Mike had seemed oddly distant. The reasons for this were nothing that Jenny could place her finger on. They both were busy and she knew Mike did not enjoy his work. She supposed he was just tired and the weather didn't encourage anyone to be lively really. She had made an effort to be more understanding and had not talked about her success or satisfaction at work. Oh well! She was looking forward to this day. She dressed quickly and as she left the bedroom she said "I'll see you at about six this evening. Have a good day yourself."

"Mmm, I will," was all the response she got from his half buried face.

Jenny had arranged to pick Pat up so she drove up the road just as Pat was arriving at her gate. "Excellent timing," she said to Jenny as she heaved herself into the car. "I'm really looking forward to this!"

"Me to," Jenny added.

Their day came up to all expectations. On arrival, having booked in, they were given the towels and robes that Jenny had imagined and were given a whistle stop tour of the facilities. After changing and snuggling into their robes they were shown to a cosy area where they were offered a glass of fizz. Jenny doubted it was champagne but they both giggled about it after the waiter had left and began to feel relaxed. "This is decadent," Jenny observed. When they were ready a lively young girl, dressed in shorts and colourful t-shirt came to fetch them and took them to the sauna. Leaving their robes on the designated hooks and dressed in their swimming gear Jenny and Pat cast each other a conspiratorial grin as they both entered the room. The girl showed them what and how to operate the steam, suggested how long they should stay and left them to it. As they sat and soaked up the heat Jenny debated whether to ask Pat how she was doing. She didn't want to bring up the subject really since this was their escape day. After a few minutes, however, Pat started to speak about the very thing that was on Jenny's mind.

"I'm hoping this separation will help Doug to see where his future lies," Pat sighed.

"If he decides he wants to come back, what will you do?" asked Jenny tentatively.

"I have to think of the boys." Pat left questions hanging in the air with her statement.

"You have to think about you as well. If this were to happen yet again you would be no good for the boys if you go under," Jenny offered.

I know, but I'm under no illusions about marriage now and under no delusions about my importance to Doug. If he comes back at least I shall be less reliant upon him, emotionally. For my own self I could do without him now, I think."

Jenny was at a bit of a loss as to how to respond to that. She knew what she thought but wasn't sure if she should be forthright and brutal enough to say it. She was quiet for a moment while she contemplated whether to speak or not.

Just then the young girl returned and suggested they might like to have a swim and then shower. "Come through to the treatment rooms when you are ready," she added and so Jenny was saved from her deliberations.

"This is just what the doctor ordered," said Pat as they stood under the streaming hot shower water a little later.

After drying off they donned their robes and went through to a calm room with soft music playing in the background. It smelt clean and delicately perfumed. Jenny had never had a scalp massage before but she decided she really enjoyed it. She felt herself sink further into the inclined chair as she turned her face to the ceiling, closed her eyes and completely relaxed. Pat was next to her and Jenny wondered if she had dozed off it was so quiet and peaceful.

As the day progressed the two friends enjoyed a light lunch with a refreshing glass of sauvignon blanc followed by a facial and hair care session. When it was time to go home Jenny said "That went so quickly but I feel much better for it."

"Oh so do I. What a fantastic idea it was Jenny. You are so clever!" responded Pat warmly. "I feel all warm and relaxed. Ready to face whatever comes next," she added wryly.

When Jenny dropped Pat off outside her gate she was feeling more positive about things too. "I'm sure you will cope with whatever happens, Pat. We're not often sent things we can't cope with at all, even if it feels like that when life throws something at us which is a nasty surprise."

"..and you?" asked Pat

"Me, I think Mike and I will be OK too. I'm more circumspect about work and give him my time as much as possible. His job will sort itself out or he'll change I suppose.

Anyway thanks for today too. I really enjoyed it."

With that, Pat got out and Jenny drove down the road.

⬜⬜⬜⬜⬜⬜⬜⬜

Mike's car wasn't there when she arrived and she hoped he had found something good to do with his day too. She entered the house, went into the kitchen and having flung her swimming stuff in the washing machine, put on the kettle for a cup of tea.

Time passed and still Mike was not home. Jenny remembered the argument they'd had the last time he was late and although she was uneasy she banished negative thoughts and busied herself with going to the bedroom and generally tidying up. She straightened the bed, smiling to herself at Mike's scruffiness. He had probably slept in she thought indulgently, as she picked his dirty clothes off the floor and carried more washing downstairs to the kitchen. Stuffing it all into the machine she switched it on and went through to turn on some music. She pushed her phone into the speaker to charge it and search for something to listen to. Then she curled up in the corner of the sofa with her book. She was blowed if she was going to do school work now. This was the book that Christopher had lent her and she was really enjoying it. The trouble was she only got a few pages read each night before she fell asleep. She really must get it finished and return it. She felt almost uncomfortable reading in the day time when there were jobs do be done, but she settled now to enjoy a guilty pleasure. Reaching over to switch on the table lamp, her mind wandered to Christopher and his attractive green eyes with the crinkles at the corners. He was so like an older version of his adorable son. Charlie had made excellent progress and was starting to come in on a full-time basis again. He was a real sweetie with his beaming smile and ready laugh; such a sunny personality. She smiled involuntarily to herself.

Just then, her mobile rang and sighing she stood to retrieve it from the docking station. "Hello," she answered.

"Oh, Jenny, it's Greg" came a slightly surprised voice.

Hello, Greg" Jenny replied "What can I do for you?"

"I wondered whether you had finished your pamper day as it's getting on a bit and I wondered where Diana was. I'm not exactly checking up, of course, but I was starting to get a bit worried as she said she'd definitely be back by four."

"Sorry Greg, I haven't seen her."

"...but I thought she was with you today."

No, Greg, she cried off; said she hadn't been well and had loads to do."

"I've obviously got my wires crossed," Greg replied. "Sorry to bother you."

"No problem, of course," Jenny said. "Let me know if she doesn't reappear won't you, but I'm sure she's just forgotten the time at the shops or something." Jenny automatically looked at her watch to see that it was well after six. Mmm all the shops in town had closed by now. "Perhaps she called in at the supermarket on her way home," she added.

"It'll be something like that." Greg said.

"Mike was really late home a little while ago," said Jenny "and I gave him hell when he got back. We had a right old ding-dong about it but it was only because I had been worried. He'd only been at the gym but I had him in a ditch or bleeding to death at the A and E. I'm sure Diana will be back soon."

"I'm sure you're right. Sorry to bother you, darling." Greg responded.

"No bother, at all. Speak soon, Greg." Jenny clicked off and replacing her mobile in the docking station she found her music.

Checking her watch again, Jenny was just feeling uneasy herself when she heard Mike's key in the door. Being reminded of her reaction the last time, having just spoken to Greg about it, she was careful to smile and ask "Hello, have you had a good day?"

"Yes, I've had a really good day," said Mike seeming very upbeat. "How about you?"

Jenny went on to give Mike the salient details of her session at the Spa with Pat. "So what did you do?" she asked.

"Oh just this and that," he answered. "I pottered around here and then went to the gym." He added turning away to leave the room. "I'm just going for a shower."

He normally showered at the gym, thought Jenny uneasily, as she started to prepare dinner.

They were eating later, when Jenny told him about Greg having called and then she added "He hasn't called back so I suppose she must have turned up. Perhaps I'll call him back after dinner and check."

"What's he checking up on her for?" was Mike's response.

Aware of their argument Jenny tentatively suggested that perhaps he was just worried about her.

A noisy sigh escaped from Mike as he begrudgingly said "Maybe. Well I bumped into her at the gym and she was fine so he's just fussing!"

"What? You saw her at the gym? That's odd because she said she couldn't join us today because she had been feeling poorly and had lots to do."

"Well, she wasn't using the gym, she was just there" he said vaguely. "Don't you start fussing too!"

🗆🗆🗆🗆🗆🗆🗆🗆

After an unremarkable week at work, with Jenny and Mike edging carefully around each other at home, the following weekend dawned bright, and clear but very cold. Jenny got up early on Saturday morning and decided to have thorough clear-out of the wardrobes. They both had old clothes and shoes cluttering the place and with Christmas fast approaching she felt she should make space and she was just in the mood for it. She knew Mike would be going to the gym as he usually did on a Saturday morning so as soon as he had left she collected bin bags and the dusters and set to work. She started on her wardrobe because she knew more clearly what was to keep, what to bag for the charity shop and what to simply bin. It was a satisfying task and by the time her half was completed she was pleased with the results of a clean and tidy cupboard. After a much needed cup of tea she decided she would make a start on Mike's and put the stuff she wasn't sure about to one side to ask him when he returned. The last time she did this he'd said how much better it was to be able to find exactly what he wanted so much more easily, but it must have been a good couple of years ago.

She found several old t-shirts and shirts and was just deciding what to do with a pair of jeans when she felt crackling in the pocket. Thinking she better check before bagging them she stuck her hand in somewhat cautiously, not wanting to find anything grim! What she found was ominous and horrible. She plonked down on the bed, her heart beating so fast she started shaking. There must be a reason for this. She tried to remember when he last wore these jeans but her mind couldn't focus. All she knew was that he and she didn't use condoms and so why were there three empty packets and two unopened ones in his jeans pocket. They hadn't done much together recently but she'd put their distance down to his stress and work though. Had he simply been relieving himself? 'Don't be stupid' she thought to herself. 'Surely there must be a sensible explanation.' She continued to sit and stare at the packets in her hands and couldn't move. Then she rapidly stuffed them back where she found them. Then, in turmoil, she retrieved them again. She thought back to the un-natural strain between them recently. She remembered the vague replies and his late return. She considered his aloofness. Oh no, surely not. He'd said he would never cheat. He'd told her that again, so recently. She's asked him directly if he would ever do that and he'd said 'no'. There must be another explanation.

Jenny wasn't sure how long she sat there shaking and disbelieving, trying hard to put a positive spin on this unwitting discovery. She sensed, rather than heard, his keys in the door, his footsteps on the stairs and still she sat, immobile, with the loathsome facts in her hands. This is how he found her.

As he pushed open the bedroom door, still she sat unmoving. He glanced at her hands and froze in the doorway.

"What are these?" she asked with a large intake of breadth.

"I think you can see that," he answered while he probably thought what to say. After a pause he continued, "You obviously went through my pockets!"

"I was doing no more than I have ever done in the past. I was going to wash you jeans before bagging them up" she said. "Last time we were both pleased with my clear-out. Why have you got them? Why have you used some?"

"Why do you think?" he responded.

"Tell me!" she raised her voice in anguish. "Tell me! Who is it?"

"You don't need to know. Jenny I'm so, so sorry"

"Tell me!" she whispered, tears springing to her eyes. "Is it Diana?"

He sank to the bed beside her and put his head in his hands. "Yes." He murmured.

"Why? What have I done wrong, or not done?" she asked.

"I don't know. Nothing. She was there."

"I was here. You said just the other week that you'd never do this. We said we'd always be honest with each other. We made promises."

"Oh Jenny, I don't know why. I love you, I really do." He went to put his arm around her. She stood quickly

"I can't do this now," she replied. "I need to be on my own."

"Do you want me to go?" he asked.

"Yes. No. I don't know. Go where? To her?"

"No, she's at home with Greg now."

"Oh no, poor Greg. Does he know?" She suddenly thought about kind, gentle, loving Greg.

"I don't think he knows. He doesn't need

to know, Jenny, unless you want to tell him. He doesn't need to be hurt too, does he?"

Jenny was suddenly mad with anger. She kicked out at the bed. You selfish, selfish sod! How could you do this? How could she. I thought she was my friend. You talk about loyalty to work colleagues. You talk about loyalty to team mates. You and your high ideals when it comes to all sorts of things. What happened to loyalty and trust with me? I'm your wife. I want you to go. I don't care where. Just go! Get out and leave me alone" her voice rose with her passion. Then she ran out of the bedroom. She hurried down the stairs. She entered the living room and slammed the door shut, flinging herself in a heap on the sofa. She clung to a cushion and heaved and heaved great gulping sobs of rejection, humility and loss.

All was quiet upstairs for a while, not that Jenny would have heard Mike moving around. After some time she began to be aware of floorboards above creaking with movements in the bedroom. Then she heard his footsteps on the stairs. The living room door opened slowly. Jenny sat up, her eyes swollen and red. Mike just stood there, looking at her forlornly. "I didn't think you'd ever find out," he said. "I didn't mean for it to be like this, to hurt you."

"Just go," she whispered.

With that he said "I'll be at Alex's. He

said I could go there for a while since he's on his own at the moment." He turned and left the room quietly and Jenny heard the front door close after him.

She sat up and, with tears still rolling down her face, watched him walk along the front path to the gate. She saw him climb into his car. He sat for a moment without moving, head down. Then she heard the engine start and the car pulled away. In the back of her mind, she hoped he drove safely. Then she adjusted her thoughts again and wryly considered that, after everything of the last hour, she still had his safety in mind.

Unaware of how long she sat, clutching the cushion to her, Jenny eventually got up and wandered aimlessly into the kitchen. Then she climbed the stairs and pushed open the bedroom door. The offending jeans had disappeared, as had all evidence of Mike's disloyalty and betrayal. She sagged down onto the bed, all impetus for action gone. She didn't know what to do. She thought of speaking to Pat but couldn't find the motivation to do even that. She just wanted to curl up and hide. Her mobile phone buzzed in her pocket. Retrieving it she saw it was Mike calling. She couldn't bring herself to answer it. It stopped but then a few minutes later it rang again. Sighing she pressed the button to answer the call. "I'm just calling to see if you are alright" he said.

"Fine," she responded briefly and cancelled the call. She certainly couldn't speak to him at the moment. She felt completely drained of all emotion and feeling not only rejection but betrayal and loneliness. She couldn't understand the selfishness of a friend's duplicity. What she thought was friendship was no more than herself being used and an object of ridicule and deceitfulness. She wondered what she had done to cause Mike's infidelity too. The more she thought about it the more she felt she must be lacking appeal, allure or attractiveness. She had never felt so rejected and useless.

CHAPTER 11

When Jenny arrived at school on Monday several people asked if she was alright because she looked tired and pale. She had spoken to no-one during the rest of the weekend. She couldn't even bring herself to speak to Pat because somehow it made it all so much more real to voice her distress and confusion. There had been no further calls from Mike either. She vaguely knew Alex, with whom Mike was reputedly staying. They had met once or twice at the occasional staff 'do' and Mike had told her some time ago that he had moved to a larger flat in that new complex behind the shopping centre.

One of the hardest things that Jenny had to do was enter the staffroom at lunchtime. She had avoided going in at playtime but she knew she couldn't dodge going there for ever. There was an informal meeting to discuss the Christmas concert arrangements so she collected a cup of tea and quietly edged her way into a seat with her back to the window. The morning had been OK, although she was finding it difficult to get motivated. She was dog-tired. There had been moments, however, when her mind had been completely engaged with the children in her care, for which she was very grateful. Sheila was reminding staff about dates for various events. The school post box would go out the following week and she was asking for a volunteer to smarten it up after its annual bashing from the previous year when the Year 6s had moved it daily to empty and distribute the contents. Concert tickets and other arrangements were discussed as well as various other aspects of the season. Lastly was discussed the more detailed organisation for Christmas lunches for children and the staff and governors' get together at the end of term. Throughout all this Jenny felt on auto pilot and mumbled responses and opinions when required. At this point in time she didn't feel in the Christmas spirit at all.

As discussion became desultory and the meeting finished people began to mill about and leave the room. Sally came and sat in the empty seat next to Jenny. "Are you not feeling too good?" she asked.

"I had a bad night. I didn't sleep too well," Jenny answered. "I'm feeling off colour today, that's all" she answered.

"Poor you. Well if you sicken for something please don't give it to me," pleaded Sally. "Between us," she spoke quietly, "Christopher has asked me out to dinner on Saturday, "she added. "I told him about that new place that's just opened up in Silver Street. My neighbour was raving about it and I was telling him after school the other day and saying how I'd love to try it."

"I don't think I'm sickening," said Jenny. "I'm just shattered."

"Oh, well I'm pleased for you, of course," Sally smiled "but I'm really looking forward to being with Christopher again. He's so kind and gentle and the way he cares for Charlie is just lovely."

"It's going alright then, your friendship?" asked Jenny.

"We get on really well, although he's quite busy, of course, and tied up a lot so we can't get together that often but we do when we can."

"Are you making progress?" Jenny enquired cautiously.

"I'm sure we are but it's hard when I have Mum to look after and he has Charlie and his work. Changing the subject, I'm really looking forward to Christmas this year. The staff and governors' do should be fun this year if we can bring partners. I shall ask Christopher of course."

"Mmm," Jenny mumbled in a non-committed way. At the moment she could think of nothing she wished to avoid more. She certainly had no Christmas mood anyway. Then she mentally tried not to feel sorry for herself. This was not a unique situation although it was for her. After all, think about Pat, she contemplated. It must be worse for her since she had the boys to consider as well as the fact that it had all happened before to her. Did that make it easier or worse? She wasn't sure. Then Jenny realised that Sally had been speaking again and she had missed what she had said completely, so great was her reverie.

"Sorry, what was that?" she asked, "I was miles away."

"I was just saying that Christopher is so conscientious. He makes sure Charlie keeps in touch with his other grand-parents as well as Christopher's own Mum and Dad. After all, it's five years since she died and he still keeps properly in touch. It must be hard. When he marries again, I'm not sure how his new wife will take to all that."

Jenny wondered if Sally saw herself in that role. She still couldn't help thinking that it sounded as though Sally was more keen than Christopher and seemed to be doing more of the running.

Just then the whistle blew in the distance and glancing at her watch, Jenny gasped and they both hurried to the classrooms to retrieve their children.

That afternoon was a full blown rehearsal for the Christmas concert. Each class had been learning songs but this would be the first time they had come together for a practice. The older children were mainly involved in singing and narrating whilst the younger ones were performing the nativity story with hosts of angels and large flocks of sheep. Whilst the 'aaah' factor always came into play amongst the parents, the staff still wanted the children to perform well. These days, with all the demands of the national curriculum, there was not much time given over to rehearsing but Graham Lockwood still believed that performing was good for children's confidence and parents really loved to come and watch. Indeed tickets were at a premium and had to be rationed to get everyone in within the insurance limits. They did an afternoon performance just for grandparents and playgroups too. The Year 6 children served tea and cakes to the older folk after that one. Generally it was a lovely festive and friendly atmosphere.

As the afternoon progressed, Jenny lost herself in the activity and encouragement of all the children to learn where they had to be and what to do. Charlie was to have been the inn keeper. She had been tempted to give him the part of Joseph. He would have charmed the audience but he was still getting tired easily. As it turned out, this

afternoon he took the part of the angel
Gabriel because that child was sent home
poorly earlier in the day. It was an
important role but not as long as that of
Joseph. Since the other child had no
knowledge of the part he had been chosen to
play and as Charlie was so good in the
designated role, Jenny decided to keep him
in that part. He was confident and cheerful
with the news he had to impart to 'Mary' and
he charmed the socks off all the staff and
the oldest children. His curly hair shone
like a veritable halo and his round face was
positively cherubic! By the end of the day
Jenny realised her work had saved her day,
literally. The afternoon had flown by as she
lost all sense of her own distress.

□□□□□□□□□

A few days later, after she had seen
the children out at the end of the day,
Jenny turned to tidy her classroom which was
slightly the worse for wear. The lack of
routine during the last session, when they
had again practised for the concert had led
to an unaccustomed disorder. By the time she
had done all that, most staff had already
left. She was in no hurry to get home. Her
classroom cleaner had finished work,
teachers weary from the slightly chaotic
nature of the afternoon had left and the
caretaker had checked all the windows and
locked all the outside doors except the main
entrance. She was reluctantly gathering her

bags and bits. She would have to be going home. She knew there was only a chilly emptiness awaiting her there and so she was putting it off. She also knew she really should go and see Pat because if her friend heard her news from elsewhere she would be devastated that Jenny had not confided in her or turned to her for support. Jenny determined to go later to see her. After all, knowing when to ask for help was a sign of strength. It was just that she was feeling so totally useless and devoid of confidence that she wasn't sure she even had the strength to take that step.

Having got her things and put her coat on, she slumped down into her chair, suddenly feeling disillusioned and totally weary. Over the last few days the same thoughts had gone round and round in her head like a nightmare carousel ride. How could a so called 'friend' have deceived and betrayed her like that. They had gone to dinner there and Diana had appeared to be kindness its-self. Abruptly crashing into her head, came the comment she had made to Mike about keeping fit and the teasing smile with which she had delivered the remark. Suddenly it took on a whole new meaning but they had all laughed at the time in what she thought was a companionable way. Jenny started to shake again with renewed shock.

Just at that precise moment of private crisis there was a knock at the internal door and Charlie's dad came in "Sorry to bother you," he said and then stopping abruptly. "Oh my goodness, are you alright? The front door was still open and Jim said it would be OK to pop down"

"Yes, of course," said Jenny rousing herself and plastering a smile on her face. "How can I help?"

"Charlie left his lunch box. My Mum is visiting for the day so she's with him and I thought I'd pop down and collect it before it starts festering!"

"No problem," said Jenny dragging herself up to show him where it was.

"I'm really sorry to bother you. You've been so kind to us, if there's anything I can help you with…."

"It's just something at home," Jenny said evasively.

"I didn't mean to be nosey," Christopher said hastily.

Jenny, already feeling fragile, suddenly desperately needed to share her burdened mind. Tears of fatigue and despair came unbidden to her eyes. She stopped her passage to the cloakroom and turning she blurted out "It's Mike, he's left. He has been seeing someone else. Sorry, sorry I didn't mean to embarrass you"

"You haven't, not at all," and after a second's hesitation he took a step towards her, extending his hand to touch her arm.

Having at last spoken the dreaded words Jenny couldn't stop letting the flood fall. "This is so embarrassing, I'm really sorry," she muttered.

"Please, don't feel awkward. I know what it's like to feel desperate and sometimes you just need to voice it. I understand, I really do," he said quietly.

Jenny immediately felt even worse. Unwittingly he had shown her that her situation was not as desperate as his had been and yet he wasn't making that point at all. "Oh goodness," she said, "I'm so sorry for making a fuss."

"Look, we all need comfort in times of stress," he added, and instinctively, it seemed, he opened his arms and she took shelter there.

After a minute or two they both quite naturally and unashamedly broke away and sat on the edge of a table in the classroom. There she told him everything. She told of her shame and shock, of her feelings of betrayal and uncertainty and of how she felt bereft of confidence and trust. She opened up to him about whom it was that Mike had been seeing and her feelings of a double betrayal by someone who was supposed to be a friend. He listened in silence and she was thankful for the lack of meaningless platitudes and banal comments that he might have made. In his silence he seemed to show that he recognised her distress. In turn she felt that she could tell him the detail of everything and he would both understand and keep the confidence. After a while her internal storm subsided, as they do, and she half smiled wryly. "I'm really sorry. I think you caught me at the wrong moment," she said looking straight into his mild, green eyes.

"Or at the right moment," he said. "Sometimes a sounding board can help."

"You've certainly helped me. Thank you. I suppose we better go. Your Mum will be wondering where you are and I suppose Jim will be waiting to lock up."

They found the lunch-box; Jenny gathered her things and they headed together up the corridor to the front door. They met Jim as they went and Jenny was grateful that he hadn't come upon them in the classroom. He might have completely got the wrong end of the stick and made the wrong assumptions. They said goodnight to him and left the building. In the car park Jenny apologised again.

"Please, I hope we count as friends," Christopher said "and what is this world if we can't help our friends."

Jenny laughed. And for a moment Christopher wondered what he had said. It dawned on him then that Jenny had been badly let down by a so called friend. Christopher joined her mirth, almost a relief of tension as they giggled together and then he added seriously, "Some friends are genuine, you know. Don't lose track of that. It's a truism."

␣␣␣␣␣␣␣␣␣␣

On her way home Jenny reflected on her outburst. She thought she should feel embarrassed but in reality she found that she didn't. With the release of emotion she found she was ready to go and see Pat to divulge to her the latest events. She decided not to go home first. There was no need she reflected grimly. Pulling up outside Pat's house she checked her watch. The boys would have had their tea by now and Pat would be in a position to chat before bath time. She determined to take the bull by the horns and share her news.

When Pat answered the door she showed mild surprise. It was rare that Jenny would call at this time of day. "Come in, come in," she welcomed warmly. "It seems ages since we chatted properly." Jenny felt Pat look at her closely but without saying more she turned and Jenny followed her down the hallway and past the living room. Jenny called hello to the two boys who were rolling on the floor in front of the television. They responded with a "Hi, Jenny" without turning. "So, what's up?" asked Pat as Jenny followed her into the familiar cosiness of the kitchen.

Jenny took a deep breath and with her voice carefully under control she dropped the bombshell. Pat turned from filling the kettle and just looked at her. Without a word she put the kettle down and gave Jenny a hug. This was so uncharacteristic that tears came to Jenny's eyes despite her resolution to remain unemotional. Typically, Pat instinctively knew what devastation Jenny would be feeling. Rummaging up her sleeve for a tissue, Jenny sat down and Pat sat opposite. "Tell me," she said simply and quietly. Having already opened up to Christopher, Jenny found it easier to tell this constant and understanding friend before her all her deepest feelings. Pat was shocked, Jenny could see; not least because it was Diana that Mike had been seeing. She'd had no idea.

"I wonder if being with Doug so much gave him ideas," she said after listening for some time.

"I just feel as if I've let him down and as for her, I don't think I'll ever forgive her. Maybe that sounds harsh but I feel so disillusioned by someone who was supposed to be a friend. It's all the lies and cheating and sneaking around. How can people who say they love treat the object of love in that way? Surely love should be unselfish and reliable. I imagine they had a good old laugh at my expense feeling they'd made plans and got away with it. I feel so humiliated."

"I'm the last person to give advice, aren't I?" Pat smiled ruefully.

"Oh Pat, what a pair we are."

Pat got up to finally put the kettle back on. "In all crises – drink tea," she smiled.

One thing Jenny had decided not to share with Pat was her breaking down in front of Christopher and the fact that he had held her and comforted her. She couldn't analyse why she didn't want to share that. After all there was nothing to it but two people, one giving comfort and the other taking much needed consolation. Christopher was becoming Sally's partner and to her he was no more than an acquaintance. Pat might get the wrong idea, although she hoped she wasn't doing her friend a disservice. She would share this in the future.

"How are you?" Jenny asked

"I'm plodding along. There are good days and bad. The boys see Doug quite regularly." She dropped her voice "They think he's on a course so can't live at home for the time being and I'm sure they believe that. It's early days yet but we're in a sort of routine. He's saying sorry all the time and making noises about coming back. He says it definitely won't happen again and that he loves us."

"Would you have him back? I know you said it's not the first time." Jenny asked.

"I'm holding out at the moment. It's too soon to decide. I haven't rationalised to myself all the humiliation and rejection yet. He can think for a bit longer and I need more time," replied Pat.

"All I can say is that now I understand and to thank you for so much" said Jenny gratefully. "I better be going and then you can sort the boys out for bed."

They stood together and in companionship and understanding headed for the front door.

□□□□□□□□□

Jenny drove down the road and let herself into her own house. The heating had come on so it wasn't chilly, but it was still seemed empty and cold. She had just put down her things when the front door bell rang. She hurriedly slipped out of her coat and flung it over the newel post of the stairs as she reached for the latch. Now what, she thought. She hoped it wasn't Mike she could not cope with any more this evening. When she opened the door she was surprised and not too happy to see who was there. "Hello, come in," she said opening the door wider.

He followed her down the hall to the living room. "Do you want a glass of wine or a cup of tea or coffee?"

"I'd love a whisky but I'll settle for a cup of tea," said Greg.

Jenny went into the kitchen and after a moment Greg followed. She turned and as he came in he scooped her into his arms. He was very tall and she only came up to his chest. He enfolded her and they stood without speaking for several moments. When he finally released her he said "Jenny, I'm so sorry."

"Greg, it's not your fault is it! I imagine you are feeling as bad as me. How did you find out?"

"She told me. She just came out with it. She said she'd rather I heard it from her than from anyone else." Then he quietly added "It's not the first time, you see. It's why we have never married. I didn't feel secure enough for that but I love her. She says she thinks it will probably be over - now that we all know! I certainly didn't see it coming though."

"She says it's over? Just like that?" asked Jenny disbelievingly. "She's caused absolute devastation and she can just walk away as if it didn't matter?" Jenny didn't understand.

"It takes two to tango, you know, Jenny" he responded quietly.

"Yes, of course," she said.

He took her in his arms again and kissed the top of her head. "Why couldn't I have met you first?" he asked.

"What a mess!" Jenny whispered into his chest. After a few moments she broke free to make the tea. "What will you do?" she asked.

"I don't know, probably nothing."

Jenny felt utterly depleted. She had been emotionally up and then down and then up and down again so many times today. They went through to the living room and she sank into the sofa willing it to envelope her and wipe away this nightmare. She just wanted to close her eyes and hide from everything and everyone. Greg looked across at her exhausted demeanour; at her whole self, crumpled in her corner and his heart wept for her. She didn't deserve this at all. "I'll always be here for you Jenny," he said. She glanced up and smiled wanly. "I know, Greg, thank you."

With that he placed his half empty mug on

the table and rose to leave, recognising that she needed to be on her own. "Please call me, whenever you need to," he said as he left. Jenny didn't get up. She didn't have the energy. She heard the front door close and Greg's footsteps fading away as he walked up the path. Tears sprang to her eyes again with the memory of his kindness, even in his own state of distress.

CHAPTER 12

Jenny was so drained and worn out that she slept very soundly that night, for which she was grateful. The new day dawned grey and windy and as she was on playground duty later she dressed warmly. She couldn't bring herself to eat breakfast but she grabbed a yoghurt, a packet of crisps and a couple of bits of fruit from the bowl just before she left the house. During the evening previously, she had made a conscious effort to pull herself together. She wasn't the first person this had happened to and she was going to cope and get back on track. She had a job she loved and a good home, for the time being, anyway. She was luckier than many! The others had always teased her for being Miss Positive and now she would pull in all her reserves and maintain that, as far as possible.

On arriving at school she got out of her car and headed speedily to the front door at the same time as Lesley. "Are you feeling better," said this half of the gruesome twosome, as Mike had christened her and Joan.

"Yes, I am," Jenny responded determinedly, "thank you for asking."

Lesley gave her a beaming smile "Oh good!" she added.

Jenny was quite amazed at the congeniality and half of her mind wondered why she was being treated to such cordiality. She found out later.

The morning proceeded much as any other. The children were starting to get tired, evidenced by the odd squabble and a little more noise than was usual. Jenny reflected at playtime outside that adults became jaded and more lifeless when they were tired but children definitely became louder and more excitable. She had tried to suggest that to Mrs. Jones at parents' evening when her Johnny was particularly wild in the classroom and especially on the playground. She had carefully suggested Johnny would benefit from a more regular and earlier bedtime. Mrs. Jones had nodded amicably and said that she would definitely give it a try. Jenny knew, however, that this had not happened because frequently Johnny had described what he had watched on television, and it certainly was late evening watching, quite often. This was definitely something she would like to tackle next term when she was in her new role for promoting positive home/ school liaison.

Lunch time came and Jenny headed for the staffroom. On this day each week, there was an informal information meeting. It was not compulsory but most staff turned up unless they had to nip out for something. It usually only lasted for fifteen or twenty minutes. Jenny collected her lunch and a drink and sitting she stifled a large yawn. The first item of information caused quite a stir. Joan had decided to leave and take early retirement. "I shan't be going until the summer," she announced which should give Mr. Lockwood plenty of time to find a replacement. Then we shan't have to have a temporary teacher. Hopefully that will be better for everyone."

Jenny smiled internally but managed to keep a straight faced expression. She imagined others would be feeling the same and Sally caught her eye from across the room. She assumed this was why Lesley had been so polite and even friendly as she had arrived that morning. If Joan was going, she would be losing her ally and so would be feeling vulnerable. Lesley had never been in quite the same category as Joan, however. Jenny remembered how she had distanced herself when Joan had made snide remarks about seeing Mike at the swimming pool. This was another remembered conversation that took on a whole new meaning and jolted

Jenny. She shivered involuntarily. This had happened before and these conversations went around and around in her mind, especially at night when she was alone in bed.

As she and Sally walked back along the corridor to their classrooms after lunch there was only one topic of conversation. Sally said "Well, she's finally going. I know the parents like her and she gets good results from the children but she can be so awful in the staffroom."

"I shan't be sorry to see her go, I admit," agreed Jenny. "I feel as if I've had my share of her spite recently."

"I imagine not getting this promotion recently gave her food for thought," Sally added.

"I suppose it must be hard with all her time in this school, to see someone like me swoop in under her nose and take it," Jenny sighed.

"You only got it because you deserve it," Sally said with conviction.

"Thanks, I need that sort of support at the moment. Things are a bit tricky at home at the moment, between you and me, but I'm looking forward to taking on that new role."

"Sorry to hear that," Sally said sympathetically. By this time they had reached their classrooms and so Jenny was thankful that put an end to conversation for the time being.

By the end of the week Jenny was thoroughly glad for a break. She had kept her brave face on at work and colleagues had not discovered the real reasons for her tiredness and lack of bounce. Mike telephoned her on Saturday morning. She hadn't been up long. Although she had woken early she had determinedly stayed in bed. First she tried to read but she found it difficult to concentrate and kept wondering what Mike was up to all weekend and with whom! She played around with the apps on her phone for quite a while and then dragged herself up and into the shower. She had just got dressed and gone downstairs when her phone buzzed as it vibrated on the kitchen worktop.

She noted on the display that it was Mike and she took a deep intake of breath to prepare herself for the call. "Hello," she responded.

"Jenny, how are you?" he asked awkwardly.

"I'm fine," she answered automatically, as we all do even though we're not. "Well, you know," she added

"We need to talk, can we talk?" he asked.

"Maybe in a few days," said Jenny cautiously, "I need space and thinking time."

"Of course," he said humbly "I understand. Jenny I'm really, really sorry. I think it's over now, anyway."

"Mike I'm not doing this over the phone," she said firmly.

"No, no, you're right, sorry. Diana asked me to say she's sorry too."

Jenny didn't know what to say to that so she said nothing. After quite a long pause Mike said "Jenny, she wants to meet you. She wants to apologise."

"No, no way!" said Jenny her voice rising. "Sorry doesn't even come close. It doesn't come into it at all. There's no way I want to speak to her at the moment. Mike I have to go. Call me towards the end of next week. Maybe we'll talk then. Bye." She added hastily, before he could argue.

"OK, but I'm so very sorry, Jenny. Go carefully. I love you. Bye"

'Yeah right,' thought Jenny as she cut the call. She paced around the kitchen both hurt and angry. Sorry really didn't even come close.

Last year at her previous school she had gone on a course for learning about the stages of loss or grief that a child might experience when a parent or sibling dies or divorce is happening around them. She reflected on this now. She reckoned she must be moving from the denial and isolation stage to that of anger. The first stage had shielded her from the immediate shock and wave of pain. Initially she had found it really hard to tell Pat and all she wanted to do was hide away. Now she definitely felt *so* angry. She understood that this was a protection against her vulnerability but being able to vocalise it to herself did not deflect this extreme emotion. She mooched about the house for quite some time swearing and talking to herself. She even kicked out at the sofa and then was consumed by remorse at her violent reaction but she couldn't quell the feeling of rage.

□□□□□□□□□

The following week were the Christmas concert performances and on the Monday was the dress rehearsal-cum-performance for the playgroups and older community. Jenny had spent the rest of her time over the weekend baking dozens of fairy cakes and biscuits for the tea party afterwards. It had been a good activity to keep her occupied. She had battered and mixed and then cooked and designed toppings and all in all she'd been very busy, which was a good thing. She had piled them onto trays and carefully conveyed them to school on the back seat of her car. She and Sally had decided to keep the children fully occupied during the morning with fairly formal learning activities so that they, too, were kept fully busy and did not get too excited prior to getting ready for their concert.

After lunch, once all the children had been to the toilet, a necessary precaution at their age, Jenny gave the children a pep talk about leaving their clothes in tidy piles. She remembered her newly qualified teacher year when she had omitted this stage of the programming and had returned from the play that year to find children with odd socks and wearing someone else's jumper at home time. It had taken ages to sort out since not all parents labelled clothing, despite the regular requests and all uniform sweatshirts looked the same. Once bitten and all that!

Several parent helpers had come in and began to get the children ready. Jenny had placed the children's costumes on the tables ready so it was all very calm and organised. True to tradition there were the normal incidents of the youngest child taking off *all* their clothes, presumably forgetting what they were doing and thinking they were getting ready for bed. It had happened several times before with different children prior to PE lessons so no-one laughed and the little one soon got himself sorted out. Then another got both feet down the same trouser leg and tumbled over. Tears were quickly mopped up and one of the parents sorted her out. Eventually everyone was ready and sitting on the carpet waiting for their call. A couple of stripy shepherds' cloths slipped off shiny, fine heads of hair and clips were found to secure them. The host of angels did not have wings as such because they would have been too much of a liability but they looked enchanting in their white, floaty costumes and silver sparkly haloes. 'Joseph' and 'Mary' were ready and waiting nervously with the innkeeper, and Charlie, as the Angel Gabriel was sitting right in front of Jenny stroking her foot. Several children of this age did that. She didn't mind. He was quiet but seemed happy and smiled up at her when she caught his eye. She smiled back at him and gave him a wink.

Then the message came and Jenny got her children ready to go into the hall. It was so hard for them to be quiet but the older children were singing a carol and so she got her class to hum the tune quietly so that they weren't chattering and spoiling the atmosphere. They entered the hall on cue and took their places. There were several 'aaahs' from the older folk and one or two children waved to their granny or grand-dad. This performance was always a little noisy since the playgroups were in to watch but it was a good chance for them to visit the vastness of 'big' school. Jenny had been finding it very difficult to feel like celebrating seasonal cheer but even with all her present tensions she took delight in the earnestness of the little ones who were trying so hard to do their best and remember their words. When they had finished and the older children had sung their last carol, Graham came to the stage and gave thanks to the entire world and his wife, or so it seemed. He invited the grand-parents and other older folk to stay for refreshments and congratulated the children for their hard work. Their next performance was the following evening for parents to come and watch so everyone had time to pick up and correct the little errors that had occurred. However, the audience all seemed to have enjoyed it and there were several comments to Jenny as she left the hall with her class. One lady grasped her hand and thanked her profusely for giving back her faith in the community which had been severely shaken after her house was broken into recently. Jenny was touched and smiled into the misty blue eyes of the old lady.

The following evening Jenny had to be back in school before six o'clock. It hardly seemed worth going home so she decided not to go back to her hollow house. Here was no reason. She stayed and ate some of her unfinished lunch in the staffroom. She sat on her own and unbidden thoughts wheedled their way into her gullible mind. She wondered what Mike was doing and with whom.

He had suggested his affair was over but Jenny was feeling insecure and vulnerable to irrationality. Fortunately, she did not have long to think like this as the time soon came for other staff to arrive back and children to start appearing. There were always some who came really early because parents wanted a front row seat. With a large intake of breath, Jenny rose and went down the corridor to her classroom. The same process as yesterday afternoon started and following a few last minute re-fixing of costumes it was not long before they were all trooping to the hall again.

As Jenny took her place at the side of the stage with her group of youngsters she had a moment to scan the hall. She saw several of her children's parents and in the second row she saw Christopher Mayhew. When Charlie came onto the stage she was struck by the expression on his father's proud face. He was more than proud, in fact. He looked jubilant, joyous. Jenny reflected on how she knew Christopher thought he might have lost him earlier in the term when the accident had happened and she was almost over-whelmed by the wonderment she could see as he gazed at his little boy dressed in the long white robe of the angel, and the light shining through his blond curly hair. She guessed it was Christopher's mum sitting next to him. There was something of a family resemblance and she saw the older lady whisper something to her son next to her. She was proved correct when, at the end of the performance this same lady came to the classroom to collect Charlie. She asked if it would be alright if Charlie showed her around the class and Jenny was only too pleased since Charlie called this lady 'Granny' and was clearly at ease with her. She stayed with them for a few minutes and then explained that she needed to take the last of the children to another class to meet an older brother.

Jenny was just returning from delivering this child to meet his Year 6 sibling when, walking through the hall, she saw Sally and Christopher at the far door. They were clearly having an in-depth conversation and Sally did not look too happy. Jenny saw her raise both hands in the air and grasp Christopher's arm. If Jenny had to guess, she thought the expression on Sally's face was pleading. She didn't linger. There was no-one else about. Most people had collected their children and left and the few who were still milling about were closer to the front entrance by now. Jenny hurried back to her classroom just as Charlie and his Granny were leaving too. "Thank you so much," said Mrs. Mayhew. She gave Jenny a sincere smile. "You must be Mrs. Lucas. Jenny, did Christopher say your name was? He was saying how very supportive and compassionate you have been. We both owe you our warmest gratitude."

"Please, no," answered Jenny. I wanted to be useful."

"More than that," she responded. "Anyway 'thank you' seems feeble for how we feel about what you did." She patted Jenny's shoulder "I feel sure we shall meet again" she said as she moved past Jenny. Charlie gave her a little wave. "Come on young fellow, my lad, time to get you home to bed. Let's find Daddy."

After they had all left and she was on her own, Jenny had time for reflection. She thought of the encounter she had witnessed between Sally and Christopher. She was suddenly overcome with envy or was it jealousy. Did she want what Sally appeared to have had or did she want Christopher. Ridiculous! What's that all about? She mentally chastised herself. She was lonely, that was all and her life was too complicated as it was. She hurriedly collected her things.

⬜⬜⬜⬜⬜⬜⬜⬜

The next morning children were tired and staff were too. At the end of the previous week Sally and Jenny had planned a day for the children that would take this into account but the day was still quite hard work to keep children on track and equitable with each other. Jenny had not slept well, having such a lot going round in her head. It seemed that Sally was feeling out of sorts too. Jenny heard her raising her voice during the morning which was something that never normally happened. Just before playtime Jenny spoke to her teaching assistant "Jodie, would you do me a big favour. Would you fetch me a cup of tea when the children go outside so that I can have it here? I've got a cracking headache," she fibbed.

"Of course," Jodie responded straight away. "Have you got any paracetamol?"

"Yes, that's fine thanks." Jenny said. She just couldn't face the staffroom this morning.

"I'll just pop next door and ask Sally if she wants one if that's OK with you," Jodie suggested. "She seemed a bit down this morning too."

Jenny nodded at her and started to organise the children into packing away their things and getting their coats on for playtime. Just as they were leaving the classroom, Jodie reappeared with a tray with two mugs of tea and a plate of biscuits. "You're a star," said Jenny gratefully.

"No problem, I'll just take this next door. Do you want me to stay and help set up for the next session?" she paused as she headed for the door.

"No, that's alright. I'm going to sit them down and have a few minutes quiet time after play so you could do it then," said Jenny. "You go on up to the staffroom and grab a rest. You've certainly earned it this morning."

After she had gone, Sally appeared. "Hi! Do you mind if I come and sit for a couple of minutes?"

Jenny imagined it might be more than two minutes and she had some idea what might be following. She was correct. Sally needed to talk.

"Christopher and I had a few words last night," she opened with. "Well, not words exactly, but I think he's backing off."

"Oh, I'm sorry," said Jenny and she meant it. Sally wanted this relationship. Perhaps that was the trouble. She had been too needy, too clinging. "Maybe it all needs to be a bit more casual," Jenny ventured. "This is his first expedition back into the dating arena since his wife died. He's probably nervous."

"Maybe I've been a bit too keen," Sally said, echoing Jenny's thoughts exactly, "but he's such a lovely guy and I'm sure we could build something good together."

They chatted for a few minutes longer. Whoever was outside on playground duty must have decided to give the children, and staff, a bit longer than the normal fifteen minutes today. There was watery sunshine and although it was cold Jenny imagined everyone would benefit. It didn't happen often, after all.

"Thanks for listening and for the advice," said Sally. "I better get cracking they'll be back in any minute now," she said "and I'll try and back off a bit."

That evening was the last of the Christmas concert performances. All was going according to plan when, just as the children were being called to the hall, there was an urgent telephone call for Sally. "You go and take it," Jenny said. "The Teaching Assistants and I can cope. All the children know what they're doing."

Sally hurried off to the office and Jenny could see the worried expression on her face. It was unusual to have an important call at this time. She knew that Sally would immediately think of her mother at home by herself and finding it difficult to do anything unassisted these days. The concert started and all was going well. The children were really trying so hard to get everything right both for their parents and for their teachers. Jenny noticed the empty chair where Sally had sat for the previous two performances and she wondered what was amiss.

After all was done and Mr. Lockwood had said his piece, again the children filed out to their classrooms to get dressed. Parents soon joined them and there was a lot of milling about, so it was a while before Jenny discovered what had happened to Sally and it was not from a direction she wholly expected. As parents and children disappeared home Christopher approached her. "Thank you so much for giving Charlie the confidence to do all that," he said. He's really flourished in your care since his accident. I'm glad his hair had grown back," he chuckled. "A bald Angel Gabriel wouldn't have had the same effect."

Jenny smiled her agreement. "He has done really well."

"I gather Sally's Mum has taken a turn for the worse," he said. "Mrs. Bagley was just telling me when I asked her if she knew where Sally was."

"Oh dear," said Jenny, "I wondered if that was the problem. There was a phone call and she didn't reappear."

"I wanted to have a word with her but it'll have to wait. She won't want me bothering her right now."

"I'm sure she wouldn't mind," Jenny considered. "She thinks a lot of you."

"We've had some pleasant times together

recently but I'm not looking for anything more yet with Sally," he said candidly. "I don't want to give her the wrong impression by pestering her when she's anxious about her Mum. On the other hand I don't want her to think I'm ignoring her." He seemed to be thinking aloud and looked restless himself in his indecision. "Sorry, I'm pestering you now with my worries!" he smiled. "I seem to be relying on your good sense yet again."

Jenny discounted and did not respond to this remark. "You might call and ask after her Mum. It would be odd not to, after all you are good friends. If Sally wants to go out again you'd probably have to say that you're not in a position to go out too much at the moment but you may find she's alright with that. I'm sure she knows you both have complicated commitments," Jenny ventured. She was wary of interfering or giving bad advice. She didn't want to just sit on the fence either. That was never helpful. Privately she was wishing that things were not always *so* complicated.

"Are you feeling any better?" Christopher asked her.

Jenny was still feeling a bit awkward at having broken down in front of him during their previous encounter. "I'm jogging along," she replied. Mike and I have some sorting out to do. He wanted to meet and talk but I asked him to ring me after these performances were out of the way. I suppose we'll do that this weekend."

"Life is too complicated sometimes," Christopher said. "Ultimately you have to do what feels right for you because if you don't it will be wrong for both of you. That's what I believe, anyway."

"I suppose so," Jenny answered, not really knowing what was right for her at this point in time.

"I must be off and get Charlie home. Come on Charlie," he called to his son who was engrossed in playing with the lego which Jenny had put out earlier.

"See you both in the morning," Jenny said, genuinely smiling as Christopher helped Charlie put the bricks away. "It will come soon enough. I think we're all tired now."

"Too true! Goodnight," he said as he left.

CHAPTER 13

As she was anticipating, there was a call from Mike early on Saturday morning. Jenny was still in bed and reached for her mobile to check the identity of the caller, although she guessed correctly who it was.

"Hello," she answered cautiously.

"Can we meet," he asked. "Please!"

Jenny was not looking forward to this at all. She hated conflict in her personal life but it was what she was expecting. "You better come round," she said.

"To the house?" he clarified.

"Yes." It was all a bit stilted.

"OK, good. When shall I come?"

"Aren't you at the gym this morning?" Jenny asked.

"Well, I would be normally," he responded "but I'd rather come and see you. I want to explain," he started.

Jenny felt it might take quite a lot of explaining but she said "Come about eleven then and we'll talk," she said.

"I'll see you later, Jenny," Mike said. "I love you."

She almost wished he wouldn't keep saying that. He wasn't usually demonstrative. "See you at eleven," was all she managed in return.

Having finished the call, Jenny felt restless so she got up, straightened the bedroom, had a shower and got dressed. She was tired and feeling cross and rebellious she really didn't want to make too much effort with her appearance. She pulled on her jeans and found a jumper. She blow dried her hair and found some earrings that matched her top. She only applied mascara and a minimal amount of lip gloss. That would have to do. It was up to Mike whether he wanted her or not. She couldn't make him. In order to keep busy she gave the bathroom and kitchen a good clean, feeling better for the occupation this provided.

Just before eleven there was a knock at the door. Jenny peeled off her rubber gloves and throwing them into the kitchen sink, she went to the front door. Mike had kept his keys as far as she knew so it was sensitive of him to knock, she supposed grudgingly as she approached the door. She could see his outline in the central glass panel and took a deep breath before opening the door.

Jenny opened the door and Mike was there holding some flowers and looking remorseful. She didn't say anything. She didn't know what to say. She stood to one side and he came past her and headed for the kitchen. He turned to her, holding out the flowers as she entered behind him. "Thank you," she said taking them and looking in the cupboard for a vase. "They smell lovely," she added burying her nose in their midst for a moment; anything to mask the awkwardness of the moment.

"Jenny…." Mike started.

"Wait," she said. "Give me a moment. Let me do these first. You could put the kettle on."

Jenny having arranged the flowers and Mike having made a cup of tea for each of them, they went into the living room with unstated understanding. After all they had lived together for years now and there were some things that didn't need to be spoken. These were the mundane things though and now, sitting on separate sofas they looked at each other. "You better go first," Jenny said quietly.

"Now I'm here I don't know what to say, where to start," Mike said hanging his head. Then after a moment he blurted "I'm so, so sorry."

"When did it start? Were you seeing her when we went for dinner that last time?" Jenny asked dispassionately.

Now he lifted his head and looked her in the eye. "Yes. I'm going to be absolutely honest with you Jenny and I'll try and answer any questions"

Tears seeped into Jenny's eyes. "Why?" she whispered. "What was I not giving you?"

"I don't know, really, I don't know. You were giving me everything."
"Yes, I thought I was," she answered forcefully. "I have been trying really hard to be understanding of your work, your mood." She was conscious of her voice rising but felt unable not to show her anger. "I felt I was bending over backwards to be understanding."

"You were so wrapped up in your work. You are so successful and enjoying it so much," Mike responded with vigour. Then more restrained he said "Maybe I was jealous of that."

"Oh Mike, if that was the case I'm really sorry but I've always *felt* you came first, always," Jenny said. She sat quietly for several moments thinking. Again she went over in her mind and asked the questions she had demanded of herself before. Had she neglected him for her work? Had she shown too much interest in the people there at the expense of her husband? She remembered other peoples' responses to these questions when she had spoken with Pat, for instance. There was Sally's answer when she had questioned her visit to Charlie in hospital. She genuinely didn't think she had thought more of her work and ignored Mike. She sighed. "Why with her? I thought she was my friend. How could she have been to disloyal, so treacherous, lying and cheating?" This came out fervently too.

"She's been unhappy at home. I felt sorry for her being bored with Greg and feeling stifled. She was there, lively and teasing. I fell for it. Jenny I wish it hadn't happened. Now, I feel like I went outside when everything was going right inside. I've ruined a good thing. I know that but *please* give me another chance. I won't let you down again."

"I feel so humiliated," Jenny murmured, tucking in her legs and curling up.

With that Mike fell to his knees in front of her and took both her hands in his. "Don't, please don't." He cried out and his eyes became moist. "It's me, not you who should feel that because I've been such an idiot." They stayed in that tableau for what seemed like several minutes, neither knowing what to say or do next. In the end Mike rose and sat on the sofa next to her. He hesitated, unsure of her and then he put his arm around her shoulder. Automatically she leaned into him for comfort. The tears that had risen before now oozed out and down her face, silently, as she wept out all the damage and anxiety that she had held in check for quite a while.

"If you come back," she said "I can't do this again and I don't know if it'll work out or not."

"It's over," Mike said. "I won't do it again. It's you I love, really"

They stayed like that for some time, the flow of Jenny's tears eventually stemmed and she dug in her pocket for a tissue. Sitting up to blow her nose she then stood. "I'm going to the bathroom," she said and ran upstairs to wash her face and calm her nerves. Her eyes were bloated – such an ugly word – and that's how she felt at that moment. Could she do this, take him back? Somehow she knew she was going to but would things ever be the same? She doubted it. She'd had that very thought about Pat and Doug when her friend had been having this dilemma recently. Jenny thought about the serious promises she had made; for better, for worse and all that. She knew she would try to understand, accept some of the blame and try to forgive even if she couldn't forget, not for a while anyway. Maybe in time, with work on both sides, she would learn to feel better about herself and gain confidence, becoming more relaxed, with Mike again.

Slowly she returned downstairs. On re-entering the living room she saw Mike with his back to her, hands in pockets looking out of the window. "You better go and get your things," she said.

He turned. "Oh Jenny, thank you," he sighed and stepped towards her. She folded her arms, sub-consciously protecting herself by retreating somewhat. He seemed to respect this and he said "I'll be back as soon as possible."

"OK," she responded and smiled wanly. She hoped this was the right decision.

□□□□□□□□□

While he was gone Jenny felt badly that she needed to call Pat. Perhaps she needed reassurance that this was the correct thing to be doing or maybe she just wanted a friendly voice to sooth her troubled and uncertain spirit. She went to the kitchen to retrieve her phone from the worktop where she had left it. When Pat answered she asked "Are you free for a quick chat?"

"Yes, fine," Pat answered.

"I haven't got long but Mike has just been round. I just needed to talk to someone. It's not the sort of thing I can talk to Mum about. I haven't even told her

Mike left. Last time she called I just said he was out."

"Oh, Jenny, she would be supportive, you know. Won't you have to tell her eventually, or are you hoping things will work out and you won't need to?"

"I know she would be there for me but I wasn't sure how things would be and so I didn't want her to worry un-necessarily and anyway I felt so bad - as if I'd failed miserably and I just couldn't bring myself to confess that"

"Jenny, no!" Pat responded quickly. "So what did Mike come round for?" asked Pat, moving the conversation forward.

"He says it's over with her, Diana, and he wants to come back. He says he's really sorry." Jenny paused as the thought passed around in her mind that Pat must have been through all this herself. She imagined that Pat could well be rolling her eyes since Doug must have voiced similar things in the past and here they were back to square one with Doug camping out at a friend's house. Almost to persuade herself that this was different she continued "He says he won't let me down again, he was virtually crying."

"Have you given him an answer?"

"He's gone back to collect his stuff and then he's coming home. I don't know if it's the right thing to be doing or not but there we are…" Jenny tailed off.

"We're all allowed to make a mistake I guess. It won't be easy for you. I think you'll have to bite your tongue a lot and not use his affair as a weapon at any point even if you are having an argument in the future. Also you will be wondering every time he goes out what he's doing. That's the hardest thing. That may last a while," Pat said knowledgeably.

"I feel like I'm swallowing a lot of pride. I feel very humiliated by this whole thing but I suppose I've been to blame too."

"Well I don't know about that but one of you has to be prepared to give a lot and he has to be prepared to be reassuring too," said Pat

"I know it's not going to be easy at first but we had such a great relationship. I really feel I should make it work. After all we both made promises at the outset. I know he's not kept his but I think I should try. We really used to have such fun together. We have been good friends." She paused and then added "Thanks for listening," said Jenny. I better go, he'll be back soon."

"Let me know how you go and remember I'm always here if you need anything at any time," said Pat

"I will let you know. I really better go. I don't want to be caught discussing all this just yet! Thanks. Speak soon," Jenny answered. "Bye."

She put her phone down and went back up to the bathroom to check on the state of her face and hair. She was determined to make an effort now. If she was going to do this she would have to do it well. After all she and Mike had been together for several years and they'd had some very good times together. It was true, they had been good friends as well as lovers.

▢▢▢▢▢▢▢▢

The first week back together was a strain on both of them. Mike was trying hard, too hard, and Jenny was trying to respond but finding it difficult. By some unspoken agreement they slept in the same bed but that was all. In the mornings before work Mike got up first and made Jenny's breakfast. For him to do so every morning was unusual and so didn't seem natural. She was polite but couldn't bring herself to be warm. She was trying to be spontaneous but was feeling numbed. Each morning on her way to school she was wondering if things would ever improve and each evening as she travelled home she was dreading Mike being late and having to worry about why. However, to be fair, she thought, by the end of that week he had been very prompt and often in before her.

On the Saturday morning she woke early and lay as still as she could in bed, frightened that she would wake him and there would be an expectation on her part to resume love-making. When he did finally stir she asked "Are you going to the gym this morning? You didn't go last week."

"I'll not go if you want me to stay here," Mike replied.

"No, that would be daft. You can't stay chained to the house and me." Jenny said.

"I'm not going to do anything I shouldn't," he responded. "It's you I love. I shan't be seeing her again."

"I know. You said. I have to learn to trust you, that's all."

"Well, I'll go but I shan't be out long."

"Stay as long as you need to," Jenny said as stalwartly as she could.

With that they got up and a normal Saturday resumed.

True to his word, Mike was not gone very long, his kit was dirty proving he had been where he said and he returned with flowers.

"They're lovely, thank you," said Jenny

as she took them into the kitchen. "You don't need to do this though Mike, although I do love them. It's not normal. We have to try and be normal."

"I just want to show you that I do care. I am sorry."

"I know," she answered.

Christmas at school was completed and Jenny finished the term pleased to have a break. She had been putting a brave face on things and trying to get into the spirit of all the celebrations with the children. She had deliberated lengthily about whether to go with the rest of the staff for their meal out. It was a tradition that all of them including the caretaker and the cleaning staff; classroom staff; kitchen helpers and dining room people as well as the headteacher all went out together in an informal and friendly way. She had liked the idea at the beginning of term but now, despite her best intentions, insidious thoughts at the back of her mind kept creeping in so that she was wondering what Mike would do all evening while she was out. She squashed these thoughts down determinedly. Either she had let him come back and she had to trust his word or there was no point. She had dressed up and gone, determinedly staying out as long as the others although there was a great temptation to make excuses and get home early. Mike was at home when she returned. He was unshaven and lying out on the sofa with a coffee and a magazine. He clearly had not been anywhere and she had to believe he had not used his phone either.

The school holidays progressed. Mike went to work and back as normal; Jenny tried to chill out and catch up with household things. There was the time when he came home with a bottle of wine and a take-away. They had a really pleasant evening and as she washed the dishes he came up behind her and put his arms around her waist and kissed the back of her neck. That was all. He reached for the tea towel to dry up and the moment passed. Jenny had felt relaxed about it and had actually enjoyed the moment of intimacy.

Before she had time to turn around, Christmas was upon them. For the last couple of years they'd woken early and exchanged main gifts in bed, normally followed by a bit of lazy lovemaking. Having had lunch together, they had gone to Jenny's Mum and Dad's for dinner. Mike's Mum and Dad lived abroad so it was a good, cosy arrangement and Jenny's Mum always said Christmas wasn't properly Christmas without seeing family so it kept her happy too. This year the practical arrangements were the same. Jenny's family knew nothing of her recent distress. She had bought all her gifts and wrapped them, stowing them in the drawer under her side of the bed as usual. She guessed Mike had done the same. This time she felt a mix of excitement, born from years and years of ingenuous enthusiasm for the season but also an amount of anxiety about how things would pan out now.

Christmas morning dawned. Recently it had been consistently grey and dank with scudding clouds and bitter winds. This morning was cold and clear with the sun already trying to push through, however. Perhaps this was an omen but then Jenny immediately chided herself for such thoughts as being too superstitious and melodramatic. She would try and get back to making her own good fortune by being positive and decisive. With that thought she kissed Mike's shoulder as he lay sleeping beside her. This was going to be a good Christmas she determined and she had to make it so. They had been excellent friends until recently and surely everyone deserved another chance especially since perhaps some of the error had been of her own making she thought resolutely. She knew that this special morning would be pivotal. He stirred awake, probably provoked by her whisper of a kiss. As he did she leant in and kissed him again, this time on his lips, sending him a clear message. "Happy Christmas," she murmured shyly.

"And back to you," he responded warmly with the ghost of a hesitant smile.

"OK, now presents?" Jenny asked trying to

sound cheerful and enthusiastic without over-doing it.

"Definitely," answered Mike. "It took me a long time to decide so I do hope you like it," he said stretching down to his own side of the bed, sliding the drawer open and pulling forth a package wrapped and beribboned. Jenny reached for her gift at the same time and as they re-met in the centre of the bed they both exclaimed, "Oh, hey!" and "Wow", followed by genuine mirth. They discovered they had both chosen the same wrapping. Jenny had used silver ribbon and Mike had chosen gold, but the paper was identical. "What are the chances," he added, smiling at her, his eyes crinkling at the corners in that oh so attractive way.

They each unwrapped their presents. Jenny held up a beautiful leather bag which she had admired from afar until recently, when disappointingly, it was no longer in the shop to be coveted. He unwrapped the new sports clothing she knew he was after "It's beautiful," she said. "I've been looking at this for quite some time, until it vanished from the shop. I didn't think I could ever afford it though. How did you know?"

"I debated with myself for ages and then I double checked with Pat exactly which one you liked," he said

My present to you is quite dull compared to this," Jenny added.

"It definitely is not," Mike said forcefully. "It's the make and style I've really wanted, you know that. Will you be able to make use of the bag?"

"I will," she said. "I will," she murmured the words again to herself that were resonant of that previous ceremony several years ago.

He put his gifts down on the floor beside the bed and as he leant back Mike turned to her and put his arm across her. "Can I?" he asked.

"Yes," Jenny replied, trying hard not to show the hesitancy she was feeling.

His hand crept under the covers in the familiar way and cupped her breast, his fingers moving, after a moment to tease her nipple. She remembered how she enjoyed this and she couldn't help but breathe out and begin to relax. Was this purely a physical thing or was she rekindling her love for him? She wasn't sure but right this moment she was enjoying this kind of attention. After initial tentativeness Mike took the lead in their lovemaking, being both tender and respectful, until the last minutes when he finally entered her and groaned his expulsion and cried her name. Completely unbidden tears oozed out of Jenny's eyes and poured down her cheeks. She tried to hide her face by snuggling into him but Mike eventually felt the wetness on his neck and asked her worriedly if he had hurt her. How could she tell him? How could she explain when she hardly knew herself? Of course she was hurting but not in the way he meant. She was trying profoundly to quash unwelcome questions. Was she better at it? Did they say the same things to each other? Did he cry her name when he came? Had he been thinking and picturing her as they made love here and now?

"No, you didn't hurt me," she said eventually when she had some control over her voice. She certainly didn't want to squeak at him. After a few moments as control returned she said "I'm sorry."

"No, it's me who's sorry." Mike responded.

The rest of Christmas day and the few days following were calm and generally restful. Mike and Jenny jogged along together, she trying to re-learn her trust and to develop her confidence in this relationship that had seemed to be firmly tight and reliable just a few short weeks ago. Mike seemed to be cruising along happily, almost as if nothing had happened. Jenny felt it was as if now he thought it was over between Diana and him and he had voiced that to Jenny everything could be completely back to normal, as if nothing had happened and her own life had not changed irrevocably. Jenny remembered some trite words from a magazine she had been idly reading at the dentist's waiting room the last time she had been; that a relationship without trust is like a car without fuel. You can stay in it as long as you like but it won't go anywhere. She tried really hard not to show him that she was wondering what he was up to every time he left the house. The thought that she had agreed to start again and forgive him this lapse of lying to her, even that she might take some of the blame was her motivation to regain the trust she had lost. To be fair to him too, he was not staying out late or going to the gym overly much. He was often in from work before her and he did as much round the house as he used to do.

CHAPTER 14

In the New Year Jenny started her increased responsibility with home/school liaison as well as continuing with her classroom role. She was extremely busy during school hours planning and implementing and time rapidly passed. She had tried very hard to keep school away from home and only worked at the weekend when Mike was at the gym. January and February were cold and generally wet but they slipped into March and quickly there were signs of the weather improving again. As part of her new role she had visited some of the families who had been identified and agreed to receive extra support. Mrs. Jones had agreed to use a positive behaviour chart at home with Johnnie and together they had identified the things that would help the most. One of these was a regular, earlier bedtime and both mother and son had agreed the rewards for success. She had also visited another parent to discuss her son's bed wetting problem because it was causing problems in school with the lad being called names since he was not always smelling hygienic! Jenny was able to suggest some strategies but also suggested that a visit to the doctor might help too. Since Charlie's dad was a single parent Jenny had also visited Christopher Mayhew. He had asked to be included in the project because he was concerned that his young son might be missing out on something further he, as a parent, should be doing. This was not such a sensitive visit and Jenny felt was probably unnecessary but she was happy to be going just to ensure that no further particular support was necessary or that there was nothing delicate that in fact Christopher wanted to discuss with her away from the school setting. Sometimes, in Jenny's experience, this did happen and a parent might disclose something important that would help a child in school. After all, every parent could be influenced by their own experiences in school for good or bad.

Christopher was welcoming and this time had tidied the house and prepared a tray with coffee and biscuits. "Last time you came I was very lacking in hospitality," he said, remembering the time that Jenny and Sally had visited following Charlie's spell in hospital.

"Not at all," Jenny laughed, "you had far more on your plate than offering us a hot drink. As I said then it was great to see you and Charlie at home and so comfortable with each other."

They spent quarter of an hour or so discussing how Charlie had recovered from his accident. Jenny reassured Christopher that he was doing all the right things for his young son especially since the lad no longer had his mother.

"It has not been easy, for sure," Christopher said, "but I think I'm moving on now. It's taken me this long to be ready to move forward after Chrissy died," he added candidly referring to the death of his wife. "If I can speak to you in confidence?" he asked.

"Absolutely," responded Jenny, thinking 'mmm this might be it!'

"Well, Sally and I have had some fun outings and pleasant times together and she gets on well with Charlie, of course. Much more, though, she has made me realise that I can be close to someone else again. The time that Chrissy and I had together was something very singular and exceptional. I know I'm a one girl type of bloke and I thought at one time that what we had was going to be unique, the only one, for me. I will never be able to replace what we had but I know now that there is someone else for me to have a very individual and extraordinary relationship with. I don't think it will be Sally," he shrugged sadly "but I'm very grateful to her for helping me to see a positive future both for me and for Charlie."

Poor Sally, thought Jenny privately. She was not too surprised though. Jenny had thought all along that Christopher was not as keen as she was.

"Anyway, I've yammered on enough. How are you doing these days? You don't look quite so drained," he asked. "Well, don't say if you don't want to. I don't mean to be nosey, just concerned," he added hastily.

She smiled warmly at his concern. "Mike has come home and swears it won't happen again. We are learning to work it out," she said. There was a pause which did not seem the slightest bit awkward. "I have to learn to trust again," she ventured. "It's not easy but I made promises and we'll have to work hard at it. Maybe I was partly to blame too." Jenny shrugged disparagingly.

"I have to say, I don't understand it" said Christopher. "I really do wish you well though. That sounds a bit trite," he frowned. "I mean so much more than that though," he said sincerely.

"Thank you, I understand," said Jenny. After a further pause she said "I really better be going," she added as she stood.

"Yes, of course. I feel we could chatter for ages but you must be so busy, sorry."

"I've enjoyed meeting again," Jenny said with an enthusiasm that surprised her.

There was a certain comfort in the year's renewal, Jenny thought as she headed for her car to return to school. Daffodil leaves were poking through the soil of the neighbouring gardens and there were buds forming in the beech hedge, although the brown leaves were still clinging to the branches waiting for the new growth to push them off. Celandines were flowering below in the dark coolness and a blue tit flew off from its shelter among the denseness. Signs of a new emergence were coming. Jenny smiled to herself, feeling relaxed and happier than she had felt in some time.

□□□□□□□□

The following weekend Jenny and Mike were due to visit her Mum and Dad for Sunday lunch. They did this on a fairly regular basis but for no reason in particular they had not been for several weeks. Jenny was certain she would receive the third degree from her Mum since she was sure her Mum had sensed her lack of complete ease with Mike, despite her best acting, the last time they had all been together. They arrived in good time for a pre-lunch drink. Her Dad was in his garage as was often the case. He always had a project on the go for one of the groups he belonged to or for something around the house or garden. Being retired had not slowed him at all. Mike went out to join him and talk 'man stuff' together. They got on well. This was another reason Jenny had not shared her marital troubles. She didn't want her parents to think less of Mike. Jenny followed her Mum into the kitchen where there was a lovely warm aroma of good food on the go. "Mmm smells like pork," she said.

"That's right," said Jean "with the usual roast potatoes and apple sauce. This time I've done some red cabbage with cranberries and apple mixed in as well as carrots and beans. It was on one of those cookery things on television and looked good."

"It sounds great. I'm famished," said Jenny.

"You always are," laughed her Mum. "Pass me the wine bottle will you, darling. I'll put a splash in the gravy."

Jenny took the bottle back after Jean had done as she said and Jenny topped up her own and her mum's glasses while she was at it.

"So what have you two been up to lately? Is everything OK?"

'Here we go' thought Jenny. "Every thing's fine and much as normal," Jenny replied, feeling this was not too far from the truth, now.

"Only I thought you seemed a little strained last time we were together," Jean continued.

"Mike and I had a bit of up and down in the autumn but everything's fine now. Probably all this winter weather getting on top of us," she finished up saying somewhat lamely.

"If you ever need to talk or want anything you know we are always here for you, darling. There's nothing you could say that would shock us. I've seen and heard it all in my time."

"I know, Mum," Jenny answered. She turned away on the pretence of replacing the wine bottle as her eyes welled up. "It's fine, really. Love you lots," she added affectionately. They might get her down from time to time but she knew that ultimately her parents would always support her in any way necessary. It was her feeling of failure that prevented her from sharing the troubles she had experienced.

Turning back, Jenny changed the subject. "What's dad up to now?" she asked.

"Oh you know him. This time he volunteered to make a penny roll table for the village Spring fayre. He's enjoyed himself talking endlessly about measurements and angles and which wood to use and now he's closeted away for hours at a time making it. I'm not sure if we'll be able to lift the thing to take it to the village hall and I really don't know where they'll store it afterwards. I suspect it'll come back here for us to store in the shed!" she laughed.

It wasn't long before she heard Mike and her dad returning to the house. "I suspect the beer glasses are empty," Jenny said.

"Probably correct," responded her Mum and sure enough as he opened the door Geoff asked "Any more where that came from?" waving his empty glass.

"Always more," laughed Jean, "but lunch is just about ready. Do you want to open the new bottle of wine instead?"

"Will do."

They spent a congenial time together and when it was time to leave her Mum managed to get Jenny alone again and whispered "remember, we will always be here for you."

"Thanks Mum. Thanks for a lovely lunch," she added more loudly as her Dad and Mike joined them in the hall. The men shook hands and Geoff gave Jenny a big hug saying

"Take care, love. Love you. Come whenever you want, you know that." This was uncharacteristically out-spoken for him and Jenny knew that her parents must have been discussing her between them.

As they went down the path she took Mike's hand, determinedly demonstrating to her watching parents that all was fine.

□□□□□□□□□

There was a surprise awaiting the staff at Holly Road School at the beginning of the following week. Jenny drove to work as usual and having parked she got out of her car and was pleased to feel a continuing touch of the forthcoming Spring in the air. She smiled to herself as she remembered the previous week when she had visited Christopher and the new growth she had witnessed there. It was the promise of warmer weather and better things to come. Again she could see bulbs pushing their greenery through the barren earth outside the front door of the school and the forsythia buds had a haze of yellow about them.

Since the health scare of her mother to which Sally had been called before Christmas, Sally herself had been away from school on several occasions to care for her parent. Whilst everyone was very supportive there was no doubt that it caused extra work for several people. Generally Graham, the head teacher, had covered the absence because money was tight and this saved on the supply teacher budget. However, Jenny had usually needed to provide him with the work to be covered and to talk him through it. This caused the least disruption for the children. After all, Graham still needed to do his own work when the day in the classroom had finished. He was working very long hours so Jenny could see this was only fair for her to do.

Sally was absent again that day, she discovered when she went down to her classroom and found Graham there, puzzling over the schemes of work documents. Later, during the information staff meeting that lunch-time he was in his office doing some catch-up work so, as his deputy, Sheila made the announcement. Sally had decided she could no longer cope with the demands of her sick mother and the responsibilities of the classroom. Senior staff and Governors had discussed with her the possibility of taking a part-time contract but she was adamant that she would prefer to leave. She and her Mum were going to move to the North to be closer to her sister, who would then be able to help out more.

There were general groans, sighs and noises of sadness at this decision. Sally was a popular member of staff and well-liked by the children and their parents. It had been decided that as soon as a supply teacher could be found, who would be able to cover longer term until a permanent replacement was appointed, she would be gone. Jenny was sad at the news on several levels. Sally had been very welcoming when Jenny had arrived. They had hit it off straight away. Sally had helped her considerably to settle in. It was Sally who had been a friend when Joan, particularly, and Lesley had been nasty to her and they had been good teaching partners, bouncing ideas against each other and working as a strong team professionally.

On a more personal level Jenny reflected upon Sally's blossoming association with Christopher. Following his disclosure to her last week she understood now that this was a relationship that was going nowhere major but she wondered if Sally had picked up on this too.

The next day her partner returned to work and before school started and the teaching assistants arrived there was the opportunity to have a quick chat about the news that had been imparted to all the staff. "Sally, I'm really genuinely sad that you have decided to go," said Jenny with feeling.

"I don't exactly want to," she replied but things are impossible at the moment. I feel I'm only doing half a job both at home and at school."

"Where will you go?" Jenny asked

"My sister lives with her family just outside Bradford in Yorkshire so we are going to rent somewhere up there while we sort out selling the house here."

Then Sally went on to answer the unspoken question on Jenny's mind. "I had hoped I might be the one for Christopher but I don't think that's going to happen either. We get on well enough but I'm not *the* one for him and he's someone who needs a lifetime soul-mate, I'm sure of that now. I think he's ready to move on, just not with me," she sighed. Then on a brighter note so characteristic of her she said "Bradford will be a new start. It's a university city with lots going on. It's probably the change I need."

"Well I'm really going to miss you," Jenny said sincerely.

"Thanks, Jenny. It's been good working with you too. I've learnt loads of stuff from you and I'm sure in time I'll get another job and use what I've done here to build upon."

With that Sally left for her own classroom and Jenny turned to get on with her morning.

❑❑❑❑❑❑❑❑

The term progressed, a supply teacher

was found and Jenny was busy helping to induct her to the school and her class. She missed Sally and her camaraderie but the new teacher, Kim Sutton, was only slightly older than Jenny's age and they seemed to get on well. Kim had a young family and was looking to get back into full time permanent teaching so she was prepared to work hard and took on board suggestions that Jenny made. Easter came and went and Jenny found she had been at Holly Road School for nearly a year. So much had happened both at school and at home that time had flown and it seemed hardly credible that summer was nearly upon them again.

Things with Mike had chugged along. Jenny was still hurting but she was determined to try and regain the trust that she had lost so bitterly. Mike was continuing as if nothing had occurred. Jenny marvelled at the ways of men. He had said it was all over and behind them so that was it, whilst she felt damaged and deeply hurt. It wasn't the act so much as what it represented. To her it was a total let down; a real betrayal; evidence of his lack of care for her and her feelings; his wishes over her need; lying and cheating to deceive her, whom he had promised to cherish whilst forsaking all others.

On Saturdays he usually went off to the gym whilst she stayed at home, often catching up on school work so that she wasn't doing so much when he was around. Sometimes he was out one evening a week but whilst she was uneasy she quelled any suspicious thoughts and to be fair he gave her no cause to doubt him. Then it happened; one little thing that should have meant nothing except that it did.

It was Friday morning. Jenny had to be at school in good time because she had a meeting with a parent before children arrived and, unusually, she was ready to leave before Mike. Normally he was gone first and so there was no need to shuffle cars about. On this morning he was still only half dressed so she took his keys from the hook as well as hers and prepared to move his car out of the way so that she could get hers out. She unlocked the driver's door and sitting in, she started the engine. It had been a cold night and her breath immediately steamed up the window. She looked in the door pocket for a cloth to wipe the window but couldn't find it. Then she remembered she had probably used it last when they had gone together to the supermarket the previous weekend. She leant over to rummage in the passenger door pocket and that's when she smelled it. She sat upright quickly, shaking slightly. Surely she was wrong. She leant over again and sniffed. She wasn't mistaken. It certainly wasn't her perfume. She pulled the passenger seat belt towards her and smelled the distinctive aroma of Diana's perfume. She was so familiar with it she was quite certain that's what it was.

Her mind was racing. There could be all sorts of explanations. Maybe Mike had given one of the office girls a lift to the bus stop or the shopping centre. Lots of people probably used this scent. She took several deep breaths to calm her shaking which was quite violent now. He had told her it was over. He hadn't been out that much lately. When had they last made love? It was at the weekend. He was out last night but not that late. He had rushed out as soon as they had eaten, though. Had he rushed or just gone out? She had to get to work. She had to calm down. There must be a rational explanation. She mustn't judge so quickly. Stop it!

She moved the cars, ran into the house to drop his keys on the worktop and shouted up the stairs to say she was going. She couldn't face this now. She must calm down and take her time to decide properly what line to take. Perhaps she should ignore it. No but she had to think what to do. She mustn't blindly accuse. There might be an innocent reason. It would not be at all helpful if that was the case and she had jumped in with both feet before hearing something totally innocuous. As she drove to work she gradually talked herself into believing there was nothing to worry about. She would think further and maybe sleep on it before asking Mike where the perfume had come from.

Following her appointment and after welcoming the children into the classroom, that morning Jenny had some non-contact time for which she was very grateful. She tried to concentrate on the planning and preparation that she knew she had to get done. For a spell her work completely stopped her mind from racing down a blind alley. During the second part of the morning Kim joined her and they continued to prepare for the following week while the higher level teaching assistants took their classes. It was good to be bouncing ideas off each other and several times they found mirth together. Jenny liked Kim and she was turning into a real asset to the school and to Jenny in particular, especially on this particular morning.

The rest of the day continued and by the end of the school afternoon Jenny was much more calm and ready to leave the talk with Mike until the weekend. She would choose her moment and not be accusatory in any way. With these thoughts in mind she drove home thinking to get a take-away she could re-heat and a bottle of wine from the supermarket. They would have a calm and quiet 'togetherness' evening. That is exactly what they did. They both chilled out on the sofa and had a relaxing evening. Jenny had to admit that Mike seemed

perfectly normal in the way that he spoke to
her and the more she thought about it the
more distant her fears seemed to be.

CHAPTER 15

The next morning, being Saturday, Mike went to the gym as usual. Jenny squashed all unwelcome thoughts and set about getting on with some school work. She hadn't been going for long when there was a ring on the front door bell. As she walked up the hallway she could see the vague outline through the glass of someone tall, so she guessed who it was and uneasily wondered why he had come.

"Hello Greg," Jenny said, smiling as best she could and standing back to hold open the door. "Come on in."

"I hope I'm not interrupting too much. I assumed that Mike would be at the gym," he started.

"You assumed correctly. Do you want a coffee?" Jenny asked, putting off the moment of asking what he wanted.

"Yes, thanks. You look great, Jenny," Greg responded, similarly hesitating to start any deep conversation.

"I'm OK," she said vaguely. "I was just doing some school work, but I haven't much to do."

"Sorry," he said. "I just needed to ask you something."

"Well, fire away." Jenny said, trying to sound enthusiastic. She was wondering what on earth Greg's query could be and wasn't sure she wanted to know at all.

"It's awkward. OK, here goes. Is everything alright again with you and Mike?"

Jenny paused in what she was doing and then put down the coffee jar. She turned and put her hand on Greg's arm. "Why do you ask?" she questioned gently.

"It's just that I thought Diana and I were getting back on track but now she seems distant again and I don't know what to do. Should I back off and give her more time; should I move out even?" he asked frowning and insecure.

"Greg, I really don't know what to say. Mike and I have been getting on better, I think." Jenny really didn't know whether to express her concerns of the day before. She finally decided not to. After all, she didn't have anything to say, did she? She had no evidence of wrong-doing on Mike's part at all.

"I'm really sorry to bother you," said

Greg frowning and awkward.

"Oh, come here," Jenny said and stepped towards him, her arms wide to console him. After all, he had been a very good friend to her and it was upsetting to see him so distressed. It seemed strange for her to be giving him a hug. He was so tall and always before it was she who had welcomed his all-enveloping, sociable embraces. He smelt lovely and he felt warm and comfortable.

"I said once before I should have met you first, Jenny," he mumbled. "You're so steadfast and genuine."

Jenny was unsure quite how to respond so she said nothing and after a moment or two more she released him and turned to finish making the coffee, saying "Maybe you need to give it more time, Greg. Or maybe you need to talk to Diana and ask her what she is feeling. I'm certainly no expert but all the professionals you read about say that communication is the biggest need and the thing that many relationships lack. I'm afraid I'm really not the person to ask. I don't seem to be very good at it do I?" she shrugged and sighed despondently.

"You're right though, of course. I should be asking Diana rather than you." Greg admitted. "Thanks," he added as he took his cup of coffee but meaning thanks for so much more.

He didn't stay long after he had finished his drink. He kissed her forehead warmly at the door and said "Do keep in touch Jenny. I should hate all this to part us as well."

"I will, and it won't," Jenny said, and she meant it.

After she had closed the front door, Jenny returned to her seat at the table and sat staring but un-seeing at her work. She realised she was chewing the end of her pencil, something she never normally did and also something that she strongly discouraged her school children from doing. With a verbal 'tch' she mentally shook herself and tried to get on. It didn't seem long after when she heard Mike's key in the lock so she started to pack away her things without really completing very much. She needed to decide what, if anything, to do and how to tackle the big question in her mind. Had Mike seen Diana again? Her opening came quicker than she expected but she was couldn't decide whether to take it or not.

"Has someone been?" asked Mike as he straightened up from depositing his gym clothes in the washing machine. He was looking in the sink where the two empty coffee cups were lying.

"Greg called round," Jenny responded.

"Oh," he paused "and what did *he* want?" Was Jenny imagining it or did Mike seem ill at ease about this. Then again, this could be a natural reaction because of past events and the uneasy relationship presumably Mike and Greg now experienced. These thoughts flitted fleetingly through Jenny's mind.

"He called round to see how I was," Jenny answered.

"Why would he do that?" Mike asked.

"I suppose because we have been friends and we haven't seen him for ages," she said.

"Mmm" Mike grunted and left the room to go upstairs.

Her opportunity passed, Jenny perversely wished she had taken it. Now she would need to let it go or engineer another opportunity. She mentally kicked herself for being so uncharacteristically feeble. Why was she like this at home with Mike when in other areas of her life, like school, she could be confident and decisive?

As she leant against the sink with these thoughts something else passed through her mind. Mike had put his gear in the machine for washing but he hadn't switched it on. Should she take it out and look at it to see if, indeed, he had used it? Oh for goodness sake! She really should not spy on her own husband, how appalling was that?

Then, on the other hand, what had caused her to act like this, if not his behaviour towards her. Without further debate with herself and against her better judgement she leant down and pulled out his shirt. It was bone dry and despite being rumpled in his bag still had the crease marks in it from when she had ironed it. Shaking, she forced herself to pull out a sock between one finger and her thumb. Again it was sweet-smelling, dry and unstained. Quickly she shoved the things back in the machine and propped herself up against the sink. She heard the toilet flush upstairs and Mike's footsteps descending the stairs. Hyper-aware of his movements, she heard him go into the living room and then she heard him approaching the kitchen. Everything in her being wanted to shrink down onto the floor and dissolve. Somehow she gripped the sink tightly, took several deep breaths and then turned to look at him as he entered the room.

"Are you alright?" he asked.

"Where did you go this morning?" Jenny asked.

"To the hotel where the gym is," Mike answered smiling, or was he smirking cleverly?

"OK," Jenny said coldly, her anger spilling out "but to use the gym or to do something else!"

"What do you mean?" he asked evasively.

"You know what I mean. Be honest with me, at least. You haven't used your gym stuff and why was Diana's perfume on your passenger seatbelt?" There she had said it.

"So you've been checking up on me have you?" he said, playing for time, probably.

"Seems like I needed to!" Jenny responded coldly. Anger exploded again, this time violently and she felt as if her whole being was being seized and dashed against the floor. She kicked the cupboard uncontrollably and banged the work-top with her hand. "You told me it was over. She was my friend, you bastard. You couldn't even make a move more distant. It's despicable" she shouted.

"Jenny, please, let me explain."

"Explain, explain, how can you explain this?" Jenny asked, sobbing now.

"She rang me last week. She needed a lift to the hospital. Her sister is really ill and Greg was away on business. She was really upset; too upset to drive safely, so I said I'd take her. She said there was no-one else she could ask. One thing just led to another. I'm really sorry, Jenny."

"Go, get out now, as soon as you can pack. I don't want to discuss this."

"Jenny please, it was a one of. It is over, really," he pleaded.

Jenny turned her back. "I want you to leave," she said.

He left the room and she heard him go upstairs. There was quite a lot of banging around and super-sensitive, a while later, she heard him descend. She had stayed where she was in the kitchen, gripping the sink. She didn't want to speak to him again at this point in time and she prayed he wouldn't seek her out again. "Jenny…" he was at the kitchen door but she didn't answer and didn't turn. She couldn't bring herself to respond. She felt rather than heard him turn away and then she heard the front door open and bang shut.

□□□□□□□□□

Later, she wasn't sure how much later, she put on her short jacket and taking her keys she headed up the road. She needed a friendly face and a warm welcome. Pat answered her front door and seeing Jenny's face, without a word she held it wide. Immediately tears welled in Jenny's eyes again. She felt as if she had been consistently down-hearted for several months. Nothing seemed to be going right.

Pat went into the kitchen and Jenny followed, sitting at the table, she put her head in her hands and cried. Pat, ever a sensitive friend, said nothing but let the flow continue. One of the boys came in and said "hello, Jenny, What's the matter?"

"Jenny's upset but she's come here and we'll make her feel better, won't we?" Pat answered him.

"Sorry Jenny," said the young lad not really knowing quite what to do.

Jenny smiled wetly at him. "Don't worry, I'll be fine when I've spoken with your Mum and had a cup of tea," she reassured him, seeing his worried expression. It was not normal to see grown-ups like this and it was dis-orientating.

"Can you go and fetch the box of tissues from the bathroom?" said Pat to her son, understanding that he needed a job to do and aiming for Jenny to have a quick moment of respite to recollect herself."

"I'm really sorry," said Jenny, slowly gathering herself.

"He'll be fine," answered Pat, understanding Jenny's contrition. She brought two mugs of tea to the table. "If in doubt or when upset, always have a cup of tea" she smiled.

"Here you are picking me up again." Jenny responded.

"Want to talk about it?"

"Yes, if you can stand another round of depression," smiled Jenny.

"We seem to spend quite a bit of time propping up each other," said Pat.

"He's gone again," Jenny said simply. "He told me it was over but clearly it wasn't, or she wasn't out of his system. He saw her again. I guessed something and then the evidence was there." Jenny explained the sequence of recent events. "He has to want me, I can't make him, and it seems he doesn't, or not within terms that I think are reasonable. It is reasonable isn't it to have a partner who is faithful and trust-worthy?"

"Some men are definitely monogamous," said Pat but it seems that more are not. It depends what you want and can accept.

"What about you?" asked Jenny.

"I have the boys to think about as well as myself, although that's all tied up together. You know Doug and I have been apart for some time now but the boys miss him and actually, so do I. I think he loves us in his way but he's basically a selfish person and his desires come first. I have to decide whether I can put up with that for the benefits I do get for having him here."

"Mmm, I see, I think," said Jenny. However, at this moment she didn't fully comprehend Pat's point of view.

Pat continued "he's good company, we do make quite a good team, especially where the boys are concerned. I miss him. Maybe for the times, he's not totally here, if you get my drift, I have to rely on my own resources more. Anyway, as he gets older I think he'll find it's hard work being deceitful and maybe not worth the effort. After all, he does have a basically lazy streak," she smiled.

Jenny found it hard to take this point of view on board but she was content to sit and soak up the atmosphere of Pat's house and to be wrapped in a friendship that she knew totally would never betray hers. Her ideas of comradeship had been shaken to the core recently but she knew beyond all doubt that Pat would never deceive her.

Having got herself under control and having shared her problems, Jenny began to feel more able to cope with the situation. Eventually she said her thanks and goodbyes to Pat. She also popped her head around the living room door and said to the two boys "I'm off now and as you see your Mum has worked her magic and I'm fine," she smiled at them. "See you soon," and she blew them a kiss.

She walked thoughtfully back along the road to her own house. When she arrived at her door there was a surprise awaiting her.

She was deep in thought. Pat had a point of view that was new to Jenny and she needed to consider what her friend had said. She nearly stepped on the small fluff bundle curled up in the corner by the door.

"Hello," she said as she bent down to stroke the cat. In fact, it was almost still a kitten and didn't even look full grown. It was a beautiful creamy white with smaller ginger patches on its ears, back and tail. "What are you doing here? You don't live with me, I'm afraid."

With that Jenny opened her front door. The young cat made to come in but Jenny knew, much as she would like to make a fuss of it, if she did it would stay forever and it must have a home somewhere nearby. It wouldn't be fair on the real owners to tempt it away. Someone would be very upset. She hardened her heart and closed the door on it. She spent a lonely evening in front of the television, feeling like having a glass of wine but resisting the temptation. Thereby ran the downward slope.

On Sunday, Jenny mooched around the house, making herself do the jobs for house and school that had to be done. She found it hard to concentrate and fluctuated between dismal depression and anger. The little cat was not there first thing in the morning but reappeared later on in the day. Again, she determined not to encourage it but she felt that she would just adore to give it some food and a gentle cuddle. It was so endearing.

On Monday morning it was there again and Jenny really thought it was looking slightly more grey and less well cared for. It mewed pitifully when she left for school and she couldn't resist bending to stroke it tenderly. "Go home, little one. I have to go to work," she whispered to it.

☐☐☐☐☐☐☐☐

After school Jenny had arranged to go and see Mrs. Jarvis. If her home life was in a mess she would take her mind off it all by throwing herself into her work, Jenny thought rebelliously. Six years old, Tina Jarvis lived with her mum in a small terraced house on the housing estate at the back of the school. Tina was a lovely little girl but was often teased for being so over-weight. One day she had been wearing a pink hand-knitted cardigan and Jenny had said to her "Tina you look like a lovely, delicious pink ice-cream. I could just eat you up." The class had laughed but their attitude to the child had changed with that one remark. Mrs. Jarvis tried hard to support Tina but did not find it easy on her own and tended to over-compensate and do far too much for her. This lady was renowned all through school for her malapropisms. These word muddles had caused quite a bit of mirth on occasions so although Jenny was really tired she didn't mind visiting and wanted to support this caring mum in her wish for her daughter to be doing well educationally. Mrs. Jarvis did everything for Tina, to the extent that the child had no idea how to organise herself, even in the simplest of activities. Jenny needed to help her to be realistic too about Tina's potential!

Sometimes Jenny took a teaching assistant with her on home visits, for her own safety or to ensure the correct outcome was recorded, but this time it wasn't necessary and when she knocked Mrs. Jarvis opened the door and beamed her bountiful smile. "'ello me duck, come on in she said in her East Midlands accent. Cuppa tea?"

"No, I'm fine," Jenny responded, not quite trusting the kitchen routines here.

"You're right on time, duck. I like good *punctuation*. Shows seriousness. Righto then, let's crack on and get down to *brass roots*," said Mrs. Jarvis lowering her ample frame into a chair that creaked ominously.

Jenny smiled at her and thought 'here we go'.

"I think we need to help Tina be a little more consistent in her timing and to be a bit more organised in her work. That way she will make better progress," Jenny started.

"Aw, I know how *erotic* she can be, never doing the same thing twice in the same way." Fortunately the second part of the sentence clarified the first few words so Jenny knew what Mrs. J was getting at.

"Is it a pigment of my imagination or is she getting a bit better though?" Mrs. Jarvis asked.

There ensued a conversation with Jenny doing her level best to concentrate on what Mrs. Jarvis meant rather than what she said. They managed to agree some short-term fairly simple targets revolving around Tina doing things for herself rather than her mum doing absolutely everything for her.

"Only I don't want her to end up like me," said Mrs. J in her flamboyant manner. "I mean my mum always said to me don't you get yourself into trouble, young lady. 'No' is the best form of *contraption* and there it was before I knew it I was in the family way," and there followed a loud guffaw. "The thought of her ending up with a kiddy at that age, well it puts the willies up me," she said. At this last remark and in this context, Jenny had great difficulty in keeping a straight face and managed to make a gentle comforting remark.

Feeling that, at least, she had made a positive contact and started to outline the problem and possible solutions, Jenny was under no illusions that this was a long-term area of work and that the same thing would need to be re-iterated many times. She considered this driving back to school.

"I thought you'd gone for the day," said Jim, the caretaker, as she entered the front door and skipped over the hoover as he pushed it back and forth across the carpet in the entrance.

"I've been to visit a parent and I just want to do a bit in the classroom for tomorrow," Jenny replied. "I shan't be too late."

"That's OK, I've got the beaver scouts in tonight, remember, so the building will be open for ages yet."

"Oh, yes, it's only Monday isn't it?" said Jenny abstractedly.

An hour or so later, she had gathered her things, collected some work to keep her busy through the evening and got in her car to drive home. On arriving she staggered under her load to the door. Putting down her bags in the dusky glow of the evening she was surprised that the little cat was, again, outside her door. This time when she turned the key and opened the door, it dived in ahead of her as she stooped to retrieve her bags. "Hey, you rascal," she called, dumping her stuff down in the hall. She hurried to find the cat which had jumped onto the sofa and looked up at her with big eyes. "Right, I can see I'm going to have to make enquiries about you."

Jenny really wanted to give it some food. It was definitely looking more ragged this evening. She sat next to it and stroked it's soft back and gently massaged the back of its neck behind its pretty ears. Immediately the little thing began to purr and Jenny warmed to it. She knew if she fed it that would be that. It would be happy to make its home with her and quite content to abandon any home it might already have. "I'm going to see if I can find out where you belong though," she said to the little cat as she carried it through to the kitchen and found a small dish in which to put a little milk. "I know older cats are not supposed to have milk but I haven't anything else this minute, and you do look very hungry."

After it had licked every drop with gentle, soft lapping sounds the young cat mooched into the living room and curled up on the floor with its back against the sofa. "Well," Jenny whispered to it, "you look very comfy, but I'm just going to nip around to the shop and put a note in their window. I'd love to keep you but if you do belong somewhere else you really better go back home or you owners might be upset if you just disappear."

With that, Jenny quickly whipped up a poster on her laptop and having printed off several copies she walked smartly round to the little parade of shops. Only the small supermarket was still open but she asked if they would put the poster in their window and left a copy for the post office which shared the same premises. Whilst returning home she wondered where else she could advertise this find.

The little cat spent the evening with her and Jenny craved something like this to give her comfort and to feel needed. "It sounds dopey, I know," she voiced her opinions to the animal, "but I really like having you here."

She felt she should put the cat outside last thing at night and then she went to bed and cried a waterfall into the pillows. Why had this happened to her? All she wanted was someone to love her exclusively as she had loved in return.

CHAPTER 16

Following her enquiries at the local shops and asking various neighbours about the little cat's ownership she had turned up no information at all. She had eventually decided that it must be a case of it having been dumped. Jenny had verified that it was a little female, so she had taken her to the local vet for a 'once over' and to organise spaying. She didn't want to end up with a whole variety of extra cats. Jenny had also bought all the accoutrements of owning a cat that she might need. The little animal's colour led to her name, Fudge. They had quickly become good companions and now Jenny couldn't imagine the house without her little friend. She was there when Jenny came home from work, purring and winding herself around her legs. The little animal kept her company during some long, otherwise lonely evenings and Jenny knew that the cat had helped to see her through some of the most difficult times of her whole life.

Spring eventually turned to summer.

Mike rang her occasionally but she had no wish to have a long and involved conversation. She was putting off the moment, she knew, and procrastinating so that painful decisions did not need to be made. He had gone back to stay with the same guy that he had gone to before but he wouldn't be able to stay there forever. However, at the moment Alex, the friend, was happy to have Mike there paying a bit towards the rent.

Jenny had seen Greg once or twice. They had gone for a coffee once and then he had called around and they had gone for a companionable walk one evening. They had talked, inevitably, about their combined situation. Diana had moved out of their shared flat and gone to live on the other side of town. That should make things easier for Mike, Jenny thought bitterly but she didn't even know if they were still seeing each other. She didn't want to know or she didn't think she did. As they strolled, she and Greg had also talked about many and varied things other than their situation though and she had enjoyed the evening.

Another time they had driven out of town on one grey, wet evening and gone for a drink at a country pub. Jenny had even found herself laughing at a tale Greg told of his work colleague who had been on a flight to Edinburgh and got into all kinds of tangles with elderly co-passengers and their carry-on baggage. He finished the long-winded story and Jenny was giggling unsure whether it was the story, the effects of two glasses of wine, or the release of months of tension. Greg then capitalised with the corniest of jokes "As migration approached, two elderly vultures doubted they could make the trip south, so they decided to go by aeroplane. When they checked their baggage, the attendant noticed that they were carrying two dead squirrels. 'Do you wish to check the squirrels through as luggage?' she asked. 'No, thanks,' replied the vultures. 'They're carrion,' " he finished.

"Greg, that's appalling," she had laughed.

"I know but I prefer that to the rude type. Probably dull but there it is, that's me," he said sardonically.

"Not dull," Jenny added and gave his arm a squeeze, thinking that he was such a nice man.

They drove home in companionable silence and when they got back to Jenny's house she was tempted to ask him in for coffee but that always had other meanings in television films and she wasn't sure how to cope anymore with situations like that. Her position was saved by Greg being practical and helpful yet again.

"If I come in for coffee" he said

smilingly, "don't worry that's all I would expect. I know how awkward this situation could become."

"Thanks, Greg. Please come in….. for coffee," Jenny laughed back at him.

They continued a pleasant evening and when it was time for him to leave Greg turned to Jenny at the front door and planted a light kiss on her lips. Jenny closed the door thoughtfully.

Having taken the empty cups into the kitchen and left them in the sink, Jenny floated off to bed and lay for a long time going over the evening in her mind and considering all kinds of possibilities. She liked Greg a lot but did she feel more than that or was she just welcoming the reassurance that his attentions gave her? She desperately needed to feel wanted and valued. Fudge lay by her feet quietly purring.

As she laid in bed Jenny's mind drifted to her parents and the time she had visited them to divulge the awful news of her and Mike's break-up. Typically her parents had rallied around and been totally supportive when she broke down in tears and told of her feelings of failure and inadequacy. Her mum had resisted calling Mike all names under the sun, despite what she was probably feeling but she sensitively understood that it wouldn't help Jenny. At that point and still, no-one knew what the future held for the pair. They were still married. Pat had taken Doug back into their home again, after all. Tears came, unbidden, yet again and Jenny determinedly dashed them away and sat up to stroke Fudge until they had gone.

□□□□□□□□□

The end of term came and the holidays started. Jenny had been at the school for a whole year. Through all the major events of that year she knew she had settled well there. She had made good in-roads into both raising standards in her classroom and ensuring progress with her particular home/school liaison responsibility. She was well respected and liked by the head teacher, other staff and parents and pupils. In May she had been invited to be involved in the interview process for Sally's replacement. This had been a new but very good experience for her. There had been three candidates, one of whom was Kim Sutton and it had been she who had got the position. Being an internal candidate was hard because there was nowhere to hide. After all, the interviewing panel knew her 'warts and all' and she was unable to tell any inflated stories. She had interviewed honestly and assuredly though, and they were confident about offering her the job. Jenny had found the experience stimulating but difficult. However, she was very pleased with the outcome, even though she was not involved in the final decision, having worked so closely with Kim.

Jenny had been fully immersed in all the end of term processes too. There were end of year parent/ teacher consultations at which she received many compliments, sports days, leavers' assembly and evening discos for the children. Then there were the oldest pupils for whom they all signed shirts and said goodbye as they moved on to the secondary school. She had been sorry to say goodbye to her own class as well. They had made good learning progress and she had exceeded her targets with them but more than that, they'd had fun and she felt close to them. She was, of course, particularly sad to say farewell to Charlie, with whom she had a special fondness which had developed quickly and especially following his accident. He had made a superb recovery and his dad was very pleased indeed with his progress; a fact that he had voiced in no uncertain terms at parents' evening and since. Still, whilst she wouldn't be responsible for them, she would see them again in September when, no doubt, they would all seem suddenly older and ready for Year 2. It had been a busy time but it had kept Jenny's mind off her home problems

When Mike had first left Jenny was in tears on a daily basis. Through late spring and early summer she had frequently taken herself for a walk, in the early evening;

just across the fields behind the house, over the bridge crossing the little brook and back along the streets. More often than not she found herself having an uncontrollably good cry. This was regularly repeated when she was alone in bed. More recently this was no longer a daily occurrence, however. Now the holidays were here and at the start she had determined to keep as busy as possible to hold the miseries at bay.

Jenny decided to go shopping during the first week. She was going to buy new bedding and determined to have a good clear-out of the bedroom. No more of this crying into pillows. She had awoken really early and so got up in good time too. It was a beautiful morning with a sky of petal colours which, with the climbing sun, shortly turned to a cerulean blue. After she had showered, she put on a light, strappy summer dress with her flat sandals. She brushed her hair and only applied a little eye makeup and a lip gloss. The sun on the playground during the last part of the term had given her a lovely clear, light colouring and she was beginning to look healthier. She decided to drive into the bigger town to look in the department store at their linen department. She wanted something simple and fresh looking.

On the shop floor there were lots of mock rooms with beautiful displays of sumptuous colours and tons of pillows and cushions on each bed. The walls of her room at home were powder blue and white so she wanted something to complement that. She wandered around the displays debating with herself whether to go for something strong and contrasting and if so what colours should she choose? On her second round she spied exactly what she was looking for. The set was plain white with small, blue embroidered flowers dotted here and there; not too many and not too tiny or too over-poweringly large. It was crisp and clean looking. She selected the size she needed and took it to the counter to pay.

Looking at her watch she decided to head for the cafeteria for a cup of tea and maybe even a scone. She felt like having a treat. She had her bag over her shoulder, her purchases in a large carrier and she was concentrating hard on balancing her tray with its little teapot, cup and saucer and plate when a voice over her shoulder said, "You look like you need another pair of hands. Can I help?" As Jenny turned to see the Samaritan her hair whipped across her eyes and a strand caught in her mouth. He gently took it and tucked it behind her ear. It was so simply done and so naturally accomplished with care that it was one of the most erotic things she had experienced for a long time. Jenny felt her tummy flip. She smiled into his eyes, those twinkling, green eyes, and managed to mumble a thank you as he took her tray. "Perhaps you would join us?" asked Christopher as he headed to a table where Charlie sat waiting patiently for his dad to return with a paper serviette to mop his young son's mouth. She followed on, mesmerised by Christopher's retreating back, admiring his broad shoulders and his shirt, slightly un-tucked from the jeans that hung from his narrow hips.

"Thank you, yes" she said vaguely, following.

"Hello, Charlie," Jenny acknowledged the little boy.

He beamed at her and asked "Are you going to sit there?" indicating the seat opposite him.

"Yes, thank you," she responded.

"We're having an away-day, my dad said" Charlie chirped. "After here we're going to the park and we're going on the train and we're going to have chips for lunch," he burbled.

Christopher smiled indulgently at his son. "How are you?" he asked Jenny.

"I'm getting there," she answered. "I'm on my own again now. I have been since the beginning of April."

"Oh, my goodness," Christopher said sincerely. "I did wonder how it was going."

"Well, it's not is the short answer," Jenny shrugged. "It all kicked off again and so there we are," she finished lamely glancing at Charlie.

"Now isn't the time for details," Christopher acknowledged, "but are you coping?"

"I wasn't for a while, but I'm starting to now," she said. "I've just been buying a new duvet cover and pillow cases, and then I thought I'd have a treat in here. Tomorrow I'm going to have a good, if late, spring clean upstairs."

"Have you any plans for the rest of today?" Christopher asked "because we'd love it if you joined us. It's not high octane but as Charlie says we're treating ourselves today, and doing some really mischievous things, like chips for lunch," he smiled and cocked his head at his son.

Jenny hesitated for only a moment. "What the heck," she said, "why not? It's only me now so I might as well please myself. I'd love to."

They finished their drinks and snacks and arranged to meet in the car park for the steam train station. They would catch the train to the country park, spend the day there, having their chips for lunch, and catch the train back again. It all sounded fun. Jenny was quite excited at the prospect.

The day was glorious, uncomplicated and relaxed. Charlie chattered non-stop and she and Christopher were much the same. The steam train stopped on its journey to let them off at the park. They went to the swings and climbing frames. Then they all three paddled in the lake and then ran around on the grass playing chase to dry their sandy feet. After their lunch Jenny and Christopher sat quietly and had a cup of tea outside so that they could watch Charlie while he fed the remains of his chips to the geese and ducks down by the water's edge. Jenny divulged her recent history and they chatted comfortably about living alone and the pros and cons of that. Jenny felt it was easier for her now that, officially, Charlie was not in her direct care at school although there was no law against having a friendship with one of the parents. The afternoon passed companionably and very quickly. So soon, it seemed, the time came to head back to the little station to catch the steam train back to where they had left their cars. As it pulled in and stopped with a loud, prolonged hiss Jenny breathed in the scent of the steam and coal. It was many years since she had taken this ride. The last time was probably when she was a child and her parents had taken her on the 'Santa Special' that the company ran to raise much needed funds. It brought back happy memories of excitement. Charlie was hopping from one foot to the other now, clearly anticipating the ride back with similar feelings.

Having returned they stood, each next to their own car, ready to head home. "This has been a lovely day," said Jenny.

"It wasn't exactly 'treating a lady' but I'm afraid it's what Charlie and I do," Christopher responded wryly.

"I've loved every minute of it. I truly have," said Jenny and she meant it.

There was a pause and Jenny was about to turn to unlock her car and say her final farewells when Christopher spoke again. "I don't suppose you would have dinner with me one night would you? It would have to be at my house because of Charlie but I'd love to cook for you. That's if you would like to of course. I quite understand if you don't feel ready …….. I mean, if you need to consider your options for longer, under the circumstances….." he trailed off, realising he was babbling.

Jenny smiled, "I'd love to," she said quickly, surprising herself.

He exhaled deeply and they both realised he had been tensed up ready to ask her but afraid of her rejection. "Well, it's Monday today, what about Wednesday? That would give me time to plan and shop."

"Wednesday it is. What time shall I come? I don't mind coming early and helping to peel or chop things."

"Absolutely not, on this occasion. I shall try to impress you with my culinary skills," he laughed. "Come about seven-thirty and then Charlie will be ready for bed and he can say good night before we eat. You won't get away with less."

"I'll see you on Wednesday, then. Thank you." She turned to Charlie and bent down to his level. "Thank you, Charlie, for a wonderful day and the best plate of chips I've had in ages."

"It was great. Thank you," he answered.

As she drove home, Jenny reflected on all that had happened. It had been a truly 'great' day, and as she pulled up outside her house she found she was grinning to herself.

That evening Jenny made up her bed with the new linen and as she lay within its coolness she was still going over the day and all that it had held, from the moment she had that overwhelming feeling as she followed Christopher weaving through the cafeteria tables, through the day at the park and all that they had shared with each other to the invitation for Wednesday evening so haltingly given.

□□□□□□□□

Wednesday evening came around quickly. The day had been sunny and warm with large white fair weather clouds in the otherwise blue sky. Jenny had done her cleaning and clearing the day before and finished off during the morning. Throughout her activities she had felt variously sad at what she'd had and was now gone and then angry at what she felt was a huge betrayal. Now, later in the day, she'd had a long, very hot shower and washed all those feelings away. She felt good, more positive and looking forward to the evening with Christopher Mayhew.

On her arrival she heard Charlie running to the front door to open it. "Hello," he cried, "come in, Daddy's in the kitchen and he said I could open the door."

As she entered, Christopher came around the corner into the hall, wiping his hands with a tea towel. Jenny could smell something delicious and her mouth started to water. Christopher sounded quite calm as he greeted her with a big smile and said to Charlie "Will you take Jenny's jacket and lay it on my bed?" although his slightly dishevelled appearance belied this.

"Daddy said if I asked you politely, you might read me a story before I go to bed," Charlie said.

"Maybe we should let Jenny get inside the door first and take a breath," Christopher laughed amiably. "Sorry. If you'd rather not…"

"Of course, I will. It's all part of bed-time, having a story," Jenny responded.

"It is here," said Christopher. "I shan't be long in the kitchen if you want to go and choose a book. Nothing too long tonight, Charlie," he added giving his son a look. "Don't let him take advantage."

"Don't worry, I won't. I've got his measure," she smiled.

"Of course you have," Christopher acknowledged.

Straight away the atmosphere was relaxed and easy. Jenny sat on the sofa and read Charlie's book with him as he leant into her. He was still very young in many ways, younger than his classmates, if not in years. He'd chosen 'Dazzling Diggers' which was a rhyming book. Before the end, Christopher joined them and sat on the other side of the little boy and looked across at the last few pages as Jenny read. When they had finished Christopher said "Righto, lad, say night-night,"

"Can't I just have one more, we quite often have two books," he said turning his large eyes to Jenny.

"That's it for tonight," she said. "Daddy said just the one so off you go," she grinned, not taken in for one moment by the appealing look he was giving her.

"OK," he said slowly. "Goodnight, Jenny," he said and stretched up to receive a goodnight kiss.

She kissed his forehead and said "Sleep tight, Charlie, see you again soon."

Soon after, Christopher returned from tucking up the little boy. "Thank you," he said. "He thinks the world of you." Before Jenny could respond, he continued, "Shall we go through to the other room."

Jenny followed Christopher through to a kitchen /dining room. The area was compact but all the toys were in a box in the corner and whilst it was over-flowing Jenny could see that Christopher had tried hard to make the room inviting, with flowers in a vase at one end of the table and a candle in the middle which cast a flickering light, although the sun was still on its descent outside. She was charmed by his efforts.

"Please, do sit down," he said, pouring Jenny a glass of wine from a bottle already on the table. "I'm just going to get our first course dished up." As she sipped the cool wine and he moved about in the kitchen they chatted easily about their activities of the past couple of days, something that had been in the news, the new building in the town centre and various other things that were undemanding and easy. Christopher placed a cold crudité of vegetables in the middle of the table between them and small dishes of different dipping sauces that he said he had made himself. "I hope you don't mind using fingers for this," he said.

"You have been very busy," she said.

"Charlie enjoyed helping, but it would pass all the health and safety regs so don't worry, I watched him carefully," he joked.

Jenny normally had a healthy appetite and she certainly did this food justice. "This is so 'more-ish'," she said "I think I'm only eating now because it's here. I love this sweet and sour sauce, and the pink one. Is that thousand island?"

"Mmm but with my own twist," he answered.

The meal continued. Christopher proved himself to be a very good cook with unflappable calm in the kitchen and Jenny ate heartily and with enjoyment. "I'm really glad you enjoyed it as he cleared away her empty plate. I wasn't sure what to cook, so I played it safe with chicken chasseur. Would you like a top up?" he indicated her glass.

"No, I better not. One glass should be

enough. Driving, and all that. It was delicious," she said "as you see by the amount I've eaten."

"Would you like a soft drink, then?" That organised, he continued "What about some cheeses or we made a gateaux ….. or both?" Christopher laughed. "Then there's coffee and we made some of our own sweets to go with it."

The evening continued leisurely and pleasurably. They didn't finish eating until nearly eleven because they were talking so much between courses.

As he cleared the table, prior to serving the coffee, Jenny watched as Christopher moved between table and sink. Earlier, she had made to get up and help but he had insisted that this time, as it was the first time, she was to remain seated and waited upon. Next time, he had said, she could help. 'Next time' she had thought to herself happily. Whilst Charlie had abundant curls, Christopher's hair had matured into appealing waves that he wore quite short. She admired his strong, capable looking hands, with their long fingers and just a few fine dark hairs that she could see moving up his arms and under his rolled up cuffs. She looked again at his broad shoulders and whilst he wasn't tall, not as tall as Mike, the thought came unbidden, he was slim hipped and attractive. His green eyes had sparkled with the candle flame as the light outside disappeared. He had enchanting green eyes, she had decided.

Jenny followed Christopher through to the little sitting room as he carried a tray with coffee, cups, cream and sugar. He put it carefully down on a table in front of the sofa and indicated that she might sit down there. She sat at one end, suddenly feeling vulnerable and awkward. He sat on the sofa too but at the other end with a respectable distance between them. Having poured the coffee and organised the more mundane aspects of what Jenny wanted in it, he seemed to sense her discomfiture because next he said "I think, maybe, I understand how you feel. It has taken me several years, until now in fact, to feel at ease with moving on with my life. I felt I was in a complete wilderness after Chrissy died. I imagine you might be feeling a mixture of guilt and unease."

"Yes, some of that," Jenny answered. "I've spent months walking in the evenings and at weekends and sometimes the weather has been joyous. There have been blue skies, birds singing, warmth and calm but I felt no joy; none at all. I began to wonder if I was depressed. That's something from which I never thought I would suffer. I am still married and I took the promises I made really seriously. Now though, I think I feel they no longer stand because of what Mike has done and then done *again* but I feel confused."

"I recognise all of that," Christopher said. "I think it can be one of the stages of break-up. I know it is one of the stages of mourning. At first I was in denial and then incredibly angry. I had my moments of crying even," he admitted. "I understand how you feel. You will find the peace of time. I just want to say that I shan't make any demands upon you until you are ready. It's just that I know how I feel and I'd like us to meet again. I value you too much to ask more than you can give. "

The moment of Jenny's awkwardness left as soon as it had come and while they sipped their coffee general chat resumed. Jenny was able to talk openly of her married life and Christopher mentioned his wife's name in general conversation with ease. The next hour passed without either of them realising the passage of the time until Jenny glanced at the clock on the mantelpiece and was shocked at how late it was.

"I must go," she gasped, "Look at the time!"

As she stood by the front door with her jacket on she thanked Christopher and in a rather lovely old fashioned way he asked if he could kiss her goodnight. As her answer she raised her face to him. He placed his hands on either side of her face and gently kissed her forehead and then lowered his lips to hers. The kiss was firm and dry and Jenny's breath slipped away with the beats of her heart.

"Ring me when you are ready, if you want to," he whispered. "Goodnight."

CHAPTER 17

Jenny did phone Christopher but she left it nearly a week before doing so. She was in a dilemma. She wanted to see him but didn't know if she should. Greg had called round the weekend following her dinner date. It was Saturday morning. She wondered why he had chosen that particular time and wondered if it was because he would know that Mike would definitely not be there. Saturday morning was his gym session and Greg would know that. Maybe, Jenny thought, she was reading too much into things. It was just that last time Greg had left he had grabbed a kiss from her and whilst it had been fairly passionless it had been aimed at her lips. This time they had chatted amiably about this and that. Jenny was beginning to speculate why he had come when he formulated his question. She took a gulp of her coffee to give herself time to think and make an appropriate response. "Dinner?" she asked. Then taking a deep breath she ploughed on "Greg, I don't think that would be a good idea. We are great friends, I hope and I wouldn't want that to change because we had complicated it with more feelings than there are." She could see from his expression that she had shot him down but sincerely hoped that he hadn't fallen too hard.

"Fair enough," he said a little too quickly. "I hoped you might be able to feel more for me as I think I do for you but I understand. Its' early days," he shrugged.

"I really do want you to be my friend, though, and I'm grateful for your support," added Jenny, at a bit of a loss to know what else to say and very aware that this sounded almost like an insult when that's the last thing she wanted. Shortly after he had headed for the door and Jenny had said "Keep in touch, Greg. This has been one whole sorry mess for us both." She reached up to kiss his cheek, feeling wretched for being unable to reciprocate. It had, however, helped to clarify her feelings for Christopher so waiting another couple of days she rang him that evening.

"I'm ringing you," she said when he answered "but I don't really know what to say, now."

"Why don't you come round for lunch tomorrow? We'll just have a picnic in the garden but it's such a beautiful day today and I think it's due to be set like this for several more. Charlie is really looking forward to seeing you again," and then he added "......and so am I."

Jenny arrived at half past eleven, in time to help prepare the meal this time. She chopped vegetables and made some sandwiches, emptied the crisps into a bowl and opened some packets of child friendly picnic snacks. Christopher opened a bottle of chilled Sancerre and found two glasses. He found a box of fruit juice for Charlie. He had spread a blanket on the lawn under a sunshade and there were a couple of chairs too. The garden was not huge and around one corner there was a bed of shrubs and some summer bedding plants, adding a little colour. Jenny was happy to sit on the rug with Charlie and so they camped down and started their meal. "This is a treat," Jenny said, indicating her glass of wine. "I don't usually go for anything so special."

Charlie helped himself to food but he was restrained in the amount that he took and he remembered all his 'pleases and thanks'.

"Have you got enough, there, Charlie?" Jenny asked him.

"Daddy always says I can have some more but I can't put it back," he responded.

"That is very wise and so true," she agreed. Turning to Christopher she added "He is such a credit to you."

"We do our best, don't we Charlie?" and

Charlie nodded his response.

Having finished and cleared away the remains, both the adults washed and dried the few dishes. Charlie had an ice-lolly from the freezer but Jenny declined. "I've already eaten a lot more than I would normally at lunchtime."

Charlie went back outside and Christopher and Jenny followed. She flopped down onto the rug and feeling completely at ease she lay down on her back. Christopher sat beside her and then lay down too. They stayed like that for a while without speaking. Charlie was playing nearby on the grass with some of his cars and a plastic garage that periodically made a variety of noises. "I think the battery may run out soon," Christopher laughed, "hopefully! He seems to have a lot of noisy toys," he added.

"I don't think it's possible to buy many children's toys that don't make a noise of some sort," Jenny agreed.

As they lay soaking up the sun they each felt sleepy but it wasn't possible to doze off with Charlie chattering to him-self and to each of them. Jenny felt warm and relaxed with the sun and after effects of two glasses of wine. Then she felt Christopher's hand creep across the space between them and he took hold of hers. He turned his head and said "Is that OK?"

"Yes it is," she answered decisively. "I've been miserable for too long. It's not just since Mike left but for months before that too." She could hear a blackbird singing its heart out and when she squinted up she saw that it was sitting on the gable end of the house. It was one of the sounds of summer and so redolent of good times.

The rest of the afternoon passed pleasantly. Jenny played, for a time with Charlie, while Christopher made coffee. When he brought it out on a tray they sat in the easy chairs and sipped it, nibbling at a biscuit too. When it was time for Jenny to go in the late afternoon, she offered her face for a repeat performance of the kiss she had experienced before. This time, though, it was lingering and full of meaning. She was happy for a second one in the gloom of the hallway and she felt his tongue exploring tentatively. "I think I better go," she whispered, "or I may find it difficult."

"We have an in-built chaperone at all times," Christopher smiled. "Take me, take my son," he shrugged.

"That goes without saying," Jenny admitted, "and I already have a real fondness for Charlie."

□□□□□□□□

There were several dates after that

gloriously relaxed afternoon. On one occasion Christopher's mum came across for the evening and they went to the pictures. Afterwards they went to the American Italian restaurant. It wasn't particularly up-market but it was stress-free and tranquil. They had chattered and laughed all through the meal. Another time they took Charlie back to the country park and fed the ducks, played on the swings and walked around the lake, holding hands and then swinging Charlie between them. As time passed Jenny began to miss Christopher on the days that she didn't see him and she missed Charlie's natural chatter. Charlie seemed to relate to her with a naturalness that charmed her. He often asked her to read his bedtime story, or to help him get a bowl of cereal before-hand. She helped him with all manner of little things and he was as easy asking her as he was asking his dad if he needed something. Jenny was very aware that she could be playing with fire. It wouldn't be fair to toy with Christopher's emotions, never mind those of Charlie. After all he had already lost his mother. If he became too reliant upon her and she disappeared that would be intolerably reckless of her. As a result, Jenny felt she was holding a little back from them both. Christopher seemed to sense this and didn't push her. However, the time came when she knew she could not prevaricate much longer. She recognised that she was placing a great responsibility on Christopher and she understood that he was finding it increasingly difficult.

"I know I said I wouldn't push you," he said one Friday evening in late autumn, "and I won't. The fact is I'd really like you to stay one night. I'm sure you know that. I want you, I want to lie all night by your side. I want to wake up with you beside me. I understand that maybe you can't trust me after what has happened to you but I think I said once before I'm a one girl guy. I know that I love you, Jenny. I have for a long, long time, long before you and Mike split up." This was a revelation to Jenny.

"What do you mean?" she asked, "How long?"

"Now I understand that it's pretty much since after you visited Charlie in hospital," he answered.

"But what about Sally?" Jenny probed.

"I was attracted to her and I realised I was ready to explore a relationship again but it wasn't meant to be with her. As I said before, I am grateful to her. She helped me to understand what I really wanted, no, needed," he said. "I want to help you find peace again, and in time, we shall."

Jenny looked at him for several long

seconds. She knew here was a genuine man; one to whom she was very attracted. She missed him when they were not together. She found herself wanting to tell him all about each day, even the minor events. Did she love him? Did she trust him? She had begun to rely on his steadfastness. She thought maybe she did. Could she commit to him? It was early days for her but then she did one of those things that was not quite in character but which determines lives.

She said "Yes. Yes, I want to be with you. Shall I come tomorrow afternoon and stay over?" she added shyly.

"I will take care of you," was Christopher's response and he kissed her gently.

□□□□□□□□□

Saturday dawned and Jenny stretched luxuriantly in bed, immediately aware of the promise of the day ahead. If she was aware of what was to follow she would not have been so animated when she spoke to Fudge who was in her customary place at the foot of Jenny's bed.

"Well, Fudge, this is it, for better, for worse." The irony of her words were not lost upon Jenny but seemed appropriate for the new start upon which she was embarking. Then suddenly she felt nervous. "What shall I take to wear?" she asked the little cat.

"My pyjamas are real passion killers. They won't set the tone at all. I think I better nip into town." With that she leapt out of bed and rushed into the bathroom, suddenly energised.

Having driven into town and looked in the meagre shops there she decided she would have to go to the department store at which she had bought the new bedding several months before. There were a couple of other smaller chain stores she could explore as well. Eventually she found what she was looking for; something not too slinky but definitely not 'practical' either! She had chosen a pale cream colour with fine straps and just above her knees. That had been a big decision too. It had to be a flattering colour but not too virginal. If it was too bright it would be garish and un-romantic, too long and it would look 'mumsy', too short and it would be 'obvious and tarty'. Decisions, decisions.

It was early afternoon before she got back home. Jenny was very aware that she had only a little time to collect herself. As she arrived she was mentally planning what she needed to do before leaving. She must leave poor young Fudge some food and check the water bowl. She considered which bag to take and what to pack. Her thoughts flowed on and on and so she was nearly at the house before she realised there was another car parked in her normal spot. It was Mike.

'Bloody Hell' was mild compared to what she was thinking. Now of all times! She could see the back of his head. He was sitting in the car presumably waiting for her to return.

She pulled up behind him and collecting her bags, she opened the car door and made to get out. Before she had one leg over the sill he was beside her. She could tell immediately that something was very wrong. He looked completely dishevelled, having not shaved. His clothes looked rumpled and his normally immaculately tidy hair was mussed and even longer than normal. It was several weeks since they'd had contact and even longer since she had seen him when he had called to collect something.

"Whatever's the matter?" she asked.

"Oh Jenny, I need you. I have some awful news. I don't know who else to tell. Please let me in so I can explain. I don't know what to do."

Jenny hurried up the path and opened the door. She led the way into the living room. She dropped her bags onto the sofa. Not sitting and not offering the ubiquitous coffee she turned to him, frowning and said "Well?" She was feeling uncharitable under the circumstances.

"The doctor thinks I've got cancer," he said putting his hands up to either side of his head.

"What?" Jenny voiced somewhat loudly. The thought flashed through her brain 'oh for goodness sake, don't be so melodramatic'. Then she instantly was sorry and asked "Why would he think that? Where are we talking about?" she asked not able to stop glancing him over.

"I went to see him last week because it's been painful going to the toilet and ...." he hesitated and took a deep breath "...and when I, you know, ejaculate. I gave a blood sample and the results came through. Apparently it measures some type of protein."

"So you're talking prostate," Jenny said.

"He didn't say I have got it but he thinks I should have some further tests. I'm using that private health care thing so I've got an appointment at the hospital on Monday morning. I think they do more examinations and maybe take a biopsy. Hell, Jenny, what's going to happen?"

Despite all this drama Jenny was desperately aware of passing time and getting panicky. Mike continued, "Jenny please can you come with me on Monday. I don't want anyone else I'm really scared."

"I'm sure I've read that prostate

cancer can be really slow growing and I'm sure you must have got into the system in good time. That's a big positive. Look, Mike, I've got to make a phone call and then we'll sit and sort out what needs to be done," Jenny said. As she left the room she found her phone in her pocket and started looking for Christopher's number as she climbed the stairs. This was certainly a call to which she didn't want Mike to be privy. Her heart was thumping as she listened to the ringing tone.

"Hello," Jenny heard his treasured voice.

"Christopher, it's Jenny,"

"I know, I recognised your number. Is something wrong?"

"Mike's here," she said

"Oh!" came the non-committal response.

"There's a big problem. He thinks he's got a cancer. He's been to the doctor and had a blood test. Christopher, he's really scared and upset. I don't know what to do," Jenny said feeling dreadful and sounding worried.

"You think you should stay with him, don't you?" Christopher asked. "I guess that's what you should do," he added. He didn't sound very pleased at all and Jenny understood why but what else could she do?

"I'm so, so sorry," Jenny said with tears springing to her eyes. "This is not what I want at all, for any of us,"

"Of course not," Christopher volunteered. " You have to stay there. Ring me when you know what's happening. Jenny, I love you. I understand this, believe me!" he added.

"Thank you," she whispered, not trusting her voice.

As she rang off, she thought, 'of course he understands'. He's been through all this. She returned to the living room where Mike was sitting with his head in his hands. As he looked up there were tears spiking his lashes. She immediately went to his side and put her arms around him. After all they had loved each other greatly and he had been her whole life for years.

"I'll have to phone Sheila Bagley. Remember, she's the deputy head at school. I'll tell her I need Monday off. It'll be the first time I've ever had a day off so there shouldn't be any problem."

"Jenny can I stay here?" Mike asked, looking pleadingly and utterly weary.

Jenny hesitated but then she said "You can stay," and after a pause she added, "but in the spare room."

"Of course," Mike responded reasonably.

"I need to go and get some stuff from Alex's."

"I'm popping up the road to see Pat while you are gone," Jenny said. She desperately needed her friend's good counsel. "Use your key, if I'm not back." She knew he still had it because she had been considering asking him to return it, recently.

"I suppose that's who you were just phoning," said Mike and Jenny did nothing to disabuse him of that idea. She couldn't possibly explain to Mike what had been about to happen when he rolled up. She saw him out and resonant of a previous occasion, again, told him to drive carefully when he had so much on his mind.

□□□□□□□□□

As soon as he had gone Jenny threw on a jacket and almost ran up the road. Just as she rang the bell the door opened and Doug was standing there. She had seen him since his return to the family home but she was no longer at ease with him and she sensed he knew this. "Hello Jenny," he said. I'm just on my way out with the boys but Pat's here. I assume it's her you want to see, though. Come on you two, hurry up!" he called, turning into the hall way, leaving Jenny to follow him. "Jenny's here, Pat," he also shouted up the stairs.

"Oh, come in Jenny. I shan't be a moment."

As Doug passed her and the boys pounded after him, with a 'hi Jenny' vaguely in her direction, Pat came down the stairs with a smile. "Sorry, I was just in the bathroom. Come on into the kitchen. Tea or coffee?" she asked"

"I'd love a quick cup of tea but I really haven't time," Jenny sighed.

"What's the latest?" Pat asked as she filled the kettle and switched it on to boil.

Jenny unburdened her soul of all that had happened. She confessed that she had been going to spend the night at Christopher's and to her great relief Pat was typically prosaic and in her straight-forward way said "I wondered what was taking you so long to get to that stage." Jenny smiled at this response. Then she embarked on the facts of Mike's arrival and the reason for that. "Well," said Pat "That's ironic!"

"What do you mean," asked Jenny.

"Ha! He who lives by the sword shall……." But she didn't finish the well-known saying. Instead she said "Sorry, that's uncalled for. I didn't mean to be so cynical. It's actually dreadful news and I'm really sorry."

They discussed possible outcomes and what might happen at the hospital. Have you looked it up on the internet?" Pat asked.

"No, not yet," Jenny responded. This has all happened within the space of less than the last hour. It's a real roller-coaster. I was just planning my first ever affair and feeling nervous and excited and then this happens to kill all that and give us a whole new set of problems instead. I can't let Mike do this on his own though, can I."

"No, you can't but it doesn't need to come between you and Christopher either.

"I don't know, I really don't know." Jenny bent her head under the weight of it all.

She left shortly after and only felt marginally less confused and upset. It had helped to share the events with Pat and she had been gratified to hear Pat's response to her developing relationship with Christopher. However, the problems were still all there. When she arrived home, her husband still had not returned and she was just about to telephone Christopher again when Mike's car drew up and he climbed out to retrieve a rucksack from the back seat. She replaced her phone into her pocket. She would phone him later though, in the privacy of her bedroom.

Instead she went to look up Sheila's number in her school diary. When Mike came in she told him she was just about to telephone the deputy. Sheila was typically affable when Jenny explained the reason for her request, despite the difficulties it would cause Sheila. "Of course you must go," she had said, volubly.

CHAPTER 18

Saturday night had been dreadful. The evening had been awkward with both Jenny and Mike avoiding the subject of his illness and watching total rubbish on television, trying to be as normal as possible. Jenny had tossed and turned all night and felt like she hadn't slept at all although she knew she must have done at some point. On Sunday morning before she got up Jenny telephoned Christopher. She had been desperately wanting to speak to him and alternately dreading the conversation. How disappointed was she? Therefore she knew how upset he would have been. She hoped he wasn't disenchanted and disillusioned or cross with her.

"It's me," she said when he answered the phone. She imagined him lying in bed, or maybe he was in the kitchen getting Charlie's breakfast ready. Then she heard a little voice in the background and what sounded like the television. "Turn it down a bit Charlie," she heard Christopher say.

Then he spoke into the phone. "Hi, how are you doing?" he asked.

"Oh Christopher, I'm so sorry, I truly am. I just can't leave him with this."

"Hey, I understand. Of all the people you know I must be the one who understands best , don't you think?" he said quietly. "I've been there, remember."

As she lay in bed with the phone to her ear she put her other hand to her forehead and tears sprang to the corners of her eyes. She said "I'm so lucky to have found you."

"Where's Mike now?" Christopher asked and Jenny sensed he was trying to sound casual.

"He's in the spare room. He asked if he could stay. He was practically crying and very frightened so I said he could stay but he has to sleep in there," she reassured.

"I miss you," Christopher whispered. "What happens next?"

"He has a hospital appointment on Monday. I've got the day off work to go with him."
"Do you know what that involves, what the next steps are?" he asked.

"No, I thought I might look it up on the internet so we know what to expect. The doctor said something about a biopsy."

"Will you let me know what happens?"

"Of course I shall, I'll ring you on Monday evening."

"Take care, Jenny. You know I love you."

"I know you do, thank you." Jenny really felt she should say it too but something held her back. She wasn't sure if it was because she wasn't yet sure enough or whether she didn't want to lead Christopher up some dead-end path.

She lay still after finishing the call and couldn't summon the energy to get up and face another day of misery with Mike or revisit her feelings for Christopher. Eventually she gave herself a sharp talking to and she told herself to stop being pathetic. It's just that she was *so* tired. Dragging herself up and coming out of the bathroom, Jenny threw on jeans and a jumper. She couldn't be bothered to use the hairdryer so tugging a brush through her wet hair, she mooched downstairs and put the kettle on. Mike had yet to appear but she got two mugs down and made to get on with the day.

Sometime later he appeared looking tired and drained too. The day was wet and windy so not conducive to feeling bright. Jenny had some school work that she needed to do and so she determined to get on with it regardless of Mike being there. This was her life too, and now she needed to be true to herself. She found it hard to concentrate and couldn't help thinking of the previous week when Christopher had come to her house for lunch and brought Charlie. She had explained that she must do a little work but they still came early. They had played in the garden and then in the living room while she had got on with it before she had then got lunch ready. He had understood that she needed to do it and was content just to be around. Charlie had brought some toys with him and he and Christopher had made a complicated set-up on the living room floor which involved cushions and ramps and cars and animals.

Now, as she got on with her work Mike put on the television and was flicking aimlessly through the channels. She felt slightly resentful of his presence if she was honest. Having been on her own, now, for several months, she found accommodating his needs more difficult. As she got on with her work she gradually managed to shut out the background distraction until he spoke directly to her. She turned to see what he was referring to and saw that he had one of Charlie's toy cars in his hand. "Who does this belong to?" he asked.

"I had some friends round the other day, for lunch. It's one of the little boy's toy cars," Jenny answered evasively.

"Oh, who was that?" Mike persisted.

Taking the bull by the proverbial horns

so to speak Jenny decided to be open. "It was Christopher Mayhew and his son Charlie." She tried not to sound belligerent.

"I see," Mike said, somewhat coldly.

"I don't think you do," she responded. "They came for lunch. Nothing could happen with a six year old in attendance, could it? They are my friends." She was really tempted to add 'besides, it's nothing to do with you!' but she refrained. With a lot more unsaid she returned to her work.

Mike eventually sighed, turned off the television and said that he was going round to the paper shop. He asked if there was anything Jenny wanted but she declined and he went out. As the door closed she breathed a large sigh.

　　　□□□□□□□□□

Sunday dragged and Monday eventually came albeit slowly. Mike's appointment was at one thirty and it would take half an hour, at least, to get to the hospital. The information had said it was alright to eat so they had an early light lunch. Mike was pacing and eager to be off. Jenny sympathised with him and felt sorry for his distress so they set off with her driving there. It was the large regional hospital and so it was busy with some people standing at the entrance in their pyjamas having a smoke, someone sitting in a wheelchair a bit further away, just taking the air and in the foyer lots of people coming and going. On arrival they found out where they had to go and headed up stairs and along corridors to the correct department. Jenny remembered the last time she had been here. It seemed and age ago that Charlie had been here and so poorly, considering how well he was now and how much had happened to Jenny since then. He had regular monitoring appointments, but to all intents and purposes he was quite healed and just as lively and enquiring as before.

Mike and Jenny found the right place and having registered their attendance they sat down to wait. Jenny had a book on her phone but she felt awkward reading while Mike was sitting staring unseeingly into the space around him. She made an attempt at conversation but quickly realised it was not the way forward so they both sat quietly and waited. Eventually Mike was called in. "Shall I wait here or do you want me to come in?" she asked.

"You better wait, I suppose," he answered but if I need you will you come?"
"Of course," she smiled at him. "It'll be fine. You will cope well."

After he had left her sitting, Jenny got out her phone and found the app with the book on it. Then it occurred to her that she probably shouldn't have her phone on at all so she switched it off and cast a guiltily glance around. She picked up a magazine from the low table in front of her and distractedly turned the pages, really only looking at the pictures and reading headlines.

It seemed an age before she was called into the room by a robust nurse in a slightly bulging, pale green uniform. The doctor who greeted her seemed very pleasant and indicated a chair. Mike was in a hospital gown and sitting self-consciously and awkwardly beside her. "Hello, Mrs. Lucas," Mr. Wakefield the consultant started. "I've done an examination of your husband and now I've been explaining to him the procedure that I am about to perform. Firstly we need to send him across for an MRI scan. Then I'm going to do a biopsy of the prostate. It is very simple and should only feel mildly uncomfortable but it would be better if he didn't drive or go to work for a few days. I'm just checking that you can take Mr. Lucas home and be with him for the rest of the today. I'm doing this now because I've just done a small internal examination which we call a DRE and I think it would be advisable to pursue the investigations to be sure we know what we are dealing with. It's only a local anaesthetic and he'll need to rest here for about half an hour afterwards." Mr. Wakefield paused to let this information sink into Jenny's mind.

She looked across at Mike and raised her eyebrows in a question. "Are you OK?"

He nodded his response.

"Do you have any questions Mrs. Lucas?" the consultant asked.

"When might the results of this biopsy be ready?" she asked.

"It should only take a few days and we'll ring as well as write so that, should it be necessary, you can make a further appointment to discuss different types of treatments that are available and we can get underway. I must stress, though, that there is usually no urgency to make a decision about that as this is not normally an aggressive disease. It may not be necessary at all, of course, but we need to be sure."

"Yes, of course," Jenny murmured.

"Do you want me to stay?" she asked no-one in particular with a slightly worried air, unsure of the protocol.

"No, that won't be necessary," Mr. Wakefield reassured her. "My nurse here will call you when we are done and you can sit with Mr. Lucas until it's time to go."

Jenny gave Mike a kiss before she left the room. After all these were fairly extreme circumstances and she was feeling a lot of sympathy for him. She wanted to be supportive and understanding of his anxiety. She was fearful of these unknowns too. This all suddenly seemed like a big deal; something that she had never considered for him or herself.

Again, Jenny sat in the waiting area and tried to calm her thoughts and her racing heart, imagining she knew not what. However, she had looked up information on the internet. There were loads of good websites which had been really informative so she knew roughly what was happening. The trouble with limited understanding was that you tended to think about worst case scenarios and so she had wanted to be more aware than that.

Eventually she got the call to go and find Mike. He was looking a bit pale but gave her a smile and said that he was fine. "It was more uncomfortable than painful," he said. "I need to wait around now to make sure everything is OK before we leave. I'm glad it's over with but I'm glad you made me look at those internet sites though. At least I knew a little of what is involved and what to expect."

"We'll be away from here soon," Jenny said reassuringly. "We'll go home and have a restoring cup of tea and I've got some cake in the cupboard too." She knew that was a small and meaningless recompense but she was at a bit of a loss to know what to say and do. "Sorry," she added "I'm useless at this."

"Thank you so much for being here, Jenny, I don't know how I would be managing without you," said Mike and he reached across and took her hand. She let her hand rest in his for several minutes and then sliding it out she fished in her handbag with the excuse of looking for a tissue. Jenny felt suddenly disorientated.

After half an hour the smiling, buxom nurse returned and the necessary leaflets were given and information exchanged to ensure Mike was fit to leave and knew of after-effects to expect over the next few days, so that he wouldn't panic if he saw some blood spotting. Jenny linked her arm through his and together they headed for the door and down the long corridor to find the lift.

That evening, as she had promised, Jenny telephoned Christopher to explain what had happened during the day. She reassured him that although Mike was staying, he was in the spare room and asked if she could call around after school the next day. She was anxious to see him and to see Charlie too. She felt she needed to explain why she had offered Mike a home again and to talk to Christopher and re-establish their rapport which she felt she must have been dented albeit unintentionally.

It felt weird having Mike living there again but not really as a full couple. Jenny reminded herself that it was only for a few days and she couldn't help planning how she would broach this with Mike if he didn't look like leaving. It all felt so complicated.

☐☐☐☐☐☐☐☐

The following day Jenny saw Christopher on the playground before school started. He waved to her and came across just as the whistle blew. "Will I still see you later?" he asked.

"Yes, please," Jenny answered. "It won't be until about five o'clock though, if that's OK. I've a short meeting after school that I really can't put off."

"Of course, that's fine." He gave her hand a surreptitious squeeze but didn't kiss her in the full publicity of the playground. Jenny felt that he knew that she was not ready for that level of advertisement yet. In fact he doubted the wisdom of her decision to stay the night last week. She knew that he sensed she had not truly crossed that line yet and so perhaps it was fortuitous as things had turned out although she also understood that it was not in his nature to wish the current circumstances on anyone, least of all Mike.

When Jenny saw Christopher after school that evening, Charlie had gone to tea with a friend and so it was just the two of them. She really felt she loved Charlie but it was a relief for Jenny on this occasion, that he was absent. Under the circumstances she welcomed the opportunity to have more of an in depth discussion with his dad and spend some time just being together. She was able to discuss how difficult she had found the visit to the hospital and how useless she had felt. She knew how scared Mike was and how she had encouraged him to find out some facts. She had believed it was better to know what might be afoot. "Do you think that was correct or do you think I should have left him to find out from the doctors at the hospital at the time?" Jenny asked Christopher.

He knew about all the feelings of uncertainty and being unable to really help ease the fear and pain too. He had been exactly where Jenny was now. Christopher had voiced that he wished intensely that all would turn out better for Mike than it had for his wife and he had meant it too. It was more likely to be positive news on that front, he had said. "Research and early discovery are the keys. Hopefully Mike has sought medical support in good time, if it does turn out to be that. I'm sure it's more usually not an aggressive form. *Please* let me know how things go, Jenny," he implored. He hoped fervently that Jenny still wanted to pursue their relationship once this was all behind her. She guessed that he was panicking slightly that she would forgive Mike again and return to him fully. They were standing in the kitchen when he had told her that he knew he had found a genuine and real love again and didn't want to contemplate what would happen if she couldn't return to him. His green eyes were sincere and imploring as they searched her face for some reciprocated emotion. "I know I shouldn't put this pressure upon you, Jenny," he had said desperately and then paused for some seconds before adding "but I need to fight for you now. I love you so much."

"Oh, Christopher," Jenny whispered and tears started to seep silently from under her lashes and slide down her cheeks. His arms came around her enveloping her in their security and she hid her face in the crook between his shoulder and neck . They stood for some minutes while Jenny wept out her misery and anxiety. Having unleashed all her pent up fears and uncertainties the tempest slowly passed. She continued to give uncontrollable reflex snuffles for some time and she just stood within his warmth but eventually she was able to pull away from him. Looking up she gave a watery smile and said "Sorry,"

"Listen, Jenny," he said, taking hold of her shoulders and holding her firmly until she looked up into his gaze, "I completely understand how you feel and the place you are in currently. I love you and will wait until you are ready, whenever that may be. Yes, I want you, more than anything but I, of all people, know what's happening right now and I'll support you in any way I can." With that he kissed her gently and released her. She kissed him back and turned to search out her bag to find a tissue. 'What an amazing man,' she thought. 'Why can't I just go to him? But Mike and I have had such a history and we have been such good friends. Perhaps I owe him my loyalty, especially now. But he's let me down so badly.' She was in such turmoil

□□□□□□□□□

The next few days passed quite quickly for Jenny because she was so busy at work. She was not home particularly early each day, having classroom preparation, meetings and a thousand other things to do. Mike was back at work and most evenings when she arrived home he was already there and had started to prepare the evening meal. Towards the end of that first week when they had attended hospital and he was staying in the spare room he welcomed her with a glass of wine when she arrived home.

"What's this in aid of?" she asked.

"Oh, nothing in particular. You seem tired that's all. You haven't to do more work tonight have you? I thought we could watch that film on TV and just chill out a bit. I feel as if I've done nothing but wait for these damn results. We both need something to take our minds off things, don't we?" he said.

"Mike, you need to go back to Alex's soon," Jenny blurted out. "This is foolish. Neither of us knows where we are at the moment."

"Please let me stay until I get the results, Jenny," Mike looked at her searchingly. "I really need you."

She put down her glass and looked at him. "You can stay until then, but that's all. I can't live like this."

"It doesn't have to be like this," Mike responded.

"It does at the moment," she said, "until we know what's happening and what we want."

"I know what I want," he said meaningfully.

Jenny turned away. "Don't!" she said. "Let's just wait for these results first."

During the following week, one morning they were each still in bed when they both heard the metallic rattle of the post box cover. They met on the landing but Mike was first down the stairs. On bending down he picked up the letters and shuffled through them until he came to the brown envelope. He grimaced and waved it at Jenny, having seen the printed logo on the envelope.

He sighed and said "This would appear to be it! I don't want to open it."

Jenny came down to stand by his side and put her hand on his arm. "Go on, do it quickly!"

□□□□□□□□□

Mike's follow up appointment to see the consultant was soon arranged and again Jenny was able to take the afternoon off work to accompany him. He was no less scared because now it was confirmed that he had the disease with that dreaded name, cancer.

Again they waited in the same area and eventually, again, the nurse with the smile and the robust figure called them in. This time Mike wanted Jenny to go with him. "I may not take it all in," he said.

Mr. Wakefield was sitting on the end of his desk with a folder open in his hands. His glasses were perched half-way down his nose and he looked over them as they entered. Taking them off he waved them at the two chairs nearby and smiled as both Jenny and Mike sat. He moved his chair to the end of the desk upon which he had just been perched. He was doing his best to remove some formality and make them feel easy, Jenny thought briefly.

"Right, well, we need to crack on and get you sorted, Mr. Lucas, and then you can get on with life, yes?" he said in an upbeat sort of way. "The good news is that from the MRI scan we can see that we are only talking prostate here and it hasn't spread elsewhere yet. I think we've got it good and early so that's a positive, yes?"

Mike nodded and on glancing at him Jenny could see he looked bewildered and worried despite the cheerful way in which Mr. Wakefield was speaking to them.

"We grade what we have found on the Gleason scale," the consultant continued. This goes from 2 to 10 and we can put yours at 7. Now we also do a 'staging'. This describes where your cancer is and whether it has progressed further. We see yours as a T2b. This means that it can be felt in more than half of one side of the lobes but not in both sides of the gland. So that's not too bad, yes? Also you get a zero for the N stage which is to do with lymph nodes and a zero for the M stage which is to do with other parts of the body. SO….this all might sound a bit technical but it means that you are at an intermediate risk.

"That sounds a bit scary," Mike said.

"I'd rather have heard low risk."

"It's not as bad as you think," Mr. Wakefield assured Mike.

"There are several courses of treatment and I'm going to outline those for you. You don't need to decide now. It's best if you go away, have a chat with Mrs. Lucas and then we'll crack on with what we think is best, yes?"

"Mmm," Mike responded quietly.

"Now, we can offer 'watchful waiting' which basically means we do nothing but monitor the growth."

Mike looked across at Jenny and grimaced.

"However, I have to say, since you are such a strapping young lad that may not be the best thing. It's extremely rare for this condition to be diagnosed this young. Now, if you were eighty years old since this type of cancer is very slow growing, chances are you'd be dead of something else long before, so 'watchful waiting' might be the best answer."

Mr. Wakefield went on to describe different treatments involving implanting low dose longer term radioactive seeds that would destroy the diseased cells, freezing and thawing treatment, high dose radiation for a few minutes at a time into the prostate gland as well as external radiation or even surgery to remove the gland altogether. Jenny's mind was buzzing. It seemed a lot to take in and she was glad that she and Mike could discuss each method at home later. They were able to ask Mr. Wakefield about possible side effects and also the advantages and disadvantages. He was so positive throughout and clearly said that Mike's chances of a full recovery were very good. Following treatment they would monitor him annually to ensure no return of the disease. By the time they had finished they were both exhausted.

▢▢▢▢▢▢▢▢

Once they were home again they both collapsed on to the sofa and sat in complete silence for some long moments. Eventually Jenny looked at Mike and said "Tea?"

He nodded his response so she rose and went into the kitchen to fill and plug in the kettle. He followed her and as she turned he drew her into his arms. For some moments Jenny felt warm inside his embrace. The smell of him was familiar and her head fitted comfortably against his shoulder. Then she gained her senses and pulled away, turning again to gather mugs, milk and to pour the hot water.

CHAPTER 19

The weeks passed. After Christmas, Mike started on his treatment. They had opted for Low Dose Radiation brachytherapy which involved the implantation of rice like 'seeds' to which the radiation could be added. The chances of problems with incontinence or impotence were reduced and in one so young that seemed a good thing. Also the seeds were aimed very precisely at the problem. Jenny had accompanied Mike for his implant treatment appointment. He had gone as a day patient. He'd had a general anaesthetic but he was fit to come home at the end of the day and had gone back to work only a few days later. After this initial therapy, Mike also returned to his friend Alex's house. Perversely, Jenny missed him to start with, not that they had shared a bedroom at all but having another person around in the evenings was becoming a habit again. She continued to see Christopher and Charlie. Occasionally at weekends she stayed to eat or as the weather got milder again they went out for the afternoon and did things that entertained a young lad. They all three got on so well and Jenny sensed that Christopher was a very loyal and completely trustworthy man. Whilst he steadfastly avoided the question of Jenny staying the night she felt very contented and relaxed with him. Thus they continued in their slightly bizarre celibates' relationship.

During the following months, once or twice, Mike had stayed in the spare room for a couple of days if he had been feeling rough or had a crisis of worry. Mr. Wakefield, the consultant, seemed to be pleased and very positive about progress though.

Spring passed quickly and summer approached. Jenny was becoming more and more convinced that she was being unfair to Christopher. She had been on the brink of being in his life fully and then all the medical complications with Mike had arisen and, despite their differences, she had felt loyalty to her husband. She really didn't know if this was misplaced or not but she couldn't leave him to cope with all that on his own. In the meantime, Christopher had been extraordinary in his patience and understanding. He frequently reminded her that he understood, having been through the same thing with his wife, although that had not turned out happily at all. He persisted in trying to reassure her that he would wait for her to be ready to accept his full love and partnership. Equally Mike was starting to press her to allow him back into her life fully. The time had come for her to make a life-affirming decision.

She had been to see her mum and dad. Whilst they had genuinely loved Mike they had been very disappointed by his behaviour because of the impact it had on Jenny. She knew, however, they would agree with whatever she decided and support her whole-heartedly. They had met Christopher and Charlie; thought Charlie was adorable and could see that Christopher was a constant and serious man who was also a devoted and caring dad; could see that his humanity, patience and good humour were good for Jenny. They really liked him. They had seen that he and Jenny got on really well and that she was very fond indeed of Charlie. However, they were also unsure if having a child from another marriage in her life was an added complication.

"It's what parents do," they had agreed when Jenny had had yet another heart to heart with her mum. "We want you to be happy and have a confident and secure life, darling. Of course whatever you decide, we'll support you," her mum had said on behalf of them both. Little snippets of conversation had informed Jenny, however, that both her mum and dad together had been having many conversations about her in her absence and were very worried for her long-term happiness.

Pat had been so supportive over the last few months as well. She understood Jenny's dilemma. After all she had her own troubles with Doug and she knew what it was like to feel let down and yet to develop a shell in order to survive that battering to her self-esteem. She hadn't told Jenny what she, Pat, thought she should do but had been there as a sounding board for Jenny's dilemmas and uncertainties.

The end of July came and school finished for the long summer holidays. Having got some energy back after a long and busy term with many evening and early morning meetings as well as working with tired and fractious children towards the end of term, Jenny made up her mind to sort out her life once and for all. She called Mike and having spoken on the phone for some time she arranged to meet him.

"When shall I come round?" he asked

"Let's meet away from here somewhere," Jenny said. "Maybe at the park, neutral territory," she added. Times and days were sorted out and she couldn't help starting to imagine how this fateful meeting would go. She hadn't told Christopher of this arrangement. She truthfully couldn't decide which way to spring and she didn't want to raise his hopes unnecessarily. She was in a fretful turmoil. The night before the meeting she had hardly slept and having finally grabbed a little broken sleep had woken early.

Jenny had parked her car and arrived early enough to walk through the park and gather her calm and her confidence. Now was the time. Now she could see Mike at the far side of the lake. Now she stepped ever closer to her destiny. She could have been feeling a sense of power over these two men in her life; two people who wanted her. This was not how she felt at all. She was feeling confusion and chaos. Pat had assured her that she would know what decision to make when she arrived and met Mike. She desperately hoped so. As she neared the bench and Mike, she could see he was pacing around rather than sitting and waiting for her. She took some deep breaths to calm her nerves.

"Hello," she waved, uncertainly, as she approached. He had not seen her before, eyes to the ground as he patrolled.

"Hi," he responded awkwardly. "Do you want to sit or walk?"

"Let's sit for a while," Jenny answered, unsure of the strength in her legs at this moment. "How are you doing since we last saw each other?" she asked.

"Really well," he said. "The radiation

should be well on its way now and finishing soon. I don't seem to have had any major after effects. I'm due for another scan in a few weeks to verify the tumours are gone. Mr. Wakefield said they'll keep me under regular review for years. I feel so lucky, Jenny." There was an awkward pause. "What have you been up to?" he asked.

Both of them, Jenny realised were putting off the moment for the root of their discussion.

"Well, we've broken up, now of course," she answered desultorily, her mind on the reason for being here. She had asked for this meeting and so she realised she would have to take the initiative. "Mike, we have to make some decisions. We can't go on like this indefinitely. Apart from anything Alex won't want you there for ever," she started.

He jumped in straight away with "No, he won't. In fact he asked me the other day what was happening. Jenny I could come back home."

"I don't know." She looked down at her hands in her lap. "I'm not sure I'm the same person and I'm not sure that you really want to be with me either."

"I do. You know I'm really sorry for what happened," Mike said. "I don't know why it did."

"I shall still need to do my school work. I shall still be earning more than you. None of that has altered."

"It doesn't matter," he insisted.

"But you promised me it was over and then you still went back for more with Diana," Jenny said quietly.

"I know but that wasn't for long anyway," Mike responded.

"What? What do you mean it wasn't for long anyway?"

"Well it wasn't. It only lasted a couple of weeks that second time."

Jenny could feel herself getting angry now. "Oh well that's alright then I suppose," she said acerbically.

"It wasn't meaningful. It wasn't important," Mike justified.

"Wasn't important to you, maybe, but you made promises to me when we got married. You broke those. Then you lied to me again after making a further promise." She sighed deeply and stood. It was Jenny's turn to pace now. "Wasn't important, you just said. It was critically important to me. Actually I'm thinking it was really wholly significant, Mike and if you think it wasn't 'important' then I don't think we can carry on." There, she had said the words that were the focal point of a decision.

All of a sudden things became distinct, crystal clear. What she saw at the key issue, to him was trifling and almost negligible – unimportant. She turned to face him. He was still sitting on the bench looking up at her with a slightly puzzled frown. The she spoke the words for the ideas that had become suddenly so well-defined. "Mike, I'm not taking you back. I'm not going to because I'm not giving you permission to lie to me and betray my trust like that."

He looked at her completely flabbergasted. "I thought you wanted to meet so that I could come home," he said after several long moments.

"If I let you come home it means I'm allowing you to think it's been OK to treat me as you have and to see what you have done as unimportant," she voiced quietly. Her anger had evaporated as quickly as it had come. Now she was feeling succinct in her thoughts and understood what there was between them.

"So there's no such thing as forgiveness in your world," he said bitterly.

"It's not a case of forgiveness," she said "It's a case of us not feeling or understanding the same thing about marriage and what it means. Mike, that's it, I'm sorry. Well actually, no I'm not. I'm just not consenting to marriage on those lines."

"I see," he said though she doubted he did. "That's it then?"

"That's it, Mike," she murmured.

The magnitude of this moment did not elude Jenny. She was sad, very sad. She had felt disappointment, failure and crushing loss over the last few months. However, more recently she had begun to see that this was not of her making but rather a fundamental difference between them in the meaning of this relationship. As she had said to Mike just now when she had said she couldn't give him permission to treat her this way, she meant she couldn't allow herself to accept his concept of their relationship. They had to part. As she stood in front of him she looked upon him and saw dawning realisation on his face that she had meant what she said and that she truly would not be changing her mind.

"That's it then," he said again, standing finally. "What do I say? See you around?"

"We'll need to sort out the house and our stuff," she said forlornly. "Ring me soon and we'll meet to discuss it. It'll have to go on the market and we'll just split it all, I suppose."

With that he kissed her cheek and without further words he turned and left. Jenny sat down again; heavily this time and with her hands in her lap she took a deep breath and lowered her head. She stayed without moving for some time. Finally she raised her eyes to the sky and closing them she sat silently, calming her pounding heart. There were the distant sounds of children who were oblivious to all but their fun and feelings in their own egotistical world; she heard the birds, unseen, in the treetops singing for the joy of a sunny warm day; she could hear the water birds on the lake arguing or just squawking for the hell of it; she smelt the balminess of the turf around her and the leaves immobile on the surrounding trees and bushes. Eventually, she raised herself from the seat and slowly moved towards the car park.

□□□□□□□□

When Jenny reached the house that, for only a short while longer, was to be her home she sat for a moment in the car and wondered what to do. She decided to simply go indoors because she didn't know what else she could or should do. She had an awful, flat feeling of anti-climax following all the emotion of the last hours. She dumped her bag and keys and just mooched around from one room to another. Then there was a ring at the front door. She jumped and immediately her heart started thumping. 'Oh no, not Mike, please no' she thought. She edged towards the door and saw, from the outline through the glass, who she thought was Pat. Momentarily she sagged against the wall, such was her relief.

"I'm afraid I was watching out of the window and saw the car. A regular curtain tweaker! The boys are out the back on the field with their bikes so they may join us quite soon, but I had to come and see you, Jenny," she smiled warmly.

"Come in, Pat," Jenny held the door wider.

"If you want to be on your own and have some space that's fine. I can go away now that I've seen you are in one piece," Pat said.

"No, it's fine. In fact, I'm pleased to see you - a bit of normality," Jenny added.

"I need to start sharing my new status although there are some key people I need to tell as well as you, so it's probably better if you keep it to yourself until I've spoken to Mum and Dad and Christopher, particularly.

"I see," Pat waited to hear more.

"We are parting," Jenny announced. "I can't let myself settle for his form of marriage. It may never happen again but I can't take that risk. He said that the second time he went back to her it wasn't important but it was." The more she thought about that the more incredulous she became at Mikes reaction. "Okay, on one level it was just a quick roll in the sack. It wasn't that act so much even. It's what that represents. It tells me that basically I'm not as significant, not that central to his life as I need to be."

"I said to you once before that I think Doug is more meaningful to Doug than I am," said Pat. Some people are more self-centred than others. They reckon two out of three men will cheat at some time. Seems we've got the two," she shrugged.

"You've found a way to cope with it but I can't," Jenny said.

"I've got two children but you haven't yet," Pat added. "Maybe that's the difference. I'm not saying it's better to stay together for the sake of them like in the old days but if I can accommodate my own feelings so that Doug and I jog along together in some fashion, without bickering and bringing up old wounds then I hope that's better for them."

"You are some special kind of person, Pat," Jenny said warmly.

With that they heard young voices at the door and going to answer the knock Jenny found Pat's two lads looking pink and warm.

"Come in, you two," she said. "You look hot and thirsty. Would you like a drink and a biscuit?"

"Yes, please," and "Mmm, thanks, Jenny" came the two responses from the boys. They pounded up the hall and into the kitchen. Ben flung his arms expansively around his mum's shoulders and meticulous Joe went to wash his hands at the sink. Jenny was pleased to have the occupation of getting them refreshments and the normality of youngsters around her. They munched the biscuits and downed the squash with the exuberance of the young. "Thanks, Jenny, they said in unison. We're going back up in the field mum," said Ben

"Alright," said Pat, "Don't go away without saying though," she reminded them.

On their own again, after the bright breeziness of the youngsters, Jenny was beginning to feel more positive than she had done for a very long time.

"So the next big question is Christopher and of course Charlie," stated Pat.

"Yes but I feel I can devote my full attention to them now," Jenny said. "I do think I've been quite selfish over the last few months but Christopher kept saying he understood and that I must get sorted with Mike's illness first. It's just been too difficult somehow while Mike was under-going treatment and staying here for such a lot of the time over the last few months. I just couldn't abandon him through all that."

"What's the latest on his medical stuff?" Pat asked

Jenny told her the positive news as she understood it from Mike.

"He's very lucky," Pat responded. "Treatments nowadays are incredible but it's a good thing, too, that he went to the doctors early." After a pause she continued "Well, I better gather up the boys and head for home to think about lunch. You've got plenty to do and think about. I'm so glad you got back safely and are okay. I've been thinking about you since you left this morning.

"Once again, I have to thank you Pat," Jenny voiced her gratitude for good friendship. "We'll talk soon."

□□□□□□□□

That night Jenny lay in bed. She was dog-tired but could not sleep. So many things were going around and around in her head. She needed a day or two to understand her own emotions and to be sure what she needed to say to Christopher before she saw him again, she thought, sensibly. Since he was unaware that she had been meeting Mike to communicate a definitive decision about her future with her husband, she felt she needed to get that out of her system before seeing him and Charlie again. Perhaps she should remain on her own and not be in a relationship at all.

Then she thought of Christopher and her tummy flipped and her heart pounded just a little faster. She missed him. She laid thinking about his gentleness, the good fun they had, his kindness and understanding, his patience, his green eyes and his strong arms, his hands. She loved his hands; his hands and his eyes. It came to her with an arresting flash. She loved him. She sat bolt upright. She loved him. Without thinking she leaped out of bed and ran downstairs. She must be mad. She loved him. She threw on her coat over her nightdress and stuffed her feet into her sandals. She loved him.

The front door banged behind her and running out to the car she wrapped her coat around her and tied the belt, not stopping to zip it up. She managed to drive, somehow. She parked the car outside on the road. She ran up the path to his front door. She knocked, breathlessly. The door opened and he stood there.

"I love you," she said and threw herself into his opening arms.

ABOUT THE AUTHOR

Now that she is retired Ros has found the process of writing utterly compelling as she has the time to research and write in this genre. Other ideas are coming fast now, too. She does NOT want to fester, wearing purple with a red hat and running her stick along the railing, in her retirement, as in the well know poem!

Her life is, probably, a mix of serendipity and (hopefully) a touch of sagacity. That happy accident mixed with a touch of (maybe) clever judgement is what she would like but there is often something that smacks her in the mouth when least expected. She remain an optimist!

Ros was encouraged by her mother, a published author with several books to her credit, to write a novel. Having worked as a headteacher for many years, writing papers and essays to further her qualifications as well as stories to which young children would enjoy listening, Ros has finally completed this work of adult fiction as she was urged   to   do.

She is currently living in France, with her husband and two dogs.

She has two daughters and four grand-daughters who also find Ros's work heartwarming and a good read.

Printed in Great Britain
by Amazon.co.uk, Ltd.,
Marston Gate.

A Guide to Zodiac Compatibility

Often, when we meet a person, we get a feeling that they are good and we take an instant liking to them. Another person, however, gives us immediate feelings of distrust, fear and hostility. Is there an astrological reason why people say that 'the first impression is the most accurate'? How can we detect those who will bring us nothing but trouble and unhappiness?

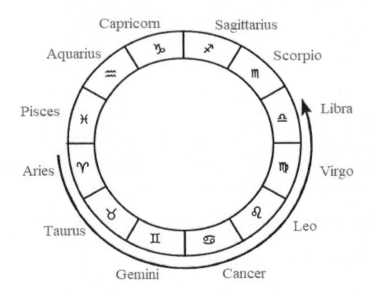

Without going too deeply into astrological subtleties unfamiliar to some readers, it is possible to determine the traits according to which friendship, love or business relationships will develop.

Let's begin with problematic relationships - our most difficult are with our **8th sign**. For example, for Aries the 8th sign is Scorpio, for Taurus it is Sagittarius and so on. Finding your 8th sign is easy; assume your own sign to be first (see above Figure) and then move eight signs counter clockwise around the Zodiac circle. This is also how the other signs (fourth, ninth and so on) that we mention are to be found.

Ancient astrologers variously referred to the 8th sign as the symbol of death, of destruction, of fated love or unfathomable attraction. In astrological terms, this pair is called 'master and slave' or 'boa constrictor and rabbit', with the role of 'master' or 'boa constrictor' being played by our 8th sign.

This relationship is especially difficult for politicians and business people.

We can take the example of a recent political confrontation in the USA. Hilary Clinton is a Scorpio while Donald Trump is a Gemini - her 8th sign. Even though many were certain that Clinton would be elected President, she lost.

To take another example, Hitler was a Taurus and his opponents – Stalin and Churchill - were both of his 8th sign, Sagittarius. The result of their confrontation is well known. Interestingly, the Russian Marshals who dealt crushing military blows to Hitler and so helped end the Third Reich - Konstantin Rokossovsky and Georgy Zhukov - were also Sagittarian, Hitler's 8th sign.

In another historical illustration, Lenin was also a Taurus. Stalin was of Lenin's 8th sign and was ultimately responsible for the downfall and possibly death of his one-time comrade-in-arms.

Business ties with those of our 8th sign are hazardous as they ultimately lead to stress and loss; both financial and moral. So, do not tangle with your 8th sign and never fight with it - your chances of winning are remote!

Such relationships are very interesting in terms of love and romance, however. We are magnetically attracted to our 8th sign and even though it may be very intense physically, it is very difficult for family life;

'Feeling bad when together, feeling worse when apart'.

As an example, let us take the famous lovers - George Sand who was Cancer and Alfred de Musset who was Sagittarius. Cancer is the 8th sign for Sagittarius, and the story of their crazy two-year love affair was the subject of much attention throughout France. Critics and writers were divided into 'Mussulist' and 'Sandist' camps; they debated fiercely about who was to blame for the sad ending to their love story - him or her. It's hard to imagine the energy needed to captivate the public for so long, but that energy was destructive for the couple. Passion raged in their hearts, but neither of them was able to comprehend their situation.

Georges Sand wrote to Musset, "*I ∙on't love you anymore, an∙ I will always a∙ore you. I ∙on't want you anymore, an∙ I can't ∙o without you. It seems that nothing but a heavenly lightning strike can heal me by ∙estroying me. Goo∙-bye! Stay or go, but ∙on't say that I am not suffering. This is the only thing that can make me suffer even more, my love, my life, my bloo∙! Go away, but kill me, leaving.*" Musset replied only in brief, but its power surpassed Sand's tirade, "*When you embrace∙ me, I felt something that is still bothering me, making it impossible for me to approach another woman.*" These two people loved each other passionately and for two years lived together in a powder keg of passion, hatred and treachery.

When someone enters into a romantic liaison with their 8th sign, there will be no peace; indeed, these relationships are very attractive to those who enjoy the edgy, the borderline and, in the Dostoevsky style, the melodramatic. The first to lose interest in the relationship is, as a rule, the 8th sign.

If, by turn of fate, our child is born under our 8th sign, they will be very different from us and, in some ways, not live up to our expectations. It may be best to let them choose their own path.

In business and political relationships, the combination with our **12th sign** is also a complicated one.

We can take two political examples. Angela Merkel is a Cancer while Donald Trump is a Gemini - her 12th sign. This is why their relations are strained and complicated and we can even perhaps assume that the American president will achieve his political goals at her expense. Boris Yeltsin (Aquarius) was the 12th sign to Mikhail Gorbachev (Pisces) and it was Yeltsin who managed to dethrone the champion of Perestroika.

Even ancient astrologers noticed that our relationships with our 12th signs can never develop evenly; it is one of the most curious and problematic combinations. They are our hidden enemies and they seem to be digging a hole for us; they ingratiate themselves with us, discover our innermost secrets. As a result, we become bewildered and make mistakes when we deal with them. Among the Roman emperors murdered by members of their entourage, there was an interesting pattern - all the murderers were the 12th sign of the murdered.

We can also see this pernicious effect in Russian history: the German princess Alexandra (Gemini) married the last Russian Tsar Nicholas II (Taurus) - he was her 12th sign and brought her a tragic death. The wicked genius Grigory Rasputin (Cancer) made friends with Tsarina Alexandra, who was his 12th sign, and was murdered as a result of their odd friendship. The weakness of Nicholas II was exposed, and his authority reduced after the death of the economic and social reformer Pyotr Stolypin, who was his 12th sign. Thus, we see a chain of people whose downfall was brought about by their 12th sign.

So, it makes sense to be cautious of your 12th sign, especially if you have business ties. Usually, these people know much more about us than we want them to and they will often reveal our secrets for personal gain if it suits them. However, the outset of these relationships is, as a rule, quite normal - sometimes the two people will be friends, but sooner or later one will betray the other one or divulge a secret; inadvertently or not.

In terms of romantic relationships, our 12th sign is gentle, they take care of us and are tender towards us. They know our weaknesses well but accept them with understanding. It is they who guide us, although sometimes almost imperceptibly. Sexual attraction is usually strong.

For example, Meghan Markle is a Leo, the 12th sign for Prince Harry, who is a Virgo. Despite Queen Elizabeth II being lukewarm about the match, Harry's love was so strong that they did marry.

If a child is our 12th sign, it later becomes clear that they know all our secrets, even those that they are not supposed to know. It is very difficult to control them as they do everything in their own way.

Relations with our **7th sign** are also interesting. They are like our opposite; they have something to learn from us while we, in turn, have something to learn from them. This combination, in business and personal relationships, can be very positive and stimulating provided that both partners are quite intelligent and have high moral standards but if not, constant misunderstandings and challenges follow. Marriage or co-operation with the 7th sign can only exist as the union of two fully-fledged individuals and in this case love, significant business achievements and social success are possible.

However, the combination can be not only interesting, but also quite complicated.

An example is Angelina Jolie, a Gemini, and Brad Pitt, a Sagittarius. This is a typical bond with a 7th sign - it's lively and interesting, but rather stressful. Although such a couple may quarrel and even part from time to time, never do they lose interest in each other.

This may be why this combination is more stable in middle-age when there is an understanding of the true nature of marriage and partnership. In global, political terms, this suggests a state of eternal tension - a cold war - for example between Yeltsin (Aquarius) and Bill Clinton (Leo).

Relations with our **9th sign** are very good; they are our teacher and advisor - one who reveals things we are unaware of and our relationships with them very often involve travel or re-location. The combination can lead to spiritual growth and can be beneficial in terms of business.

Although, for example, Trump and Putin are political opponents, they can come to an understanding and even feel a certain sympathy for each other because Putin is a Libra while Trump is a Gemini, his 9th sign.

This union is also quite harmonious for conjugal and romantic relationships.

We treat our **3rd sign** somewhat condescendingly. They are like our younger siblings; we teach them and expect them to listen attentively. Our younger brothers and sisters are more often than not born under this sign. In terms of personal and sexual relationships, the union is not very inspiring and can end quickly, although this is not always the case. In terms of business, it is fairly average as it often connects partners from different cities or countries.

We treat our **5th sign** as a child and we must take care of them accordingly. The combination is not very good for business, however, since our 5th sign triumphs over us in terms of connections and finances, and thereby gives us very little in return save for love or sympathy. However, they are very good for family and romantic relationships, especially if the 5th sign is female. If a child is born as a 5th sign to their parents, their relationship will be a mutually smooth, loving and understanding one that lasts a lifetime.

Our **10th sign** is a born leader. Depending on the spiritual level of those involved, both pleasant and tense relations are possible; the relationship is often mutually beneficial in the good times but mutually disruptive in the bad times. In family relations, our 10th sign always tries to lead and will do so according to their intelligence and upbringing.

Our **4th sign** protects our home and can act as a sponsor to strengthen our financial or moral positions. Their advice should be heeded in all cases as it can be very effective, albeit very unobtrusive. If a woman takes this role, the relationship can be long and romantic, since all the spouse's wishes are usually met one way or another. Sometimes, such couples achieve great social success; for instance, Hilary Clinton, a Scorpio is the 4th sign to Bill Clinton, a Leo. On the other hand, if the husband is the 4th sign for his wife, he tends to be henpecked. There is often a strong sexual attraction. Our 4th sign can improve our living conditions and care for us in a parental way. If a child is our 4th sign, they are close to us and support us affectionately.

Relations with our **11th sign** are often either friendly or patronizing; we treat them reverently, while they treat us with friendly condescension. Sometimes, these relationships develop in an 'older brother' or 'high-ranking friend' sense; indeed, older brothers and sisters are often our 11th sign. In terms of personal and sexual relationships, our 11th sign is always inclined to enslave us. This tendency is most clearly manifested in such alliances as Capricorn and Pisces or Leo and Libra. A child who is the 11th sign to their parents will achieve greater success than their parents, but this will only make the parents proud.

Our **2nd sign** should bring us financial or other benefits; we receive a lot from them in both our business and our family life. In married couples, the 2nd sign usually looks after the financial situation for the benefit of the family. Sexual attraction is strong.

Our **6th sign** is our 'slave'; we always benefit from working with them and it's very difficult for them to escape our influence. In the event of hostility, especially if they have provoked the conflict, they receive a powerful retaliatory strike. In personal relations, we can almost destroy them by making them dance to our tune. For example, if a husband doesn't allow his wife to work or there are other adverse family circumstances, she gradually becomes lost as an individual despite being surrounded by care. This is the best-case scenario; worse outcomes are possible. Our 6th sign has a strong sexual attraction to us because we are the fatal 8th sign for them; we cool down quickly, however, and often make all kinds of demands. If the relationship with our 6th sign is a long one, there is a danger that routine, boredom and stagnation will ultimately destroy the relationship. A child born under our 6th sign needs particularly careful handling as they can feel fear or embarrassment when communicating with us. Their health often needs increased attention and we should also remember that they are very different from us emotionally.

Finally, we turn to relations with **our own sign**. Scorpio with Scorpio and Cancer with Cancer get along well, but in most other cases, however, our own sign is of little interest to us as it has a similar energy. Sometimes, this relationship can develop as a rivalry, either in business or in love.

There is another interesting detail - we are often attracted to one particular sign. For example, a man's wife and mistress often have the same sign. If there is confrontation between the two, the stronger character displaces the weaker one. As an example, Prince Charles is a Scorpio, while both Princess Diana and Camilla Parker Bowles were born under the sign of Cancer. Camilla was the more assertive and became dominant.

Of course, in order to draw any definitive conclusions, we need an individually prepared horoscope, but the above always, one way or another, manifests itself.

Love Description of Zodiac Signs

We know that human sexual behavior has been studied at length. Entire libraries have been written about it, with the aim of helping us understand ourselves and our partners. But is that even possible? It may not be; no matter how smart we are, when it comes to love and sex, there is always an infinite amount to learn. But we have to strive for perfection, and astrology, with its millennia of research, twelve astrological types, and twelve zodiac signs, may hold the key. Below, you will find a brief and accurate description of each zodiac sign's characteristics in love, for both men and women.

Men

ARIES

Aries men are not particularly deep or wise, but they make up for it in sincerity and loyalty. They are active, even aggressive lovers, but a hopeless romantic may be lurking just below the surface. Aries are often monogamous and chivalrous men, for whom there is only one woman (of course, in her absence, they can sleep around with no remorse). If the object of your affection is an Aries, be sure to give him a lot of sex, and remember that for an Aries, when it comes to sex, anything goes. Aries cannot stand women who are negative or disheveled. They need someone energetic, lively, and to feel exciting feelings of romance.

The best partner for an Aries is Cancer, Sagittarius, or Leo. Aquarius can also be a good match, but the relationship will be rather friendly in nature. Partnering with a Scorpio or Taurus will be difficult, but they can be stimulating lovers for an Aries. Virgos are good business contacts, but a poor match as lovers or spouses.

TAURUS

A typical Taurean man is warm, friendly, gentle, and passionate, even if he doesn't always show it. He is utterly captivated by the beauty of the female body, and can find inspiration in any woman. A Taurus has such excess physical and sexual prowess, that to him, sex is a way to relax and calm down. He is the most passionate and emotional lover of the Zodiac, but he expects his partner to take the initiative, and if she doesn't, he will easily find someone else. Taureans rarely divorce, and are true to the end – if not sexually, at least spiritually. They are secretive, keep their cards close, and may have secret lovers. If a Taurus does not feel a deep emotional connection with someone, he won't be shy to ask her friends for their number. He prefers a voluptuous figure over an athletic or skinny woman.

The best partners for a Taurus are Cancer, Virgo, Pisces, or Scorpio. Sagittarius can show a Taurus real delights in both body and spirit, but they are unlikely to make it down the aisle. They can have an interesting relationship with an Aquarius – these signs are very different, but sometimes can spend their lives together. They might initially feel attracted to an Aries, before rejecting her.

GEMINI

The typical Gemini man is easygoing and polite. He is calm, collected, and analytical. For a Gemini, passion is closely linked to intellect, to the point that they will try to find an explanation for their actions before carrying them out. But passion cannot be explained, which scares a Gemini, and they begin jumping from one extreme to the other. This is why you will find more bigamists among Geminis than any other sign of the Zodiac. Sometimes, Gemini men even have two families, or divorce and marry several times throughout the course of their lives. This may be because they simply can't let new and interesting experiences pass them by. A Gemini's wife or lover needs to be smart, quick, and always looking ahead. If she isn't, he will find a new object for his affection.

Aquarians, Libras, and Aries make good partners for a Gemini. A Sagittarius can be fascinating for him, but they will not marry before he reaches middle age, as both partners will be fickle while they are younger. A Gemini and Scorpio are likely to be a difficult match, and the Gemini will try to wriggle out of the Scorpio's tight embrace. A Taurus will be an exciting sex partner, but their partnership won't be for long, and the Taurus is often at fault.

CANCER

Cancers tend to be deep, emotional individuals, who are both sensitive and highly sexual. Their charm is almost mystical, and they know how to use it. Cancers may be the most promiscuous sign of the Zodiac, and open to absolutely anything in bed. Younger Cancers look for women who are more mature, as they are skilled lovers. As they age, they look for someone young enough to be their own daughter, and delight in taking on the role of a teacher. Cancers are devoted to building a family and an inviting home, but once they achieve that goal, they are likely to have a wandering eye. They will not seek moral justification, as they sincerely believe it is simply something everyone does. Their charm works in such a way that women are deeply convinced they are the most important love in a Cancer's life, and that circumstances are the only thing preventing them from being together. Remember that a Cancer man is a master manipulator, and will not be yours unless he is sure you have throngs of admirers. He loves feminine curves, and is turned on by exquisite fragrances. Cancers don't end things with old lovers, and often go back for a visit after a breakup. Another type of Cancer is rarer – a faithful friend, and up for anything in order to provide for his wife and children. He is patriotic and a responsible worker.

Scorpios, Pisces, and other Cancers are a good match. A Taurus can make for a lasting relationship, as both signs place great value on family and are able to get along with one another. A Sagittarius will result in fights and blowouts from the very beginning, followed by conflicts and breakups. The Sagittarius will suffer the most. Marriage to an Aries isn't off the table, but it won't last very long.

LEO

A typical Leo is handsome, proud, and vain, with a need to be the center of attention at all times. They often pretend to be virtuous, until they are able to actually master it. They crave flattery, and prefer women who comply and cater to them. Leos demand unconditional obedience, and constant approval. When a Leo is in love, he is fairly sexual, and capable of being devoted and faithful. Cheap love affairs are not his thing, and Leos are highly aware of how expensive it is to divorce. They make excellent fathers. A Leo's partner needs to look polished and well-dressed, and he will not tolerate either frumpiness or nerds.

Aries, Sagittarius, and Gemini make for good matches. Leos are often very beguiling to Libras; this is the most infamous astrological "master-slave" pairing. Leos are also inexplicably drawn to Pisces – this is the only sign capable of taming them. A Leo and Virgo will face a host of problems sooner or later, and they might be material in nature. The Virgo will attempt to conquer him, and if she does, a breakup is inevitable.

VIRGO

Virgo is a highly intellectual sign, who likes to take a step back and spend his time studying the big picture. But love inherently does not lend itself to analysis, and this can leave Virgos feeling perplexed. While Virgo is taking his time, studying the object of his affection, someone else will swoop in and take her away, leaving him bitterly disappointed. Perhaps for that reason, Virgos tend to marry late, but once they are married, they remain true, and hardly ever initiate divorce. In bed, they are modest and reserved, as they see sex as some sort of quirk of nature, designed solely for procreation. Most Virgos have a gifted sense of taste, hearing, and smell. They cannot tolerate pungent odors and can be squeamish; they believe their partners should always take pains to be very clean. Virgos usually hate over-the-top expressions of love, and are immune to sex as a mean s of control. Many Virgos are stingy and more appropriate as husbands than lovers. Male Virgos tend to be monogamous, though if they are unhappy or disappointed with their partner, they may begin to look for comfort elsewhere and often give in to drunkenness.

Taurus, Capricorn, and Scorpio make the best partners for a Virgo. They may feel inexplicable attraction for Aquarians. They will form friendships with Aries, but rarely will this couple make it down the aisle. With Leos, be careful – this sign is best as a lover, not a spouse.

LIBRA

Libra is a very complex, wishy-washy sign. They are constantly seeking perfection, which often leaves them in discord with the reality around them. Libra men are elegant and refined, and expect no less from their partner. Many Libras treat their partners like a beautiful work of art, and have trouble holding onto the object of their affection. They view love itself as a very abstract concept, and can get tired of the physical aspect of their relationship. They are much more drawn to intrigue and the chase- dreams, candlelit evenings, and other symbols of romance. A high percentage of Libra men are gay, and they view sex with other men as the more elite option. Even when Libras are unhappy in their marriages, they never divorce willingly. Their wives might leave them, however, or they might be taken away by a more decisive partner.

Aquarius and Gemini make the best matches for Libras. Libra can also easily control an independent Sagittarius, and can easily fall under the influence of a powerful and determined Leo, before putting all his strength and effort into breaking free. Relationships with Scorpios are difficult; they may become lovers, but will rarely marry.

SCORPIO

Though it is common to perceive Scorpios as incredibly sexual, they are, in fact, very unassuming, and never brag about their exploits. They will, however, be faithful and devoted to the right woman. The Scorpio man is taciturn, and you can't expect any tender words from him, but he will defend those he loves to the very end. Despite his outward control, Scorpio is very emotional; he needs and craves love, and is willing to fight for it. Scorpios are incredible lovers, and rather than leaving them tired, sex leaves them feeling energized. They are always sexy, even if they aren't particularly handsome. They are unconcerned with the ceremony of wooing you, and more focused on the act of love itself.

Expressive Cancers and gentle, amenable Pisces make the best partners. A Scorpio might also fall under the spell of a Virgo, who is adept at taking the lead. Sparks might fly between two Scorpios, or with a Taurus, who is perfect for a Scorpio in bed. Relationships with Libras, Sagittarians, and Aries are difficult.

SAGITTARIUS

Sagittarian men are lucky, curious, and gregarious. Younger Sagittarians are romantic, passionate, and burning with desire to experience every type of love. Sagittarius is a very idealistic sign, and in that search for perfection, they tend to flit from one partner to another, eventually forgetting what they were even looking for in the first place. A negative Sagittarius might have two or three relationships going on at once, assigning each partner a different day of the week. On the other hand, a positive Sagittarius will channel his powerful sexual energy into creativity, and take his career to new heights. Generally speaking, after multiple relationships and divorces, the Sagittarian man will conclude that his ideal marriage is one where his partner is willing to look the other way.

Aries and Leo make the best matches for a Sagittarius. He might fall under the spell of a Cancer, but would not be happy being married to her. Gemini can be very intriguing, but will only make for a happy marriage after middle age, when both partners are older and wiser. Younger Sagittarians often marry Aquarian women, but things quickly fall apart. Scorpios can make for an interesting relationship, but if the Sagittarius fails to comply, divorce is inevitable.

CAPRICORN

Practical, reserved Capricorn is one of the least sexual signs of the Zodiac. He views sex as an idle way to pass the time, and something he can live without, until he wants to start a family. He tends to marry late, and almost never divorces. Young Capricorns are prone to suppressing their sexual desires, and only discover them later in life, when they have already achieved everything a real man needs – a career and money. We'll be frank – Capricorn is not the best lover, but he can compensate by being caring, attentive, and showering you with valuable gifts. Ever cautious, Capricorn loves to schedule his sexual relationships, and this is something partners will just have to accept. Women should understand that Capricorn needs some help relaxing – perhaps with alcohol. They prefer inconspicuous, unassuming women, and run away from a fashion plate.

The best partners for a Capricorn are Virgo, Taurus, or Scorpio. Cancers might catch his attention, and if they marry, it is likely to be for life. Capricorn is able to easily dominate Pisces, and Pisces-Capricorn is a well-known "slave and master" combination. Relationships with Leos tend to be erratic, and they are unlikely to wed. Aries might make for a cozy family at first, but things will cool off quickly, and often, the marriage only lasts as long as Capricorn is unwilling to make a change in his life.

AQUARIUS

Aquarian men are mercurial, and often come off as peculiar, unusual, or aloof, and detached. Aquarians are turned on by anything novel or strange, and they are constantly looking for new and interesting people. They are stimulated by having a variety of sexual partners, but they consider this to simply be normal life, rather than sexually immoral. Aquarians are unique – they are more abstract than realistic, and can be cold and incomprehensible, even in close relationships. Once an Aquarius gets married, he will try to remain within the realm of decency, but often fails. An Aquarian's partners need uncommon patience, as nothing they do can restrain him. Occasionally, one might encounter another kind of Aquarius – a responsible, hard worker, and exemplary family man.

The best matches for an Aquarius are female fellow Aquarians, Libras, and Sagittarians. When Aquarius seeks out yet another affair, he is not choosy, and will be happy with anyone.

PISCES

Pisces is the most eccentric sign of the Zodiac. This is reflected in his romantic tendencies and sex life. Pisces men become very dependent on those with whom they have a close relationship. Paradoxically, they are simultaneously crafty and childlike when it comes to playing games, and they are easily deceived. As a double bodied sign, Pisces rarely marry just once, as they are very sexual, easily fall in love, and are constantly seeking their ideal. Pisces are very warm people, who love to take care of others and are inclined toward "slave-master" relationships, in which they are the submissive partner. But after catering to so many lovers, Pisces will remain elusive. They are impossible to figure out ahead of time – today, they might be declaring their love for you, but tomorrow, they may disappear – possibly forever! To a Pisces, love is a fantasy, illusion, and dream, and they might spend their whole lives in pursuit of it. Pisces who are unhappy in love are vulnerable to alcoholism or drug addiction.

Cancer and Scorpio make the best partners for a Pisces. He is also easily dominated by Capricorn and Libra, but in turn will conquer even a queen-like Leo. Often, they are fascinated by Geminis – if they marry, it will last a long time, but likely not forever. Relationships with Aries and Sagittarians are erratic, though initially, things can seem almost perfect.

Women

ARIES

Aries women are leaders. They are decisive, bold, and very protective. An Aries can take initiative and is not afraid to make the first move. Her ideal man is strong, and someone she can admire. But remember, at the slightest whiff of weakness, she will knock him off his pedestal. She does not like dull, whiny men, and thinks that there is always a way out of any situation. If she loves someone, she will be faithful. Aries women are too honest to try leading a double life. They are possessive, jealous, and not only will they not forgive those who are unfaithful, their revenge may be brutal; they know no limits. If you can handle an Aries, don't try to put her in a cage; it is best to give her a long leash. Periodically give her some space – then she will seek you out herself. She is sexual, and believe that anything goes in bed.

Her best partners are a Sagittarius or Leo. A Libra can make a good match after middle age, once both partners have grown wiser and settled down a bit. Gemini and Aquarius are only good partners during the initial phase, when everything is still new, but soon enough, they will lose interest in each other. Scorpios are good matches in bed, but only suitable as lovers.

TAURUS

Taurean women possess qualities that men often dream about, but rarely find in the flesh – they are soft, charming, practical, and reliable – they are very caring and will support their partner in every way. A Taurus is highly sexual, affectionate, and can show a man how to take pleasure to new heights. She is also strong and intense. If she is in love, she will be faithful. But when love fades away, she might find someone else on the side, though she will still fight to save her marriage, particularly if her husband earns good money. A Taurus will not tolerate a man who is disheveled or disorganized, and anyone dating her needs to always be on his toes. She will expect gifts, and likes being taken to expensive restaurants, concerts, and other events. If you argue, try to make the first peace offering, because a Taurus finds it very hard to do so – she might withdraw and ruminate for a long time. Never air your dirty laundry; solve all your problems one-on-one.

Scorpio, Virgo, Capricorn, and Cancer make the best matches. A relationship with an Aries or Sagittarius would be difficult. There is little attraction between a Taurus and a Leo, and initially Libras can make for a good partner in bed, but things will quickly cool off and fall apart. A Taurus and Aquarius make an interesting match – despite the difference in signs, their relationships are often lasting, and almost lifelong.

GEMINI

Gemini women are social butterflies, outgoing, and they easily make friends, and then break off the friendship, if people do not hold their interest. A Gemini falls in love hard, is very creative, and often fantasizes about the object of her affection. She is uninterested in sex without any attachment, loves to flirt, and, for the most part, is not particularly affectionate. She dreams of a partner who is her friend, lover, and a romantic, all at once. A Gemini has no use for a man who brings nothing to the table intellectually. That is a tall order, so Geminis often divorce and marry several times. Others simply marry later in life. Once you have begun a life together, do not try to keep her inside – she needs to travel, explore, socialize, attend events and go to the theater. She cannot tolerate possessive men, so avoid giving her the third degree, and remember that despite her flirtatious and social nature, she is, in fact, faithful – as long as you keep her interested and she is in love. Astrologists believe that Geminis do not know what they need until age 29 or 30, so it is best to hold off on marriage until then.

Leo and Libra make the best matches. A relationship with a Cancer is likely, though complex, and depends solely on the Cancer's affection. A Gemini and Sagittarius can have an interesting, dynamic relationship, but these are two restless signs, which might only manage to get together after ages 40-45, once they have had enough thrills out of life and learned to be patient. Relationships with a Capricorn are very difficult, and almost never happen. The honeymoon stage can be wonderful with a Scorpio, but each partner will eventually go their own way, before ending things. A Gemini and Pisces union can also be very interesting – they are drawn to each other, and can have a wonderful relationship, but after a while, the cracks start to show and things will fall apart. An Aquarius is also not a bad match, but they will have little sexual chemistry.

CANCER

Cancers can be divided into two opposing groups. The first includes a sweet and gentle creature who is willing to dedicate her life to her husband and children. She is endlessly devoted to her husband, especially if he makes a decent living and remains faithful. She views all men as potential husbands, which means it is dangerous to strike up a relationship with her if your intentions are not serious; she can be anxious and clingy, sensitive and prone to crying. It is better to break things to her gently, rather than directly spitting out the cold, hard truth. She wants a man who can be a provider, though she often earns well herself. She puts money away for a rainy day, and knows how to be thrifty, for the sake of others around her, rather than only for herself. She is an excellent cook and capable of building an inviting home for her loved ones. She is enthusiastic in bed, a wonderful wife, and a caring mother.

The second type of Cancer is neurotic, and capable of creating a living hell for those around her. She believes that the world is her enemy, and manages to constantly find new intrigue and machinations.

Another Cancer, Virgo, Taurus, Scorpio, and Pisces make the best matches. A Cancer can often fall in love with a Gemini, but eventually, things will grow complicated, as she will be exhausted by a Gemini's constant mood swings and cheating. A Cancer and Sagittarius will initially have passionate sex, but things will quickly cool off. A relationship with a Capricorn is a real possibility, but only later in life, as while they are young, they are likely to fight and argue constantly. Cancer can also have a relationship with an Aries, but this will not be easy.

LEO

Leos are usually beautiful or charming, and outwardly sexual. And yet, appearances can be deceiving – they are not actually that interested in sex. Leo women want to be the center of attention and men running after them boosts their self-esteem, but they are more interested in their career, creating something new, and success than sex. They often have high-powered careers and are proud of their own achievements. Their partners need to be strong; if a Leo feels a man is weak, she can carry him herself for a while- before leaving him. It is difficult for her to find a partner for life, as chivalrous knights are a dying breed, and she is not willing to compromise. If you are interested in a Leo, take the initiative, admire her, and remember that even a queen is still a woman. Timid men or tightwads need not apply. Leos like to help others, but they don't need a walking disaster in their life. If they are married and in love, they are usually faithful, and petty gossip isn't their thing. Leo women make excellent mothers, and are ready to give their lives to their children. Their negative traits include vanity and a willingness to lie, in order to make themselves look better.

Sagittarius, Aries, and Libra make the best matches. Leos can also have an interesting relationship with a Virgo, though both partners will weaken each other. Life with a Taurus will lead to endless arguments – both signs are very stubborn, and unwilling to give in. Leos and Pisces are another difficult pair, as she will have to learn to be submissive if she wants to keep him around. A relationship with a Capricorn will work if there is a common denominator, but they will have little sexual chemistry. Life with a Scorpio will be turbulent to say the least, and they will usually break up later in life.

VIRGO

Virgo women are practical, clever, and often duplicitous. Marrying one isn't for everyone. She is a neat freak to the point of annoying those around her. She is also an excellent cook, and strives to ensure her children receive the very best by teaching them everything, and preparing them for a bright future. She is also thrifty – she won't throw money around, and, in fact, won't even give it to her husband. She has no time for rude, macho strongmen, and is suspicious of spendthrifts. She will not be offended if you take her to a cozy and modest café rather than an elegant restaurant. Virgos are masters of intrigue, and manage to outperform every other sign of the Zodiac in this regard. Virgos love to criticize everyone and everything; to listen to them, the entire world is simply a disaster and wrong, and only she is the exception to this rule. Virgos are not believed to be particularly sexual, but there are different variations when it comes to this. Rarely, one finds an open-minded Virgo willing to try anything, and who does it all on a grand scale – but she is rather the exception to this general rule.

The best matches for a Virgo are Cancer, Taurus, and Capricorn. She also can get along well with a Scorpio, but will find conflict with Sagittarius. A Pisces will strike her interest, but they will rarely make it down the aisle. She is often attracted to an Aquarius, but they would drive each other up the wall were they to actually marry. An Aries forces Virgo to see another side of life, but here, she will have to learn to conform and adapt.

LIBRA

Female Libras tend to be beautiful, glamorous, or very charming. They are practical, tactical, rational, though they are adept at hiding these qualities behind their romantic and elegant appearance. Libras are drawn to marriage, and are good at imagining the kind of partner they need. They seek out strong, well-off men and are often more interested in someone's social status and bank account than feelings. The object of their affection needs to be dashing, and have a good reputation in society. Libras love expensive things, jewelry, and finery. If they are feeling down, a beautiful gift will instantly cheer them up. They will not tolerate scandal or conflict, and will spend all their energy trying to keep the peace, or at least the appearance thereof. They do not like to air their dirty laundry, and will only divorce in extreme circumstances. They are always convinced they are right and react to any objections as though they have been insulted. Most Libras are not particularly sexual, except those with Venus or the Moon in Scorpio.

Leos, Geminis, and Aquarians make good matches. Libra women are highly attracted to Aries men - this is a real case of opposites attract. They can get along with a Sagittarius, though he will find that Libras are too proper and calm. Capricorn, Pisces, and Cancer are all difficult matches. Things will begin tumultuously with a Taurus, before each partner goes his or her own way.

SCORPIO

Scorpio women may appear outwardly restrained, but there is much more bubbling below the surface. They are ambitious with high self-esteem, but often wear a mask of unpretentiousness. They are the true power behind the scenes, the one who holds the family together, but never talk about it. Scorpios are strong-willed, resilient, and natural survivors. Often, Scorpios are brutally honest, and expect the same out of those around them. They do not like having to conform, and attempt to get others to adapt to them, as they honestly believe everyone will be better off that way. They are incredibly intuitive, and not easily deceived. They have an excellent memory, and can quickly figure out which of your buttons to push. They are passionate in bed, and their temperament will not diminish with age. When she is sexually frustrated, a Scorpio will throw all of her energy into her career or her loved ones. She is proud, categorical, and "if you don't do it right, don't do it at all" is her motto. Scorpio cannot be fooled, and she will not forgive any cheating. Will she cheat herself? Yes! But it will not break up her family, and she will attempt to keep it a secret. Scorpios are usually attractive to men, even if they are not particularly beautiful. They keep a low profile, though they always figure out their partner, and give them some invisible sign. There is also another, selfish type of Scorpio, who will use others for as long as they need them, before unceremoniously casting them aside.

Taurus is a good match; they will have excellent sexual chemistry and understand each other. Scorpio and Gemini are drawn to each other, but are unlikely to stay together long enough to actually get married. Cancer can be a good partner as well, but Cancers are possessive, while Scorpios do not like others meddling in their affairs, though they can later resolve their arguments in bed. Scorpio and Leo are often found together, but their relationship can also be very complicated. Leos are animated and chipper, while Scorpios, who are much deeper and more stubborn, see Leos as not particularly serious or reliable. One good example of this is Bill (a Leo) and Hillary (a Scorpio) Clinton. Virgo can also make a good partner, but when Scorpio seemingly lacks emotions, he will look for them elsewhere. Relationships with Lira are strange and very rare. Scorpio sees Libra as too insecure, and Libra does not appreciate Scorpio's rigidity. Two Scorpios together make an excellent marriage! Sagittarius and Scorpio are unlikely to get together, as she will think he is shallow and rude. If they do manage to get married, Scorpio's drive and persistence is the only thing that will make the marriage last. Capricorn is also not a bad match, and while Scorpio finds Aquarius attractive, they will rarely get married, as they are simply speaking different languages! Things are alright with a Pisces, as both signs are emotional, and Pisces can let Scorpio take the lead when necessary.

SAGITTARIUS

Sagittarius women are usually charming, bubbly, energetic, and have the gift of gab. They are kind, sincere, and love people. They are also straightforward, fair, and very ambitious, occasionally to the point of irritating those around them. But telling them something is easier than not telling them, and they often manage to win over their enemies. Sagittarius tends to have excellent intuition, and she loves to both learn and teach others. She is a natural leader, and loves taking charge at work and at home. Many Sagittarian women have itchy feet, and prefer all kinds of travel to sitting at home. They are not particularly good housewives – to be frank, cooking and cleaning is simply not for them. Their loved ones must learn to adapt to them, but Sagittarians themselves hate any pressure. They are not easy for men to handle, as Sagittarians want to be in charge. Sagittarius falls in love easily, is very sexual and temperamental, and may marry multiple times. Despite outward appearances, Sagittarius is a very lonely sign. Even after she is married with children, she may continue living as if she were alone; you might say she marches to the beat of her own drum. Younger

Sagittarians can be reckless, but as they mature, they can be drawn to religion, philosophy, and the occult.

Aries and Leo make the best matches, as Sagittarius is able to bend to Leo's ways, or at least pretend to. Sagittarians often end up with Aquarians, but their marriages do not tend to be for the long haul. They are attracted to Geminis, but are unlikely to marry one until middle age, when both signs have settled down. Sagittarius and Cancer have incredible sexual chemistry, but an actual relationship between them would be tumultuous and difficult. Capricorn can make a good partner- as long as they are able to respect each other's quirks. Sagittarius rarely ends up with a Virgo, and while she may often meet Pisces, things are unlikely to go very far.

CAPRICORN

Capricorn women are conscientious, reliable, organized, and hard-working. Many believe that life means nothing but work, and live accordingly. They are practical, and not particularly drawn to parties or loud groups of people. But if someone useful will be there, they are sure to make an appearance. Capricorn women are stingy, but not as much as their male counterparts. They are critical of others, but think highly of themselves. Generally, they take a difficult path in life, but thanks to their dedication, perseverance, and willingness to push their own limits, they are able to forge their own path, and by 45 or 50, they can provide themselves with anything they could want. Capricorn women have the peculiarity of looking older than their peers when they are young, and younger than everyone else once they have matured. They are not particularly sexual, and tend to be faithful partners. They rarely divorce, and even will fight until the end, even for a failed marriage. Many Capricorns have a pessimistic outlook of life, and have a tendency to be depressed. They are rarely at the center of any social circle, but are excellent organizers. They have a very rigid view of life and love, and are not interested in a fling, as marriage is the end goal. As a wife, Capricorn is simultaneously difficult and reliable. She is difficult because of her strict nature and difficulty adapting. But she will also take on all the household duties, and her husband can relax, knowing his children are in good hands.

Taurus, Pisces, and Scorpio make good matches. Aries is difficult, once things cool off after the initial honeymoon. When a Capricorn meets another Capricorn, they will be each other's first and last love. Sagittarius isn't a bad match, but they don't always pass the test of time. Aquarius and Capricorn are a difficult match, and rarely found together. Things are too dull with a Virgo, and while Leo can be exciting at first, things will fall apart when he begins showing off. Libra and Aquarius are both difficult partners for Capricorn, and she is rarely found with either of them.

AQUARIUS

A female Aquarius is very different from her male counterparts. She is calm and keeps a cool head, but she is also affectionate and open. She values loyalty above all else, and is unlikely to recover from any infidelity, though she will only divorce if this becomes a chronic trend, and she has truly been stabbed in the back. She is not interested in her partner's money, but rather, his professional success. She is unobtrusive and trusting, and will refrain from listening in on her partner's phone conversations or hacking into his email. With rare exceptions, Aquarian women make terrible housewives. But they are excellent partners in life – they are faithful, never boring, and will not reject a man, even in the most difficult circumstances. Most Aquarians are highly intuitive, and can easily tell the truth from a lie. They themselves only lie in extreme situations, which call for a "white lie" in order to avoid hurting someone's feelings.

Aquarius gets along well with Aries, Gemini, and Libra. She can also have a good relationship with a Sagittarius. Taurus often makes a successful match, though they are emotionally very different; the same goes for Virgo. Aquarius and Scorpio, Capricorn, or Cancer is a difficult match. Pisces can make a good partner as well, as both signs complement each other. Any relationship with a Leo will be tumultuous, but lasting, as Leo is selfish, and Aquarius will therefore have to be very forgiving.

PISCES

Pisces women are very adaptable, musically inclined, and erotic. They possess an innate earthly wisdom, and a good business sense. Pisces often reinvent themselves; they can be emotional, soft, and obstinate, as well as sentimental, at times. Their behavioral changes can be explained by frequent ups and downs. Pisces is charming, caring, and her outward malleability is very attractive to men. She is capable of loving selflessly, as long as the man has something to love. Even if he doesn't, she will try and take care of him until the very end. Pisces' greatest fear is poverty. They are intuitive, vulnerable, and always try to avoid conflict. They love to embellish the truth, and sometimes alcohol helps with this. Rarely, one finds extremely unbalanced, neurotic and dishonest Pisces, who are capable of turning their loved ones' lives into a living Hell!

Taurus, Capricorn, Cancer, and Scorpio make the best matches. She will be greatly attracted to a Virgo, but a lasting relationship is only likely if both partners are highly spiritual. Any union with a Libra is likely to be difficult and full of conflict. Pisces finds Gemini attractive, and they may have a very lively relationship – for a while. Occasionally, Pisces ends up with a Sagittarius, but she will have to fade into the background and entirely submit to him. If she ends up with an Aquarius, expect strong emotional outbursts, and a marriage that revolves around the need to raise their children.

Tatiana Borsch